The Circle of Sappho

The
Circle
of
Sappho

A REGENCY
DETECTIVE MYSTERY

DAVID LASSMAN & TERENCE JAMES

The
Mystery
Press

For

Sophie and Rory

Original cover photograph courtesy of Terence James.

First published 2016

The Mystery Press is an imprint of The History Press
The Mill, Brimscombe Port
Stroud, Gloucestershire, GL5 2QG
www.thehistorypress.co.uk

© David Lassman & Terence James, 2016

The right of David Lassman & Terence James to be
identified as the Authors of this work has been asserted
in accordance with the Copyright, Designs and Patents Act 1988.

British Library Cataloguing in Publication Data.
A catalogue record for this book is available from the British Library.

ISBN 978 0 7509 6296 4

Typesetting and origination by The History Press
Printed in Great Britain

PROLOGUE

'Tell me about Sappho and Atthis again.'

'You really love that story, don't you?'

The young girl nodded. 'I love hearing you tell it, as well. The sound of your voice makes me feel happy inside.'

The older woman smiled and momentarily held the girl's gaze with her own. She positioned herself crossed-legged on a weaved mat she had brought to place on the stone floor and let her adolescent companion lay her head upon her lap; the girl's long auburn hair, free of its restrictive school cap, flowing out over the woman's thighs. A slight chill penetrated the enclosed space, bringing a biting air to the late morning, but its inhabitants were too engaged in the moment to feel it.

'In ancient times there was a beautiful poetess called Sappho. She lived in a place called Mytilene, on the Greek island of Lesbos. She was tutor to many girls whose parents had sent them to her from not only other parts of the island but, as her reputation grew, from throughout Greece. Her school became known as "the home of the servants of the muses". One day, a girl arrived from an island far away. Her name was Atthis. Like the rest of the pupils she was instructed in dancing, poetry and the other disciplines the muses are said to have inspired. Sappho loved all her girls equally, but Atthis became special.'

'Like me to you?' said the girl, grinning.

'Yes, like you to me,' said the older woman, leaning forward and kissing the girl's forehead.

'And then what happened?'

'Eventually Atthis finished her studies and had to leave the island.'

'I do not want to leave, I ...'

The girl raised herself up onto one elbow.

'What is it?' asked the woman.

'I thought I heard someone outside.'

'Do not worry, there is no one. I am the only teacher on duty; the others are with the girls at church, in the village. As for Tom, he's probably asleep in his flowerbeds by now.'

'I do not want anyone to find us and make me leave. I want to be alone with you in this place, forever.'

'That is why I brought you here. Now, drink this, it is a special drink I have made to mark the occasion. It will keep you warm.'

The girl accepted the small wooden cup and drank the liquid. The woman then refilled the cup and drank it herself. The girl relaxed back into the older woman's lap, gazing up contentedly as her hair began to be stroked.

'Tell me about the poem Sappho wrote for Atthis.'

'Well, the poem she wrote was a unique one. When the girls at her school left her tutelage it was usually to marry and so Sappho would compose for them a marriage song. For Atthis, however, she wrote one especially for her alone.'

'I love it when you recite it.'

The older woman did not smile this time.

'Beyond all hope,' she began, 'I prayed those timeless days we spent might be made twice as long. I prayed one word: I *want*. Someone, I tell you, will remember us, even in another time.'

In the four years the older woman had been at the school, and the numerous pupils that had passed through it under her guardianship, she had never before come across a student so befitting her vision of Atthis and what she believed Sappho must have felt for her. On a number of occasions she thought she had found it, but she had been wrong. Those had been infatuations, imitations, illusions. This time it was different. This time it was real. This time it hurt at the thought of losing her. She wanted to kiss the rest of the girl's head, her face, her neck, her body. She knew only too well though that however far her passion was allowed to go unbridled, even this would not be enough to quell the all-consuming feeling of sheer terror she felt, knowing of her imminent loss. But she knew she would never let her go from her heart. An eternal place had been carved there. She had spent every waking moment since learning the girl's news hoping for some kind of reprieve. Hoping beyond all hope that her parents would change their mind and decide they did not want their daughter to accompany them, after all, on her father's foreign posting.

That hope now looked in vain and so she knew what had to be done. She had planned it to the last detail. Now was the time. As Sappho could not live without Atthis, so she could not live without her own 'special' love by her side.

'Do you think Sappho killed herself for Atthis?' the girl asked, her voice a little slurred from the drink.

The woman nodded.

'Yes. Even though it is said that Sappho killed herself over Phaon, a boatman she is supposed to have fallen in love with, I believe this version to have been invented by men who could not endure the thought of one woman loving another so completely and passionately. If she did take her own life by throwing herself off the cliffs at Lefaka, I like to think it was because of Atthis. In my mind, Sappho heard Atthis had died and, unable to bear the grief of her passing, or the thought of being alone forever, ended her own life. In that way, they were reunited in another place to enjoy their love eternally.'

'Will you still love me after I go away?'

'You'll never leave my side or my heart, I promise you.'

The girl started abruptly and looked again in the direction of the entrance.

'I am sure I heard something, did you not hear it that time?'

The older woman took the younger one by the arms and held them gently but firmly. 'I told you my love, we're quite alone here. I have prepared it that way.'

CHAPTER ONE

Jack Swann sat at his usual table in the White Hart Inn and contemplated the morning ahead. He had three appointments scheduled, which in itself was not unusual. Swann liked to arrange what he called 'obligations, duties and favours' for the first part of the day, as this allowed him, when not working on a case, to pursue other interests. These comprised mainly of walking in the countryside that lay outside the city boundaries or else climbing the hills surrounding them. From these latter vantage points he could look down and gain a perspective on the place he had begun, after almost six months, to think of as home. He had yet to return to London since arriving in Bath the previous October, but at present there were no outstanding matters to be dealt with and anything that did need attention was being taken care of by his lawyer, who kept in contact through regular correspondence.

Swann had to confess he was enjoying his first season in Bath; the period of time in the city between October and May that encompassed all manner of social events and activities, created solely to occupy the masses arriving here seeking either restitution for their health or entertainment alone. Not that he had taken part in any of the more extravagant displays of socialising, such as promenading or balls, but instead had attended several concerts and a number of performances at the Theatre Royal in Old Orchard Street – accompanying his sister, Mary, on the majority of these occasions. The physical experience of the theatre, despite having their own box, had left a lot to be desired – the extraordinary heat generated by so many bodies confined in one place made the atmosphere oppressive and stifling – but the plays they had seen were worth each sweltering moment of discomfort. He had also enjoyed an exhibition of Gainsborough's work that had been held to celebrate his time in the city and which had made the now famous painter's reputation. Another highlight he particularly remembered was a recital by Rauzzini, the famous Italian castrato, who had enthralled the assembled patrons with a repertoire consisting of Mozart, Handel and Haydn.

It had to be admitted, therefore, and much to Mary's amusement during one such conversation on the subject, that his perception of Bath as merely a frivolous and super-ficial place had changed, or at the very least been tempered. There was a cultural element to the city he could now observe, which he himself enjoyed immensely. Nevertheless, as he went about his daily business the shallower aspects of the place and its inhabitants were still visible; exemplified none more so than by the never-ending stream of parents who travelled to Bath in order to engage in match-making for their unmarried daughters. Their sole purpose here, therefore, being to find their offspring a suitable husband – the term 'suitable' being merely a euphemism for 'rich'.

There was, of course, also a darker side to the city, absent from the guidebooks, and it was this element that kept Swann in Bath; pervading his waking hours and haunting his dreams and to which theatrical, musical or artistic excursions were only temporary distractions. It was now more than twenty years since his father had been murdered while trying to protect his employers' London house from two burglars. In gratitude for this act these employers, the Gardiner family, had adopted Swann and brought him up alongside their daughter, Mary, as their own. The two criminals, however, had never been caught and Swann had sworn to bring them to justice. The man he had watched deliver the fatal blow was called Malone – at least this was the name cried out by his accomplice as the red-hot poker, held by Swann's father, had seared his right cheek. That accomplice, due to what would now be a permanent mark acquired from that murderous night, was referred to by Swann as the Scarred Man. His quest had brought him to Bath for a short visit the previous autumn, but after catching sight of what he believed to be this very person, he had decided to stay on. Swann had yet to see the man again but instinctively felt the key to his quest lay in the city; and that somehow, although he wasn't yet sure in what way, there was a connection between the Scarred Man and the local crime boss, Wicks.

Swann now had a drawing of how the Scarred Man would currently look. He had found an artist in Bath who had the unique ability to 'age' a subject, which made it possible to see what they would look like in ten, twenty, even fifty years time. It took only a small leap of the imagination for Swann to realise he could commission a portrait of the Scarred Man as he now looked, from the description scorched in Swann's memory from all those years ago. Although the portrait had been destroyed and the artist murdered before Swann could take possession of it – he suspected Wicks of the crime – he had seen enough of the picture while it was being painted to employ his adoptive sister's artistic skills to produce an acceptable likeness, from which she then made a copy. The first drawing Swann had kept, while the other had been given to George and Bridges, the two thief-takers he employed in the city on a semi-permanent basis to help him in his quest to find the Scarred Man.

Unbeknownst to Swann, however, Mary had produced another copy for her aunt, Lady Harriet Montague-Smithson, who requested it after hearing of his ingenuity. Mary did not exactly know why she wanted it, but felt her aunt was not someone she could refuse.

And of course there was Lockhart. Swann believed the man now engaged to Mary was also, in some way, involved with Wicks, although he had as yet not been able to prove this belief. As frustrating was the fact that Lockhart's past, prior to arriving in Bath only a few weeks before Swann, seemed non-existent, or at least nothing which could be verified. The only fact he could be certain about was Mary's continuing blindness in matters of the heart; for all her intelligence, discernment and self-regard, she had accepted Lockhart's proposal of marriage less than three months after being first formally introduced. He was determined to unearth the truth about this man, and as no date for the wedding ceremony had yet been arranged, he still had time on his side. Lady Harriet seemed to be of the same opinion and so he felt he had an ally in his intention to stop this marriage from taking place.

Only the first appointment that morning was related to any of these matters. He was waiting at the White Hart for George and Bridges. They had become his eyes and ears in the notorious Avon Street district, the centre of Wicks' crime activities, and where Swann believed he had sighted the Scarred Man. Hopefully the pair would have news that would help in his search for him. In terms of trust, he believed he could depend on them with his life; indeed, they had already as good as saved his life during an assassination attempt made on him not long after he had arrived in the city. In terms of punctuality, however, this was a different matter. There was always a good reason for their lateness, most relating to 'trouble' which had seemingly found them, like bees to honey. And yet even within this irregularity there was a pattern. As Swann had come to realise, whatever hour an arrangement had been made, the time between that appointment and their appearance at the White Hart's entrance always allowed just enough time for a second cup of coffee to be drunk. If this was to be true today, he mused, they would arrive after his next mouthful.

His thoughts briefly turned to the other appointments. The later one, with Henry Fitzpatrick, was to discuss a matter he had been told required the 'utmost discretion'. He had grown fond of Fitzpatrick whilst in Bath and the local magistrate had proved himself a trustworthy companion, above corruption and with a moral centre that could be relied upon in any manner of situations. If George and Bridges were two men you would want beside you in a street fight, then Fitzpatrick was a man you would wish in a legal one. And even though his calm demeanour and emotional self-restraint was not at the level of a top card player, his ability as a moral compass was beyond question.

Then there was the remaining appointment, slotted in between the other two, which had led Swann to cancel returning home for breakfast with Mary. The urgent request for the meeting had been in the form of a hand-written letter that had been posted through the door of the house in Great Pulteney Street earlier that morning. There was no signature, but the paper on which the communication had been written was embossed and expensive. There was a familiarity to the handwriting, but he had not been able to yet recall what it was. It mentioned a matter of national security but other than the time and place, no other details were forthcoming. No doubt all would be revealed at the appointed hour, he thought. He then lifted his cup and drank the remaining contents of his second cup of coffee.

'Mr Swann, sir, I know we are late but we were detained,' shouted George as he entered the White Hart. 'We just heard news about what you've been asking us about.'

George hurried over to where Swann was sitting, as Bridges came through the door. Although he had given them money for clothes and footwear, on top of their usual pay, they still wore their usual shabby attire, which stood in marked contrast to the well-dressed clientele of the coaching inn. At least they were no longer barefoot, as they had been the first few times he had met them. No doubt George, although having a penchant for spending money on more pleasurable pursuits, knew the benefits of thick boots during the winter months in the city.

'Do you mean the Scarred Man?' asked Swann quietly, as George stood next to his table like a pupil being addressed by a teacher.

'Yes, sir, 'im.'

George produced the copy of the drawing he had been given. Unlike Swann's still pristine original, this was creased in several places, dirt-stained and had one corner torn.

'What is the news, George?'

Bridges had joined his companion. He was deaf and dumb but could lip-read and sign. For some reason, Swann observed, he was doing neither at present.

'He is in the city again.'

'Someone has seen him?'

'Yes, sir, or so they say. That is why we're late. There was a message at the Fountain, saying a man we know wanted to see us. We went to his stall in Horse Street but he wasn't there. Then we came here. We'll go later.'

'This is the same stallholder as before?'

George nodded. When they had begun showing the drawing around the market traders and stallholders in 'the hate', as the Avon Street district was known locally, one of them had recognised its subject. He had seen him a few times in the area, so he said, during the past couple of years. He always remembered him from an incident near his stall. The man had a long scar on his right cheek and had been walking with the previous crime boss, before Wicks, when three men had attacked them. One of the attackers had been killed outright by this Scarred Man, who had produced a short bayonet and stabbed him. The crime boss had despatched the second man and wounded the third. As this third man lay on the floor the crime boss put his boot on the man's bleeding leg and began to press down. The man screamed in agony but wouldn't say the name of the person behind the attack. After more of the same, along with a promise his life would be spared if he told them, he did so. The Scarred Man then stepped forward and thrust the already bloodied bayonet through his throat. He had only said a few words during the incident but it was enough to know he came from London.

The last time the stallholder had seen him, however, was sometime last year, possibly October or November, he said. He had been alone with his head down, but it was definitely him. This last sighting, around the time Swann believed he had seen him, confirmed in his mind that the man he had been searching for all these years had been in the city. And with the stallholder wanting to see George and Bridges it might be that he was back; that he was somewhere in the city at this very moment. Swann had the urge to leave the White

Hart and take to the streets looking for the stallholder or even the Scarred Man himself, but he had two more appointments to keep and George and Bridges had promised they would look for the stallholder as soon as they left.

'Devote all your time to this George until you find him,' said Swann. 'I will make sure it is worth your trouble, both of you.'

'Yes sir!' said George.

'I have a couple of appointments to keep this morning but leave a message at my office if you find out anything more. Otherwise I suggest we meet at the Fountain Inn this evening at the usual time.'

George nodded, although Bridges' gaze showed he was still elsewhere. As well as noticing he had not been lip-reading or signing, Swann had also observed he had a black eye. This was not an unusual sight for the pair but it was normally George, through an altercation with an angry husband or suchlike, who bore it.

'Is something wrong with Bridges?' enquired Swann. 'His attention seems elsewhere.'

'He is thinking about a woman, sir. That's how he got his black eye.'

'Ah, I see,' replied Swann, somewhat surprised.

'No, Mr Swann, it's nothing like that. I'll tell you about it tonight.'

Swann nodded.

George tapped Bridges on the arm and brought him back to the present. As soon as the men left, Swann paid his bill and departed. It was not yet ten o'clock but already the morning had provided enough mystery for the whole day.

CHAPTER TWO

Swann came out of the White Hart and turned right down Stall Street. A light drizzle was falling. If there was such a thing as a typical early spring morning, this was not it. The sky was a dark winter grey and threatened heavier rain.

Opposite the White Hart and across a large courtyard stood Bath Abbey; its west front magnificent even in inclement weather. There had been a Christian church on or near the site for more than a thousand years, while elements of Christianity in the area could be traced back to the Roman occupation. At this time worship had been undertaken in secret, for fear of persecution, and, after the Romans left, became submerged into Celticism through the Irish invaders who arrived in the city. Somehow the religion survived and throughout the Anglo-Saxon, Norman and medieval periods, various structures had been erected, destroyed, restored or rebuilt. The present-day abbey had undergone major restoration prompted by Elizabeth I, who instigated a national fund to pay for the work and then, in 1583, decreed it should become the parish church of Bath.

Swann had been researching Bath Abbey and its west front for a chapter to be included in a guide to the city, to be published later in the year. It was really a favour for Richard

Huntley, his literary agent acquaintance, whose client and original author of the book had died three chapters short of completion. When asked if he would write the chapter, Swann had immediately said yes. Not that he was overtly religious, but the chance to discover more about the carved figures scaling the ladders on its west front, which he often stopped to admire, was too good an opportunity to pass up.

The truth was, he had actually been given the option of writing all three outstanding chapters, but 'A Discerning Ladies' Guide to Shops and Shopping' and 'Balls, Banquets and Bathing', which would serve as introductory chapters giving an overview of the highlights awaiting visitors arriving for the season, had been quickly declined. He had briefly mentioned it to Mary, but as she was already involved in her own piece of writing – although she did not disclose what it was – she turned them down as well.

As he walked down Stall Street Swann briefly entered the Three Tuns, which acted as collection point for the Royal Mail coaches. He came out empty handed though, as no post had arrived for him from London that morning. There were rumours about the inn being in financial difficulty and that it might possibly close, but in Bath rumours were as much a currency in social circles as money. If it was true, it would no doubt soon become public notice.

Swann now took a circumvent route into the southern part of the city, to ensure he was not being followed. He had made that error once and the artist who had painted the Scarred Man's portrait had lost his life through it. He was heading into the centre of the Avon Street district, but now felt the urge to turn right and go to Horse Street, to see if the stallholder had arrived. As he realised he did not know what the man looked like, a nearby city clock started striking the hour. He carried on deeper into the maze of alleyways of the notorious area with another thought now rising within him: what if it was a trap? Despite the officialdom the letter had seemingly carried with it, as soon as he had seen the address where the meeting was to take place, the possibility of it being a trap and the possibility of it being permeated by Wicks had entered his mind. It had been temporarily supplanted by his meeting with George and Bridges, but now re-entered his thoughts as the reality of the incongruity of his surroundings and the letter became visibly apparent.

With regular flooding, along with the vermin and stench, it was easy to see why its inhabitants knew this place as 'the hate', especially with the ever-present threat of violence and death palpable in the air. Street names here were almost non-existent but Swann's knowledge of the area, gleaned from numerous trips he had undertaken, most of them in disguise, plus information he had picked up from George and Bridges, meant there were very few streets, alleys or passageways that were not known to him. He turned the corner and bumped into a figure coming the other way. He was momentarily taken aback, but then realised who it was.

'Lockhart!'

'Swann?'

In the next moment they had composed themselves and without another word continued on their separate ways. For his part, Swann could not afford to stop and converse, however curious he might have been to discover the reason behind Lockhart's presence in this nefarious district.

Swann reached the street in which the address on the letter was located. The winter flooding had receded, but one could see the water mark, above the ground-floor windowsills, where it had risen this particular year. He reached the building and looked around. The door looked secure and could not be pushed open. Although the exterior seemed rundown, the locks on display showed the length which someone had gone to secure the interior. He turned the door handle habitually and to his surprise found it unlocked. He opened it cautiously and stepped inside.

'If you would be so good as to close and lock the door behind you, Mr Swann,' a male voice spoke from one of the landings above, 'and then make your way up the staircase to the third floor.'

Swann did as he was instructed. The voice sounded too educated to be one of Wicks' men, but nevertheless the possibility remained in Swann's mind and so he checked his pistol was easily retrievable from inside his jacket. The stairs were not pristine but in good enough order. As he climbed the first two flights he observed that the doors which ran the length of the hallways, leading off from the landings, were all closed. He carried on up to the third floor, where the man who had spoken awaited him. This time he did not speak but merely gestured for Swann to follow him along the hallway. He was well dressed and clean-shaven. If this was part of Wicks' empire, then Swann had dramatically underestimated him.

As they continued along the hallway, Swann noticed a door slightly ajar and looked in as they passed it. Much to his surprise, he saw a desk and a gentleman lent over it, writing, as though this was an office in London or in the city's upper town. Two doors along, the man in front now stopped. He knocked on the door, opened it and gestured for Swann to go through. As he did so the door closed behind him, the man staying outside.

The room was sparsely furnished but looked as if it functioned as another office. Across the room, looking out of the window up at Beechen Cliff, was a figure he immediately recognised, even from behind. It was the second time in a matter of minutes he found himself in the company of a person he would not expect to see in this part of the city.

'Thank you for coming, Swann,' said Lady Harriet as she turned to face him. 'As I mentioned in the note to you, this is a matter of the utmost urgency.'

'I was intrigued by the summons, even more so now I know who is behind it.'

'Hardly a summons, more a request I hope.'

'I did not realise you had a presence in the city.'

'This building is used by an organisation I occasionally undertake work for.'

'I would not have believed this existed here.'

'Which is exactly why it does,' replied Lady Harriet. 'It is prone to flooding during the winter, but the rooms on the ground floor and basement are hardly ever used. Still, I do not want to bore you with distracting details. I have requested your attendance here to undertake a case for me. I prefer to tell you the particulars in my carriage, if you care to join me for a journey out of the city.'

'I have an appointment in an hour's time, which I wish to keep.'

'This may well take longer,' replied Lady Harriet, 'but if the urgency and importance of this matter was not adequately conveyed within my communication, then I am stating it now.'

'Then you have my agreement, Lady Harriet, although I wish a note to be sent to the magistrate, Henry Fitzpatrick, stating I have been unfortunately detained and will meet him at his Guildhall chambers as soon as I am able.'

Harriet nodded and took a sheet of paper from a desk drawer. She handed it to Swann. As he wrote his message to Fitzpatrick, Lady Harriet returned to the window, picked up a plant pot with a black flag in it and placed it on the floor.

'Come, my carriage will be waiting outside by the time we are downstairs.'

Swann followed Lady Harriet out into the corridor, where she handed the note he had written to the well-dressed man still standing there. He took it obediently and gave an almost imperceptible bow. Lady Harriet and Swann descended the three flights of stairs he had recently climbed, but instead of leaving by the front entrance they descended another flight that led to the basement. From here they walked along a corridor toward the farthest room. Lady Harriet lifted a flaming torch from outside the room and went inside, where a curtain hung on the opposite wall. She lifted it and Swann saw a door behind. Lady Harriet unlocked it with a key she had on her person and gestured for Swann to go through first. Stepping inside herself, she followed him through, then closed and locked the door. The passageway in front was now cast into light from the torch. Lady Harriet went ahead again as they moved along another corridor, this one made of earth. It smelt damp but the floor beneath Swann's feet was thankfully dry. If this part of the building had flooded, someone had done a good job of clearing it up. Swann measured about two streets' worth of passageway until they reached another door. Again Lady Harriet unlocked and relocked it. There was now a flight of stairs heading up. Given the fact Swann had entered the building from the south, with the river behind him, and that the subterranean route they had taken was north, this meant, if his calculations were correct, that they were now under Peter Street. They climbed the staircase and passed through an unlocked door into the stock room of a shop. Swann followed Lady Harriet through the shop itself, where none of the workers or customers gave either of them a second glance, and outside on to the road he had correctly predicted: Peter Street. No sooner had they emerged than a four-horse carriage pulled up and its driver jumped down to open a door; Lady Harriet and Swann stepped in. The carriage then sped off.

'I assume moving the black flag in your plant pot is what summoned your driver,' said Swann.

'That is most observant of you, Swann, but from your reputation nothing less is to be expected. Yes, the driver waits with the carriage at Beechen Cliff and when I remove the black flag and plant pot from the window, he knows I wish to be collected. We have it down to a fine art, as you have experienced. But as for the urgent matter with which I require your assistance, it is in connection with a girls' school a little way out of the city at Grove Park. It is a private establishment run by a close acquaintance of mine. An incident has taken place there which I wish you to investigate.'

'What kind of "incident" and why do you think I can help?'

'The bodies of a teacher and one of the pupils were discovered yesterday in the grounds and I want you to ascertain exactly how they died.'

'They were found together?'

Lady Harriett nodded.

'I want to engage you professionally, Swann. As I said, it is my understanding that you have acquired a reputation for solving several crimes since being in Bath.'

'Your message mentioned national security,' queried Swann.

'I will give you more details after we have been to the school; which is where we are heading now.'

'If I do take this case, there will be two provisions.'

Lady Harriet said nothing but waited for Swann to continue.

'I carry out the investigation in my own way. No interference from the school, yourself or anyone connected with the Alien Office, back in Avon Street.'

Lady Harriet smiled.

'My compliments, Swann. How did you know?'

'I did not for sure, Lady Harriet. It was an educated assumption. I have been aware of their existence for a number of years, as my work with the Bow Street Runners in London occasionally brought me into contact with their agents; one of whom I believe I recognised at a desk on the same floor as your office just now. Given that their *raison d'être* is being the authority through which all foreigners entering England have to register, I still cannot quite understand what they, and therefore you, are doing in Bath; unless, of course, the River Avon has now been assigned as a point of entry.'

'I am obviously not at liberty to discuss anything you witnessed this morning, but I do agree to your first condition. There will be no interference.'

Swann nodded.

'You mentioned a second one?'

'Yes,' replied Swann. 'I would like to know exactly what it was that you and Lockhart were discussing at the meeting you both had, not long before I arrived.'

'Lockhart? I have not seen him since I gave my blessing on his engagement with Mary. I really do not know what you are talking about, Swann.'

'Then forgive me Lady Harriet, I must have been mistaken.'

Although outwardly accepting her answer, the momentary flicker of her eyes only confirmed his suspicion that it was her office from which Lockhart had been leaving when they had bumped into each other. It had only been a hunch and almost on a whim he had made the suggestion to gauge Lady Harriet's reaction. Her response had been enlightening enough for now.

The remainder of the journey was undertaken in silence. The carriage made its way out of the city, up its steep northern slope and onto the expanse that was Lansdown. They drove past the former residence of Henry Gregor-Smith, the man whom Swann had saved from the gallows only a few months before. As good as his word, the author had subsequently moved to the continent and put his gothic novel-writing days behind him. He continued to look out of the carriage window as they travelled along the top of Lansdown and down the other side, into the valley beyond. As the carriage came round one corner, an estate with extensive grounds and a huge lake came into view. The main residence was impressive, but Swann's attention was immediately drawn to the small island situated in the centre of the lake. Instinctively, he knew this estate was where they were headed and that whatever the 'incident' involved, it had occurred here.

CHAPTER THREE

'I opened the school eleven years ago, Mr Swann. Each year we welcome girls from respectable and distinguished families from all across England and each year the authorities attempt ever more elaborate and ludicrous ways to try and close us down because they do not like what my school represents. As you can see they have not succeeded and I consider their attempts an indication that I must be doing something right in my educational outlook.'

Catherine Jennings looked exactly how she spoke: forthright, determined and readily prepared for an argument.

'So why have they failed, if you do not mind my asking?' asked Swann. 'My understanding of such men is that they are not the type easily defeated.'

'I work hard to ensure we remain open, Mr Swann. Although I can always rely on help from acquaintances in high places,' she said, acknowledging Lady Harriet.

'And is the crowd at the entrance when we arrived part of their attempts?'

On arriving at the front gates, Lady Harriet's carriage had been met by a small group, the majority of them male, who made a show of protest as they drove through. Although their words were lost between the wind and the carriage's wheels on the gravel, their gestures and expressions showed they were not advocating an endorsement of the school.

'I have set ideas on the way to educate the girls here and one of those is that they should learn French. A pamphlet has recently been circulated by an author or authors unknown, although it is not hard to assume its origination, which suggests, given we are at war with Napoleon, this is unpatriotic and should be stopped immediately. It is this pamphlet which those outside have responded to with their protest. They call me a traitor. I am a patriot, Mr Swann, but first and foremost I am the guardian of my girls' education and one day this war will end and if the girls have not learnt French, their lives will be the poorer for it. I would be doing a disservice to their parents, who have entrusted their daughters' futures in my hands, if I did anything less. French is, after all, the language of Fénelon, Voltaire and Rousseau.'

'I wholeheartedly agree with you, Miss Jennings, although I am not familiar with the first of those you mentioned.'

'Fénelon? His most famous work is the book *Les Aventures de Télémaque, fils d'Ulysse*, which was published at the end of the seventeenth century. His views on education were ahead of its time and many of his principles I have adopted for my school.'

Swann remained silent for a few moments.

'Is something wrong, Swann?' asked Lady Harriet.

'It is just that I have heard of the book Miss Jennings mentioned, but could not remember its author. But as for the reason I am here,' said Swann, now addressing Miss Jennings, 'Lady Harriet has told me there have been two deaths at the school.'

'Yes, Miss Leigh, the school's classics teacher and one of the pupils under her tutorage, Miss Grace Templeton, were discovered yesterday afternoon.'

'Where are their bodies now?'

'They have been placed in our chapel. Lady Harriet said you might wish to view them before they are taken away.'

Lady Harriet acknowledged Swann's raised eyebrow as Miss Jennings led them through the maze of corridors that made up the main building of the school and outside into a small courtyard. Across the yard was a small chapel, outside of which sat a girl, sitting on a chair and reading. When she saw them, she stood up.

'This is Elsa Timmins. She is head girl here at the school. The other girls are in lessons but I asked her to be here as a precaution, as the chapel is used for individual prayers if any of the girls so require it.'

Swann nodded his approval.

Miss Jennings addressed the girl. 'Elsa, can you enquire of cook if the delivery of lamb has been made yet? With that mob outside, I want to make sure it has arrived safely.'

Elsa curtsied and left.

'What have the girls been told about the deaths?' asked Swann as Miss Jennings opened the chapel door.

'That it was a boating accident, which is what we also intend to tell the local authorities.'

'They have not yet been informed?'

Miss Jennings looked towards Lady Harriet.

'We wanted your opinion before we made any announcement,' said Lady Harriet.

Swann entered the chapel and immediately saw the two bodies laid out on makeshift tables. He moved closer. The teacher was thirty-four, Miss Jennings said, while the girl had turned sixteen the previous year. The latter – Grace – had a beautiful face, Swann observed, with classical features which seemed not to have diminished in death. The older woman, though clearly showing signs of aging, nevertheless retained a youthful exuberance about her person. Swann leaned in to take a better look at a bloodied mark on her forehead.

'Do you know how this wound happened?' asked Swann.

'From all indications,' replied Miss Jennings 'it looks like Miss Leigh killed the girl by stabbing her in the heart, but in the struggle Miss Templeton inflicted that wound with a sharp stone. There are no other wounds on either of the bodies. Miss Leigh then killed herself by taking poison. This was found beside her.'

Miss Jennings handed Swann a small bottle, which had been on a shelf next to the bloodied knife and the stone used to inflict the wound to Miss Leigh's forehead. He took it and held it to his nose. 'Am I to assume this held the poison?'

'That is what we believe,' said Miss Jennings.

Swann finished his examination. 'I cannot see anything which would disagree with what you have told me, but I would like to see the place where the bodies were found,' he said.

Ten minutes later, Swann, Miss Jennings and Lady Harriet were in the middle of the lake, being rowed towards the island by Thomas, the school gardener. Miss Jennings informed Swann that it had been Tom, as everyone called him, who had found the bodies on the island. The wooden boat was just about large enough to carry the four of them but it felt as if the boat might capsize; the motion of the oars moving the craft almost as much from side to side as it did forward. However, they reached the island's small jetty on the far side of the islet, dry and upright.

Tom stepped off the boat and then tied it to a small wooden pillar. Swann followed him onto the jetty and the two men helped the women ashore. Tom requested to stay with the boat, to which Miss Jennings agreed. Swann and the two women made their way to the spot where the bodies had been discovered. It was at the end of one of the many paths and trails that crisscrossed the relatively large island, which was otherwise covered in trees, now starting to bud in the spring air.

They reached the end of the trail and in front of them stood a stone structure. It was about twenty feet high and the same wide, with a pair of Doric columns adorning the entrance.

'I believe it is a temple dedicated to the goddess Aphrodite,' said Miss Jennings.

'It cannot be seen from the house,' observed Swann.

'That is correct. For whatever reason the builder designed it that way. The island is completely isolated and can only be reached by the boat on which we just arrived. One could swim across but the edges of the island are too steep to climb out onto and there are many sharp rocks, deliberately placed, just under the surface of the water. The builder certainly took steps to ensure that the island was difficult to access.'

'I do not understand,' said Swann. 'If Miss Leigh had already brought the boat across to the island, how did Tom gain access to it?'

'He swam across, pulled himself up onto the boat and then stepped onto the jetty and island that way.'

Swann nodded as they went inside the temple. It took a few moments for his eyes to adjust to the change of light but once he became accustomed to it he could see that the interior went back about twice the length of its height and width.

'Do any of the other teachers or girls come over here?'

'No, Mr Swann, the island is out of bounds to everyone in the school.'

'Why do you think Miss Leigh went against your orders and came across?'

'I assume she wished privacy to carry out her abominable crime, although I still cannot understand why she wanted to kill Grace. On the occasions we discussed the girl's progress, Miss Leigh spoke of her with great regard.'

'Do you know any reason why anyone else would want them dead?'

'No one else was involved; of that I am certain.'

'Miss Jennings,' said Swann, 'if it was that simple, I am sure my services would not have been engaged to investigate. I would suggest that either you or Lady Harriet believe it to be something else or otherwise …'

'Swann, if I may,' interrupted Lady Harriet. 'I asked you here today for your expert judgement in asserting it was as described by Catherine. I am sorry if I misled you to think it was anything else.'

Swann immediately realised Lady Harriet was lying but for the moment remained silent on the matter. Instead he glanced around the temple's interior and said: 'If I may, I would like a few minutes to look around on my own.'

Lady Harriet nodded.

'Catherine and I will be at the jetty, once you have finished.'

'Thank you, Lady Harriet,' replied Swann.

As soon as Lady Harriet and Miss Jennings left the temple, Swann positioned himself in the middle of the room and closed his eyes. He began to imagine the sequence of tragic events, as he had been told them, which had unfolded within it. He could see the two female figures, perhaps sitting or kneeling upon the woven mat that had been used to cover part of the uneven earthen floor. On what pretext had the girl come across to the island with her teacher, knowing it was forbidden. For the moment Swann had to imagine it was through her own free will. It was therefore a harmonious scene, or had at least started that way. Perhaps an argument or a disagreement had taken place and they began to fight. The girl had grabbed one of the stones that lay about the temple and hit out at her teacher, making the cut Swann had observed in the chapel. The teacher then stabbed the girl, killing her instantly. Possibly out of remorse or through the realisation that she would no doubt hang for the crime, she took out the bottle of poison and drank it. There was no suicide note, so he assumed it was not premeditated. Swann opened his eyes and began to apply his 'system' to the scene; a method of investigation which relied on a series of 'givens' and the 'assumptions' deduced through them.

'I shall begin from here,' Swann said to himself as he stepped outside.

Given that the island could not be accessed by swimming and the boat Tom rowed them across in was the only one in the grounds, or so he had been told, it had to be assumed that no one else was involved. And yet, despite the difficulties and danger swimming entailed, Tom had done exactly that to enable him to discover the bodies. After searching the grounds for the two missing women and finding the boat missing from its usual mooring, on the house side, he had been ordered across by Miss Jennings on her return, with the rest of the school, from church. He had swum across and then managed to haul himself up into the boat, to get onto the jetty. If someone else other than Tom had swum over though, why had they not returned in the boat?

It was still a possibility that someone else was involved in the deaths, but given that a knife and a bottle of poison had been found near the bodies, the assumption had to be made that, whether or not Miss Leigh had decided to kill the girl before coming across to the island, she was certainly prepared for that eventuality. Given that there was no note, Swann was left to assume it had been a spontaneous act. He went back inside the temple and crouched down to look more closely at the bloodstains on the floor and surrounding rocks. They seemed to be conducive with the sequence of events he imagined had occurred. Only one bloodstain seemed out of place. This was near the back of the temple, upon a large rock. It appeared to Swann to be a bloodied handprint, or at least part of one. From what he could determine from its size, it belonged to the girl. Perhaps she had not died straight away but had staggered to the back of the temple before succumbing to her wound. The bodies had been found together on the mat, according to Tom, but perhaps the teacher had brought the girl back there, before killing herself.

Swann's attention was now caught by an object near to where the bodies had been found. It lay discarded, in the shadows. As he picked it up he saw it was a small wooden cup. Had the teacher used it to drink the poison? He lifted the cup to his nose and thought he smelt a familiar aroma of almonds. If it had been used for that purpose, she had sweetened its bitterness with red wine. He placed the cup in his pocket, took another look around the interior and then went to go outside. As he passed through the opening, he saw there was an inscription above the doorway. It was in Latin and he recognised it as being from Virgil's *Aeneid*. It read *Procul, o procul este, profani* – 'Be gone, be gone you who are uninitiated'.

Swann made his way back to the boat, where Lady Harriet, Miss Jennings and Tom were waiting. The return journey across the lake was undertaken in silence. Once back on the other side, Swann requested to see where the teacher and pupil had slept. The girl, Grace, had been in a dormitory with seven other girls, and a quick glance at her possessions revealed nothing. There were a few textbooks, including one by Dr Borzacchini called *The Parisian Master or A New and Easy Method for Acquiring a Perfect Knowledge of the French Language in a Short Time*, but nothing which struck him as being relevant to her death. He smoothed his hand across the bed and then briefly knelt down and slipped his hand under the mattress. There he felt something. He brought it out. It was a book of poetry by Sappho, a name Swann vaguely remembered from his Classical literature studies during his own schooldays and from a work by his favourite author, John Donne. She was a poetess in ancient Greece who killed herself over a boatman, if he remembered correctly. Swann could recall little about her poetry though. He had no idea if the book was significant, but the fact Grace had chosen to hide it meant Swann swiftly seconded it about his person, before going across the corridor to where Miss Jennings and Lady Harriet waited outside Miss Leigh's room.

'Miss Leigh slept across the corridor as she was responsible for the wellbeing of the girls in this dormitory,' explained Miss Jennings.

The irony of her statement was not lost on Swann. Once in the room, there was again nothing which seemed to him as being significant. Several books on a shelf were duplicated with those from Grace's possessions, but these were Classical texts and to be expected. Swann spotted a book behind the others. He pushed a couple of volumes aside and pulled it out.

'Did Miss Leigh cover Sappho in her teaching?' asked Swann as he held up the book of poetry to show her.

'No,' Miss Jennings replied, 'that was definitely not on the curriculum.'

The rest of the room was an exemplar of neat and tidiness. A stack of papers lay on a small table; these were essays waiting to be marked Swann observed, as he briefly scanned through them. A bed, a wardrobe and a chair completed the room's furnishing. There was nothing to suggest anything sinister or out of the ordinary. She was there to do a job and for all intents and purposes, up to the point she disobeyed a school rule, murdered a pupil and then killed herself, she seemed the ideal teacher.

They walked down the stairs of the main building and out of the front entrance. It was twelve o'clock and the girls were coming out from their morning lessons. As Lady Harriet said her goodbyes to Miss Jennings, Swann noticed a girl standing at the top of the school steps. She was around the same age as the dead girl and stood watching intently, as if waiting for an opportunity to approach him. But then Elsa, the head girl, came along and appeared to chide her for staring; taking her by the arm and leading her away.

Swann and Lady Harriet got back into her carriage and departed. It had begun to rain heavily, but the protesters were still outside the gates as they left.

CHAPTER FOUR

'Elizabeth Singer was born in the Somerset town of Ilchester, in 1674, the eldest daughter of a dissenting minister. She began writing at the age of twelve and her work, consisting mainly of poetry and novels, is still popular today.'

Mary Gardiner sighed despondently, stood up from her writing table and went across to the bedroom window. Outside her Great Pulteney Street house the sky was a dark grey and rain pattered against the glass panes. The day was as dull as the words she had just read, written in her own handwriting, which began the booklet she was completing for Lady Harriet. It was to be one in a series her aunt was having published, which was to be entitled *Incredible Women Authors of Bygone Ages*, with each volume concentrating on a particular female writer. Mary had been allocated Elizabeth Singer Rowe; the 'Rowe' in her name having been added on marriage. The publication would consist of two parts; the first, a biographical 'sketch', as Lady Harriet had called it, detailing the writer's life, this being what Mary had recently completed, while the second would be a compilation of the subject's poems or prose pieces.

Mary had compiled the biographical section from numerous books, periodicals and unpublished papers her aunt

Harriet had lent her from her own library, located at her residence near Frome, and consisting as it did of seemingly every book printed on the subject of women's education and equality of rights with men. The collection was housed upon numerous huge bookcases which stood ceiling to floor around the room and among which were long out-of-print works, limited editions, first editions – some as old as two centuries – and stacks upon stacks of unpublished essays, articles, journals and diaries that were the envy of several universities and museums. It seemed every female writer who had anything worthwhile to say about their own sex and their position in life was represented, from Aphra Behn to Mary Wollstonecraft, Catharine Macaulay to Hannah More.

Mary had read the biography, she had written, for the third time before going to the window and overall was pleased with it; in so much as she felt justice had been done to the life she had to portray in prose. It seemed Elizabeth Singer Rowe had been, at least towards the end of her long life, a pious, religious woman, whose righteousness had subsequently been held up by certain clergy as an exemplary mode of living to be followed. Mary felt, however, that there had also been a more feminine, radical woman underneath this veneer and had tried to balance this in her profile. If there was a problem with the piece though, it was the opening paragraph. Having read it a number of times Mary felt it lacked the impact her subject required, perhaps even demanded. It was competent enough and would no doubt be satisfactory to the majority of readers, but it was not inspirational; so not reflecting the premise behind her aunt's series. She had been trying to rewrite the opening all morning and had yet to find her own inspiration. The weather did not look inviting, but she was now determined to venture out into it in the hope of gaining a different perspective on her writing.

The need to rewrite the manuscript's opening had clouded Mary's morning as completely as the ones in the sky. It was doubly frustrating as she had been really looking forward to the morning, ever since her brother had announced he would not be returning at ten for breakfast. It was not that she found Jack's company disagreeable; on the contrary, she very much enjoyed his companionship and their stimulating conversations – but when she was in the middle of an artistic endeavour, one which demanded complete concentration, the presence of another person, even if there was no dialogue between them, always lead to distraction. So when Jack announced he would not be returning to the house that morning she had looked ahead to several uninterrupted hours' work. She could now see though that to continue would be counter-productive and so, from the moment she made her decision to leave the house and walk the short distance to the entrance of her chosen destination – the nearby Sydney Vauxhall pleasure gardens – only twenty-five minutes had passed.

Throughout the eighteenth century, promenading had become popular in many towns and cities in England. From this fashionable pursuit of social walking the concept of pleasure gardens developed; either in the centre of these metropolises or, more often, on their outskirts. Here, an area of land would be set aside for the planting of tree-lined avenues or other agreeable vistas, so as to give a formal setting and framework for socialising. In Bath, this had originally taken place among the rows of trees in Orange Grove, in view of the Guildhall, and then later on land near the river.

The Sydney Vauxhall pleasure gardens had opened in 1795 and when Mary's father had retired to Bath eight years earlier and bought their house in Great Pulteney Street, she had been fortunate enough to arrive in time for the pleasure garden's inaugural gala and a visit by the Prince of Wales. The pleasure gardens of Sydney Vauxhall were like a familiar and beloved acquaintance to Mary. She had sought solace here after her father's death, more often than not in the company of her mother, but now alone, since she too had also passed away. When the family had all been together, they would spend countless afternoons strolling in the grounds and trying to find their way out of the labyrinth, which was one of the central features of the gardens. Mary smiled as she recalled her mother and herself hopelessly lost within the maze, only to hear the sound of laughter above and, looking up, seeing her father on the swing, which had been erected at the labyrinth's centre and whose occupant, it was advertised, could 'look down upon all the lost souls'. From his vantage point, he would then tell them where they were going wrong and attempt to guide them to the centre. They came here in all weathers, at least when it was open, and enjoyed all the seasons equally; each having its own atmosphere. It was now spring, and despite the gloominess of the day Mary could see clematis and honeysuckle beginning to bloom, finding the surface again after winter.

Her solitary figure had become a regular sight to the gardeners and groundkeepers, although Mary was not the only person to enjoy such walks. She had not been in the gardens long when her name was called from behind. She turned and saw a familiar face.

'Oh, Mary, it is you!'

'Jane, what a lovely surprise!'

Jane was around five years older than Mary and like her was unmarried. Unlike her, though, there was no fiancé in her life. In fact, Mary could not remember Jane ever talking about any romantic attachments in the three years she had known her. This did not concern her though, for although Mary did not see Jane often, each time they met she always came away feeling enlivened from their encounter.

'How is your mother?' Mary asked. 'I understand she has been unwell.'

'Yes, she has been quite ill. So much so we thought we were going to lose her. Mr Bowden, our apothecary, was of the same opinion, but she has shown great fortitude and has come through unscathed. She is so recovered, in fact, that she has written a humorous poem about the whole experience!'

'I am so glad to hear she is better. It must have been stressful for your father.'

Jane nodded.

'Father is not in the best of health either. He has taken to using a walking stick and finds, at times, even the journey to Mr Bowden's premises in Argyle Street to be tiring. Mother's illness has shaken him into activity, however. We have a few months left on the lease of our house, but father has decreed we are to leave the city for the seaside, at least as a temporary measure.'

'Oh, you are to leave Bath?' said Mary, surprised. 'When?'

'As soon as arrangements can be made, I believe. I will enjoy the sea air, but I admit I shall miss the city and its walks, in these gardens and in the countryside. I have come out today to take as much advantage of them as our time left in the city affords. I may even attempt a longer walk before we leave, although I do prefer a companion for those.'

'My brother and I are going to walk to Swainswick this Friday, if the weather is fine; we are to visit my mother's grave. You are most welcome to join us.'

'That would be most agreeable,' replied Jane, visibly excited. 'And I can pay our family's respects at the same time. Mother was very sad she could not attend the funeral, as we all were, being in Lyme Regis at the time. Can I enquire as to the way you intend to walk there?'

'We have not discussed the exact route yet.'

'Then may I propose we go through the village of Charlcombe on the way. It is a charming little place, with wonderful views.'

'That does sound wonderful. I am certain my brother will not mind which way we go.'

'Then it is set,' said Jane, smiling. 'Now, would you care to join me in a walk around the gardens, or shall we continue in our solitudes!'

'Together would be most agreeable,' replied Mary.

As they walked through the gardens they passed a board advertising the foods available for the public breakfast, which took place at the Sydney Hotel each day.

'I must confess,' said Mary, seeing the board, 'I am quite hungry. I did have breakfast but did not eat much of it, as I was occupied with a piece of writing.'

'I can appreciate that feeling,' replied Jane. 'I can miss several meals at a time when my prose is in full flow.'

'I did not know you wrote,' said Mary. 'Have you had anything published?'

'No. A manuscript was bought by a publisher last year. He even advertised the book as being for sale, but so far it has yet to see the light of day.'

'What is it about?' enquired Mary.

'Let us retire to a table for breakfast and I shall enlighten you.'

Once they had been seated, Jane continued. 'It concerns an unusual heroine who finds herself within a drama of her own making. The first part of the book is set in the city. I had the idea for it when I first visited Bath a few years ago. And what about your own writing, Mary?'

Mary told her companion about the booklet and how she was having trouble writing an inspirational opening paragraph.

'You must draw the reader in like an old friend,' said Jane, 'and whet their appetite for a story.'

'This is not a story,' said Mary, 'it is about someone's life.'

'Then you must make their life feel as though it is a story. In that way the words will come alive for the reader.'

'I will try. Thank you,' said Mary.

They finished their breakfast together and made their way back to the Sydney Hotel entrance. Outside the gardens they parted, Jane crossing the street to her house in Sydney Place, Mary carrying on up Great Pulteney Street. Whatever else the morning had been, she thought, it had reacquainted her with a friend and also given her a female companion for the walk to Swainswick on Friday. As much as she was endeared to her brother, the opportunity to have an extended conversation with another female, of similar age and intelligence, was something to relish and anticipate.

Mary arrived home and went upstairs to her bedroom. She took out her writing paper and began to rewrite the opening paragraph; the words flowing as if they had always been there but had simply been waiting for the chance to be set down. She sat back on her bed, read what she had written and felt deeply satisfied. It had been a productive morning after all.

For a moment she wondered what matter had kept Jack from returning home for breakfast, but she knew better than to enquire.

CHAPTER FIVE

'So what are your thoughts as to this unfortunate matter, Swann?' enquired Lady Harriet as they returned in her carriage to the city.

'From what I have observed, Lady Harriet, it seems to be murder in the case of the pupil, perpetrated by the teacher, followed by self-poisoning. But if this is the situation, I do not understand why you have engaged my services; unless, of course, there is information not yet disclosed to me.'

'In all likelihood, a murder and suicide is exactly what these two deaths are,' replied Lady Harriet. 'However, I cannot risk overlooking the possibility that more sinister forces are at work, especially given the situation the country is in at present.'

'What do you mean?'

'Now we are at war with France again, Napoleon Bonaparte will do anything to gain an upper hand, to secure an advantage.'

'I am lost, Lady Harriet. I do not understand how being at war with France can be connected to these two deaths.'

'What I am about to tell you must not go outside this carriage.'

Swann instinctively moved forward in his seat. 'You can be assured of my utmost discretion, Lady Harriet,' he said.

Lady Harriet seemed satisfied by this assurance.

'For a number of years, even during the period of the Amiens peace, both our government and the French have been involved in the drawing up of plans to gain victory against the other. Bonaparte's are variations on how to invade us, while our plans focus on his removal from power, the belief by our government being that it would be easier to win the war against France if Bonaparte, as the First Consul, was not in office.'

Swann was silent for a few moments, deep in thought. He then spoke.

'Well, given the fact that French troops are stationed on their own coast, and have been for several months, but are still led by Napoleon, it seems neither plan has yet been successful.'

'It is not through lack of fortitude on our part. We have, for instance, recently enlisted the help of several dissident French generals sympathetic to our cause. They have their own agenda, of course, that of restoring the monarchy, or else assuming power themselves, but one of them came close to assassinating the First Consul four years ago.'

'Cadoudal?'

Lady Harriet was surprised. 'We refer to him simply as Georges, but you know of him?'

'Only by reputation,' said Swann. 'French politician and military General turned assassin and rebel. As leader of the *Chouannerie* he organised a failed uprising against the First Republic. Arrested, he managed to escape and took refuge in England and has been waging his own war against Napoleon ever since; most famously, as you have mentioned, in the attempt on the First Consul's life in December 1800. I have no further information, but assumed he had returned to England.'

'You are right in your assumption,' replied Lady Harriet. She shook her head, remembering. 'They came so close in the Rue Sainte Nicaise, where the bomb was planted; if only Bonaparte's carriage had passed the cart two minutes later.'

'It is said that Napoleon was sleeping in his carriage and did not even wake when the explosion occurred.'

Lady Harriet nodded.

'If it had succeeded, our concerns would have been over. As for this current plan, it began last summer when several royal insurgents, including Georges, along with many of our own men, were secretly landed on the coast of France. Reinforcements were sent at the beginning of this year. The aim was for them to travel to Paris, where they would assemble to undertake the task of kidnapping the First Consul and so removing him from power. We expected surveillance by their police, but we believed luck would be with us this time. It seems, however, one of the insurgents disclosed the plan, most probably under torture, although we are not discounting the possibility of a double agent within our midst. Either way, one by one, all of the main protagonists have been arrested. Georges, as we have recently learnt, was arrested two weeks ago. The plan has failed.'

'And this is somehow related to the two deaths?' asked Swann.

'Possibly,' replied Lady Harriet.

'But how?'

'As soon as we learned of the first arrests, a second plan, using less distinguished personnel, was made ready. I cannot divulge details, only to say that it involves our agents travelling to France, this time assuming the cover of French families and hopefully drawing less attention to themselves.'

'Do I presume Miss Leigh and the girl were part of this plan?'

'No, only the girl; she was to leave yesterday afternoon to join her family and then travel to France in the next few days.'

'I find it hard to believe the French would go to so much trouble to kill a girl? And besides, how would they have known?'

'I share your opinion, Swann, but there are spies and informants everywhere; Bonaparte has a network of them operating throughout the country. Thankfully, through our own channels, we know many of them and several have now started to work for our own government. We even sent one of these agents to protect the girl at the school, while at the same time helping her to improve her spoken French and learn the culture.'

'So if you thought they may have been murdered, why did you allow their bodies to be taken off the island before I could observe the scene?'

'The longer they were allowed to remain there, the greater the possibility of word leaking out as to the truth, whatever that may be. Bringing the bodies to the chapel immediately and reporting it as an accident saves a lot of unnecessary complications.'

'What will be listed as the cause of death?'

'A *reliable* doctor was summoned and performed his duties accordingly.'

'Isn't that doing a disservice to the two victims and their families?'

'As I thought you would be aware by now, Swann, there are bigger issues at stake. This is why I have engaged your services.'

'If this is a matter of national security, may I enquire as to why you are not dealing with it yourself or assigning men from the Alien Office?'

'I have my reasons,' she said.

Swann glanced out of the carriage window and saw they were heading along the top of Lansdown.

'As I have said, Lady Harriet, if I do agree to this case then I have to be allowed to undertake it in my own way.'

Lady Harriet nodded.

'I would also like the answer to the following question. Where was the girl's "protector" when she was murdered?'

'According to his report, she climbed out of the dormitory window some time during the morning, as he stood outside her room. He then did not see her again until her body was discovered.'

'And you believe him?' asked Swann.

'I do not know what to believe, which is why I want you to find out exactly what happened.'

Swann nodded. 'It does seem slightly improbable he would have murdered the girl and then not left the grounds.'

'All I know is that our plan to remove Bonaparte has failed and will now give him the resolve to increase his preparations for invasion. He refers to the English Channel as "a ditch that can be leapt by the bold" and he is becoming bolder by the hour. We have reason to believe he is planning a three-pronged attack; from above, by sea, and subterranean.'

'A tunnel under the Channel? Could they achieve such a feat?'

'Our government believes it is possible.'

'And how would the invasion from the air occur?'

'We understand they would use hot-air balloons.'

The military's application of an activity previously undertaken for pleasure did not come as any great surprise to Swann.

'Bonaparte will not be able to move until May, of course,' continued Lady Harriet, 'as the currents and weather are against him until that time. The Admiralty has given its assurance that our navy is still unbeatable but nevertheless we have to be alert and watch his preparations. Especially as our domestic affairs are in a delicate state, what with the King ill again and the current Parliament seen as ineffective.'

'What is wrong with King George this time?'

'He was apparently inspecting his troops and caught a severe chill. But it is worse than that – his mind is not as it should be. He is apparently giving orders that make no sense. Whether the two deaths at the school are in anyway part of all these various states of affairs, I do not know, but I need to find out one way or another as I have to confess a personal interest. When news of these deaths becomes public knowledge, if it is seen as anything other than a tragic accident, Catherine's school may have to close down.'

'I will be honest, Lady Harriet, I feel there is information which is being kept from me and if I am not in possession of all the facts, I am not sure I can take this case.'

'Yes, there are things of which you have not been informed, Swann, but I cannot reveal them to you; all I can say is that there is more at stake than you can possibly realise. The entire future of the country's liberty is at stake and I have sworn to protect that at whatever cost. I am asking you as a personal favour to take this case.'

The carriage entered the city and headed towards the Guildhall, where Swann had requested to be taken.

'I will take the case, then,' said Swann.

'Thank you,' said Lady Harriet, gratefully. 'I shall arrange for you to go to Frome the day after tomorrow. Miss Leigh came from the town and she has a sister who still lives there. You will be taken to visit her by an acquaintance of mine, Mr Thomas Bunn. I want you to talk to this woman and find out what kind of person her sister was, who she was acquainted with and where her sympathies lay.'

Swann looked puzzled.

'I understand Miss Leigh spent some time abroad,' explained Lady Harriet. 'This can sometimes have an effect on one's patriotism, let us say. Before then, I have arranged with Catherine for you return to the school tomorrow, to talk to those who shared the dormitory with the deceased girl.'

'Could I not have questioned them today?'

'Catherine wished to prepare the girls, to allow them to take in the news; and besides, I believe you have another appointment, one to which you desired to attend at the earliest opportunity.'

The coach arrived outside the Guildhall's front entrance. Swann went to leave the coach, but Lady Harriet held his arm.

'Remember Swann, not a word of this matter to anyone, not even Mary. This could involve national security.'

Swann nodded and then stepped down onto the pavement. The sky had turned darker. His instinct told him there was something not right with this situation, but he had agreed to take the case as it would give him the opportunity to spend time with Lady Harriet and, if nothing else, allow him to find out about her connection with Lockhart.

As Lady Harriet's carriage drove off his attention turned to the steps in front of him, which lead up to the Guildhall and Fitzpatrick's chambers.

CHAPTER SIX

He placed the index finger of his left hand on the right side of his face and let it run down the length of the scarred tissue. It was now more than twenty years since he had received the wound to his cheek, from a searing-hot poker, and in that time it had come to define his life; no, more than that, it had *become* his life. If it had not happened he would never have been as close to Malone as he was, enjoying the benefits and protection that came with being second-in-command to one of the toughest crime bosses in London. He would never have become involved in the lucrative activities that provided him with more wealth than he could ever have imagined achieving if still on the streets. And he certainly would not have travelled to places like Dublin, Bristol and Bath, along with other towns and cities in England and Ireland connected with Malone's empire.

He thought back to *that* night, as he had done many times before. They had let themselves in with no trouble at all. An old, decrepit latch on a first-floor window at the back of the house had been their means of entry; with Malone's shoulders providing the platform he needed to prise open the window, the latch breaking apart as he did so. Once they were inside, the house was quiet, as if empty. But then they hadn't expected anyone, at least no one to fear. They had been told there would only be a near-deaf woman and young boy, whose resistance, had they been discovered, would have been of little trouble. Instead they had found a male servant who had taken it upon himself to defend the property. Having been surprised by this servant, the ensuing struggle had seen them both tumble into an adjoining room, in which, at the far end, was a glowing fire and a poker. At the memory of the agonising pain he had felt as the scorching metal seared the flesh on his cheek, he winced, even after all this time.

After entering the house Malone had gone straight upstairs, as agreed, while he had stayed on the first floor. He was looking for anything portable, valuable, saleable; the three elements that made any object worth taking. He was no expert in these matters, at least not then, but anything gold or silver would always be lifted. Depending on the property you could usually tell whether jewellery was real or imitation. This house was definitely the former and he had been able to fill his bag at least half-full before heading downstairs. The information they had received was correct, the owners were obviously rich and could afford the real thing. It was as he reached the bottom of the stairs things had gone wrong. As he turned the corner he knocked a table, which sent a small bronze statue falling to the ground. It was not damaged but had made a loud noise as it thudded onto the marble floor. He cursed under his breath and would have prepared for the worse, but given the nature of the occupants who were supposed to be in the house, he knew they could easily be overpowered. It was therefore a complete shock when a few moments later the male servant had come charging toward him and a struggle had ensued.

He and Malone had been sent out of the city by their gang leader as soon as the reward for their capture was announced. For this he would always be grateful, as their boss could easily have been another Jonathan Wild and betrayed them for the money. But then the crime boss looked on Malone as a son, and possibly even successor to his criminal empire, having taken him under his wing not long after he joined the gang.

The two of them passed through Bath in the middle of the night, on their way to Bristol. The journey took less than twelve hours and once at their destination, they waited at the docks to board the first ship that would take them across to Ireland; Malone's homeland. They had spent most of the fourteen months they were away in the country's capital, Dublin, except for two visits to County Wexford and the village where Malone had been born.

It was during his time in Ireland he had been converted to the 'cause'. Through Malone and the men they were in contact with he learnt about the history of the Irish people and their oppression by the English invaders. He had been told about centuries of dispossession, prejudice and persecution, how Protestantism was introduced into this Catholic country, and how lands belonging to Irish families were seized and given to the newly arrived English settlers. Malone's own family had been wealthy and owned land around County Wexford, but during his grandfather's time they had lost everything through legislation, which amounted to little more than theft. He had also learnt that this constant reduction of Irish land and their unsuccessful attempts to resist it merely allowed each failure to be used as an opportunity to confiscate even more; so much so it was believed that while a hundred years earlier Catholics owned two thirds of all cultivated land in Ireland, now it was just one twentieth.

And then there were the Penal Laws, introduced from 1703, which, he was told, discriminated so heavily against the Catholics it was feared the whole population would end up as beggars. Not only that, they were excluded from all public life, as well as engaging in any private activity. Catholic education was made illegal, as was the buying of land. If the Irish people were dispirited, they were certainly not defeated and it did not take long before numerous gangs of men roamed the countryside, under the cover of darkness, seeking retribution and revenge by destroying livestock and buildings held by settlers.

As soon as Malone was old enough he had joined one of these gangs and took part in ham-stringing cattle and burning haystacks and barns, along with levelling houses and firing shots through the windows of those buildings left standing.

A little more than a year after their departure from London, they received the news informing them they could go back. By now though, with passions ignited by thoughts of bringing about an independent Ireland once more, and supporting those who might achieve it, they made the journey changed men.

It did not take long for Malone to assume control of the gang on their return to England – murdering his former protector and 'father' with a sword brought swiftly across his throat – and subsequently start to send money from their activities across the water to the increasing number of Irishmen united in their desire for revolution. The intended rebellion had not succeeded six years earlier, in 1798, due mainly to the troops sent by Napoleon landing on the wrong coast of Ireland and thus not able to assist the Irish before their defeat at the hands of the English army; this failure ultimately leading to the Act of Union, in 1801, and abolishment of the Irish Parliament, so bringing the whole of the country under the subjection of the British.

It had not succeeded the year before either, in 1803, with the uprising led by Robert Emmett. But these defeats had only made Malone more determined and plans were already being put into action for the next attempt at insurrection; so determined was Malone, in fact, that he had ordered the murder of his own brother, whom he suspected of betraying the last uprising to the English government.

They had passed through Bath on their return from Ireland, back in 1785. It had been only a brief stay, a day and a night, but that was enough for Malone to realise the city could provide much in terms of funds and manpower for the cause – its population containing a large number of poor Irish immigrants – and perhaps act as a strategic base outside the capital, and prying governmental eyes, from which to operate. Not long after he had taken control of the gang in London, Malone had also 'taken over' as crime boss in Bath as well. He had then brought his brother over from Ireland, so as to run his 'interests' in Bath. Everything had gone as planned until the previous year. Thomas Malone seemed as loyal to the cause as anyone else, so why he had chosen to betray his fellow countrymen, his own *brother*, was a question which remained unanswered. He knew he could not ask Malone about it, either. As close as he felt to his boss, there were certain subjects he knew you did not raise in his company.

Malone did not seem affected by his brother's death, but he rarely showed emotion; it was what made him so dangerous. He had only once seen any kind of emotional response from Malone and that was while they were in Ireland. A member of the gang Malone had been connected with had reminded him of a 'carding' he had given a man against whom he had held a longstanding grudge. A smile had formed on Malone's face as details of the attack were vividly relayed. Malone had drawn a steel-tooth comb, the type used in the wool industry to prepare the yarn for spinning, across the face of his victim, lacerating the skin on both cheeks. He then sliced off a piece of the man's ear, before cutting his throat.

Somewhere in his mind, however, he could not believe Malone's brother Thomas had been an informant. He himself had been the connection between the brothers and on his trips to Bath had not witnessed any lessening of the desire for Irish independence from the younger Malone. And yet what the elder Malone ordered had to be obeyed and so he set up a meeting with Wicks, who, it became apparent, was the most suitable person to execute the murder and assume control of the top position. The fact he was English could be overcome, like it had with himself, and, after all, it seemed being Irish did not stop you from betraying your own countrymen.

Since taking over in Bath, Wicks had proved his worth to the cause; he had sent money from the blackmail scheme they had recently set up and had given haven to United Irishmen on the run from the English authorities.

Wicks had also informed him of the portrait of his present-day self which had been painted, and about the man who had commissioned it. This man, intent on tracking him and Malone, was the son of the servant they killed all those years ago, when he received his scar. When Wicks had first told him that there was a man asking questions, he had not taken much notice; he had covered his tracks sufficiently, he believed, and what with Malone's position, felt he was powerful enough to see off any reminders from his past. When the portrait had been completed the matter became more urgent. It was too accurate. Even with the artist now dead and the portrait destroyed, there were still images of him being shown around the city, or so he had been told. The easiest thing, of course, would be to have this man, who he now knew to be called Swann, eliminated, but for some unknown reason Malone would not allow it.

The Scarred Man looked out the carriage window and gazed back at the city he had just left. He had not long finished a meeting with Wicks and was on his way to Bristol, to talk with the Bath crime boss's counterpart there. The blackmail scheme they had begun in London was proving even more successful in Bath and Bristol; there seemed to be plenty of gentlemen in the two cities who wished to retain their reputations. He would come back through Bath in a few days, on his return to London, and would briefly meet with Wicks again. Everything seemed to be going well and he afforded himself a self-congratulatory smile; one which would not have been so forthcoming if he had known what was in store during the next few days.

CHAPTER SEVEN

Swann stood on the pavement outside Bath's Guildhall and looked at the steps in front of him. He thought back to his arrival the previous October and of seeing Tyler at the top of them, the petty criminal having just emerged a free man from the courtroom inside the building – courtesy of corrupt magistrate Kirby. Tyler had been his introduction to the murkier side of the city. He remembered how he had chased the criminal into the notorious Avon Street district after having witnessed him pickpocket Fitzpatrick and then again, later, after his failed assassination attempt of Swann. On this occasion, during a struggle down near the river, a fatal gunshot had been fired and Tyler's body had fallen into the water and been swept away downstream towards Bristol.

It was, of course, while following Tyler on a separate instance that he encountered the Scarred Man. As he often did, Swann thought about this man. What had happened in the years since the murder of Swann's father? Did the Scarred Man ever think about *that* night? Did the killing play on his conscience? And did the Scarred Man stay with Malone, his father's murderer, afterwards to engage in a life of crime? The answers to these questions, and the many others that had played on his mind over the years, would never be forthcoming until he came face-to-face with this man. And that, for now, remained the foremost reason for his being in Bath.

Lady Harriet's carriage was gone and Swann walked up the steps into the building. He entered and approached a clerk behind a large wooden desk. Swann was directed toward Fitzpatrick's chambers where, if the morning's court session had finished on time, the magistrate would be residing. Swann made his way along a corridor and knocked on Fitzpatrick's door.

'Swann, it is good to see you,' said the magistrate warmly as Swann entered the room. 'Is everything well with you?'

'Thank you, Fitzpatrick, although please accept my apologies that my previous appointment occupied me longer than expected. I am also sorry if my message was somewhat vague.'

'What message is this?'

'You were not informed I would be delayed but would call on you later?'

Fitzpatrick shook his head.

'Then I am profoundly sorry my friend, as I believed a message regarding my enforced lateness was to be relayed to you.'

'Do not worry,' replied Fitzpatrick. 'My duties in court this morning have also seen me delayed; in fact, I only arrived back in my chambers a few minutes ago and, as you can observe, I have yet to change out of my magisterial attire.'

This brought relief to Swann's guilt regarding his own lateness, but did not diminish his annoyance at his message having not been sent.

'So,' said Swann, returning his attention to Fitzpatrick, 'I understand there is a delicate matter you wish to discuss?'

'Yes, but I contend it is not a matter to confer about here. I suggest we return to my office.'

Swann nodded.

After Fitzpatrick had changed from his official robes, they left the Guildhall. It was always interesting to walk with the magistrate through the streets of Bath as he would, more often than not, be forthcoming with interesting facts about the city. This journey proved no different and as soon as they stepped outside of the municipal building, Fitzpatrick began to relate historical information.

'Did you know that at one time the city's Guildhall was over there,' said Fitzpatrick, pointing to the middle of the High Street. 'Just imagine the chaos that would ensue if traffic still had to manoeuvre around it today.'

As Swann looked across at the relevant spot: the constant stream of carriages, barouches and other horse-drawn vehicles gave validation to Fitzpatrick's image. Nearly thirty years before, when the new Guildhall had been completed, leaving the former to be demolished, the amount of vehicles using this main route into Bath from the London Road had been enough to necessitate the move. In the years since, the volume of traffic had increased exponentially to the point where the two men now found difficulty in crossing the street. Eventually, however, they succeeded and safely reached the far side; although not without an outburst of verbal obscenities from the driver of a curricle, whose progress had been momentarily impeded by this pair of troublesome pedestrians.

The pavements were likewise crowded as they made their way towards Fitzpatrick's office in Queen Square, but the journey was a pleasant enough one, especially with the magistrate as companion and tour guide. The route they walked took them past the site of the North Gate, which had been the entrance to the city for those travellers coming from the direction of the London Road but had been demolished half a century before, and then up the slight elevation to Upper Borough Walls. This thoroughfare boasted the largest remaining section of the medieval wall, complete with crenellations, which once surrounded the city, the rest of the wall having all but been dismantled through the 'rage for building' and expansion which had taken place since Queen Anne vested her presence at the beginning of the eighteenth century.

'In its time,' said Fitzpatrick, as they came parallel to the remains, 'the circuit of the city's medieval wall was one of the smallest in the country and it is said that it was built on its Roman predecessor. The Romans were attracted here for the same reason as the majority of today's visitors; the spa water. When they left though, the wall fell into disrepair until it was rebuilt in the Middle Ages.'

'It certainly looks impressive,' said Swann.

'When the wall was completed it stood twenty feet high and at its base it was ten feet wide. John Leland wrote about it, when he visited during his travels, as did Samuel Pepys.' The pride in Fitzpatrick's voice now assumed a sadder tone. 'Eventually though, the walls began to be pillaged for its stone or demolished by developers.'

This historical vandalism had begun in 1707, four years after Queen Anne's second visit, when clothier George Trymme had requested the demolishment of certain sections of the wall to facilitate his development of a new route into the city. Permission was granted by the Corporation – the body of men who ran the affairs of the city – apparently without difficulty, but then this was not surprising given Trymme was a prominent member of that particular organisation. Later in the century, a right of way through the walls was granted to assist speculative building, leading ultimately to the creation of several large through-roads, including Milsom Street in 1763, while further sections of the wall had been irretrievably lost when Westgate Buildings had been built, along with developments outside the original city boundaries.

The first of the main gates, which were the major entrances into the city, had been demolished in the mid-1750s, when the North and South Gates were pulled down by the Corporation to aid private developers; while the West Gate had been taken down later, during development of that particular section of the city.

The part of wall Swann and Fitzpatrick now passed had only survived through its location in Upper Borough Walls to a hospital opposite. After the building was opened, it had been decreed that land would be set aside for the burial of those patients who died there. This cemetery was located beyond the remaining section of wall, residing in the ground immediately below it, in what would then have been outside of the city. When expansion of the city took place throughout the eighteenth century, the cemetery and its adjoining wall were left untouched.

After they had turned the corner, out of sight from the wall, it was a relatively straight route to Fitzpatrick's office in Queen Square. On arriving at the building they entered, went up the flight of stairs and into Fitzpatrick's consulting room. Once there, both men sat down.

'As I mentioned,' said Fitzpatrick, as soon as they were seated, 'it is a delicate matter for which I must ask your service.'

'Then please tell me what it is and what I can do,' replied Swann.

'It is the nephew of an old acquaintance of mine. He has become the victim of blackmailers. He makes frequent visits to … well, perhaps I do not need to elaborate on the details at this moment; suffice to say he has engaged in activities that have left him open to criminal elements taking advantage for nefarious gain. Believe me Swann, I do not condone his behaviour, but I have been approached by this acquaintance to obtain your assistance in this matter. Your reputation has become well known to those wishing your services and I was able to vouch for your discretion in this matter. The nephew is apparently a rising star within the Tory Party and there is every possibility he will become a Member of Parliament in the near future. He has ambitions of a ministerial position in government and there are those who would see him achieve these ambitions as soon as possible.'

Swann nodded but said nothing for the moment.

'He is also married and has a young son. Any public airing of his indiscretions, therefore, would certainly lose him not only any political standing but the good name of his family. His father is very well known in certain circles.'

Swann nodded but still did not answer immediately, preferring instead to let his thoughts return to the blackmail cases he had investigated in the last few years, including the most recent one, which he had undertaken in London prior to arriving in Bath. It was always the same: someone, usually male and involved in politics, would indulge in activities that, as Fitzpatrick said, left them open to blackmail should they be discovered. They would then bemoan the fact when they became entrapped. It was a matter that Swann could do without at the moment, especially as he had now taken the case for Lady Harriet and also had the pursuit of the Scarred Man to occupy his time. As much as Fitzpatrick was a valued friend, and Swann really did not wish to refuse his request, his instinct told him if he took the case it would bring nothing but trouble.

'I value your friendship and would like to be able to assist your acquaintance's nephew, Fitzpatrick, but I must decline. There are two other investigations which require my attention and I do not believe there is anything I would be able to do to help. I am sorry.'

'I completely understand, Swann,' replied Fitzpatrick. 'Do not concern yourself any further over this matter.'

'To be honest,' said Swann, feeling he owed it to the magistrate to elaborate on the reasoning behind his decision, 'I have reached a point in my life where these types of cases are not something I wish any longer to consider. The last one of this nature, in fact, which I undertook for the Bow Street Runners in London, was a similar case and its outcome was most unfortunate. I believe there is nothing I can do to assist and so would rather say at this present time than to give hope where none exists. My only regret is that I have to disappoint you. You are a true friend, Henry. I was due to meet you this morning at eleven o'clock and yet did not arrive at your chambers until after midday. I am then informed you did not receive my message and yet not once have you enquired of me as to where I was or what I was doing.'

'I merely assumed if you could enlighten me you would have done so,' replied Fitzpatrick, 'and whatever it is, it is obviously important enough to postpone our meeting; something I know you would not have undertaken lightly.'

Swann smiled at his friend's affability, shook his hand warmly and then left the magistrate's office for the city bustle once more. Outside, Swann headed directly into the centre, walking along Wood Street and Milsom Street and then turning right to make his way down towards Bath Abbey courtyard, with its mixture of wonderful flagstones; a combination of local Pennant Sandstone and Caithness, from the far north of Scotland. There were a number of facts he wanted to verify concerning his chapter on the abbey, and this ensured his walk through the heaving crowds of shoppers was a brisk one.

The sun, at last unencumbered by cloud, brought with it a heat to the early part of the afternoon and as he made his way towards the abbey and felt the warmth on the back of his neck, Swann felt strangely content.

CHAPTER EIGHT

Despite the death of the leader of their group, along with one of its members, the girls assembled at the appointed time and place. They had each received handwritten confirmation during the day, in the form of notes surreptitiously placed inside their textbooks, stating that the evening's gathering was to take place as arranged. As they came together in the corridor outside the school library, there was a curiosity as to how this would actually happen given the absence of their leader, along with a need to share their collective but as yet unspoken grief over their loss.

As the library clock began to chime the hour, a realisation spread throughout the girls that there were only seven of them, meaning that another girl, in addition to the one who had died, was missing. This was Elsa, the head girl who, at nineteen and a half, was the eldest of the group. There was nothing that could be done about her non-appearance though and so they made their way into the library and across its floor toward the secret doorway, located behind one of the many bookcases. As preordained, the girls went through the gap, one by one, before the chimes finished and descended a stone staircase into semi-darkness; the last girl through having pulled a handle attached to the rear of the bookcase to close it behind them. On reaching the bottom of the steps, a passage stretched out before them into complete darkness.

Each of them carried with her a ceremonial candle, which remained unlit, while the front girl carried an additional lit one, the glow from which guided the rest as they made their way along the passage. When they reached a certain point in the passageway, a second light, further off in the distance, could be seen. They continued towards it, cautiously at times, over the uneven flagstone floor, their bodies reacting with goose bumps to the damp air and earthen walls; the thin material of their nightdresses inadequate for keeping the occupants warm.

The girls approached the second light, which emanated from inside a chamber at the end of the passageway. They passed through the wooden arched entrance in single file, and once inside lit their ceremonial candles from one of the many already there and that had been responsible for the distant light. The girls then took their allotted places in the circle of stone seats surrounding a large oblong-shaped altar, as they had done so on several occasions before, and placed their lighted candles in holders next to each seat. If their actions had been performed almost by rote, automatic and devoid of any true emotional input, now that the girls were seated the remaining empty seats became a stark, visual reminder of the events of the last thirty-six hours; the loss of Miss Leigh, their favourite teacher and leader, along with their friend, Grace, and more recently the mystery of Elsa, who had inexplicably failed to appear for the meeting. Had the head girl found her grief too much to bear and decided not to come, or had something tragic also happened to her? As they sat there in their thoughts, it suddenly dawned on them that if Miss Leigh was gone, who had summoned them here? They did not have long to wait for the answer. From behind a curtain which partitioned an annex room, a figure wearing a violet cloak and gold encrusted domino mask emerged. In spite of the mask, which covered the top half of her face, the girls knew her identity immediately.

'What are you doing?' exclaimed one of them.

'I have assumed the Circle's leadership,' said Elsa, as she sat down in the place normally reserved for their teacher. 'It is what Miss Leigh would have wanted.'

'How do you know that?' replied another girl.

'Because if it were not so, why would she have given me this for safekeeping?'

As Elsa held up a large golden key, candlelight reflected along its entire length. There were audible gasps but silence quickly followed.

'With my elevated position,' said the head girl and now group leader, 'there are now *two* empty places in the Circle to be filled in order to make it complete again. We will begin this evening with the initiation ceremonies. The first of our new members has already undergone the cleansing ritual, it therefore just remains for you all to acknowledge her as a fellow muse.' As Elsa said this, a girl stepped out from behind the curtain. The group immediately recognised Gretchen, the head girl's closest companion in the school.

A murmur went around the circle. 'By what authority is she here?' one asked.

'By mine,' replied Elsa. 'As leader, I alone have the power to invite neophytes to the Circle and oversee their initiation. I have therefore decreed it that Gretchen takes my place within the nine. She will assume the role of Melpomene. You will all acknowledge her as such and receive her as one of your number.'

Reluctantly the girls responded in unison: 'We acknowledge you, Melpomene, revered muse of tragedy, and receive you into this Circle of Sappho. Keep our secrets close to your heart and your way will be joyous and light, but speak of them outside the Circle and your way will be dark and filled with torment.'

Elsa smiled. 'Good. Before Melpomene takes her seat amongst you, we have to initiate and receive Erato.' At this the head girl nodded to her companion, who immediately went back behind the curtain. She returned a few moments later with another girl, which again the seated girls instantly recognised; that of Anne, who had been the best friend of Grace, the previous Erato.

'I have prepared her for initiation,' said Elsa, 'which we shall undertake here, before performing our main ceremony outside.'

Gretchen brought Anne forward, within the circle of seated girls, disrobed her and laid her naked, on her back, upon the oblong stone altar.

'Begin the initiation,' said Elsa, standing up.

As the seated girls watched in silence, Gretchen brought a bowl from a nearby table and set it down on a metal stand by the stone altar. She cupped her hands and scooped out some of the mixture in the bowl and applied it to the front of Anne's body. Elsa's expression was one of delight as she observed her companion spread the oil first onto the girl's naval, and then her shoulders, legs, thighs and arms. She then began rubbing the oil onto the breasts and *mons pubis*, which earlier had been shaved of its hair by Elsa in preparation for the ceremony.

Each of the seated girls had undergone the cleansing ritual on joining the Circle and each had undergone it within full view of the others. There was a provision for it to be under-taken without the gathering, where it would be carried out by the leader alone, and on her sanction, but Gretchen's exemption was only the second time it had occurred in the group's history. The Circle itself consisted of nine pupils – a trio of girls from each of the final three years of the school – deliberately equivalent to the number of muses in Classical Greece. On becoming part of the Circle an initiate would take on, or rather become, the essence of a specific muse chosen by the group's leader; herself being the essence of Sappho, the famous Greek poetess who was known from antiquity as the 'Tenth Muse'.

With the ritual cleansing part of the initiation ceremony now completed, Anne was brought down from the altar, her robe put back on, and led a few steps forward to the spot where she was to be acknowledged. After a prompt from their leader, the group, again in unison, acknowledged and received Anne, who as Erato represented the muse of erotic and lyrical poetry. The Circle was once again complete.

With the initiations concluded, Elsa donned the hood of her cloak and went towards another curtained entrance. Here she drew back the large crimson-red material to reveal a large sturdy wooden door. She placed the golden key into the lock and turned it. Once opened, she led the way through into another passageway. She took a lit torch from its fastening on the wall and proceeded in the direction of another set of stone steps in the distance. Gretchen followed her, carrying various accoutrements, and then the rest of the girls followed behind, with a couple of them helping Anne negotiate the flagstone floor which continued in this passage too, as her eyes were glazed and her walking unsteady. On reaching the far end of this passageway, the procession climbed up the steps and stopped at the large stone at the top. Gretchen, along with the two others from the final year, put their bodies against it and, without too much effort, pushed it aside, revealing the island temple bathed in light from the full moon.

Once outside the temple, the Latin inscription above the entrance having been adhered to, the group turned right and made their way through the trees, along a trail to a clearing. Here, another circle of stones acted as seating, while in the middle was another, much larger, altar. The sky held patches of cloud but the moon was not obscured, as it fully bathed the clearing in its silver glow. Although well lit, the spot was out of sight of the school and grounds, across the lake, as had always been the intention of its original builder.

The nine 'muses' sat down on the circled stones, while their leader moved into its middle and stood by the altar. The items brought by Gretchen and the others had been left on a wooden table beside the altar and Elsa began making preparations for the ceremony that was about to be conducted. She picked up a container and took off its top. She poured its contents into several small wooden cups and then handed them around. She kept a cup for herself and, holding it up, tipped some of the liquid onto the altar. After this libation, she began an incantation.

'Oh, goddess Aphrodite, we honour you in the name of Sappho. Look down on us tonight, this night of the full moon, and see us for who we are – your devoted servants, made flesh to perform acts to venerate your honour and take part in devotional recreations that bring glory to your name. We ask you in all your wisdom and reverence to accept our latest additions to our Circle and thus return our number to its whole.'

Elsa tipped a little more of her cup's contents onto the altar and then drank the remainder. She turned to observe the Circle, as each girl mirrored her actions. Once this had been completed, honey cakes were placed on the altar and burnt; the sweetly scented smoke permeating the air, rising upwards towards the goddess. The liquid the girls had drunk now began to make them feel woozy and light-headed, yet at the same time, liberated. It was not an unpleasant feeling and any earlier anxiety or fears they may have had disappeared with the smoke.

At each gathering, it was tradition that one of the 'muses' gave a performance appropriate to the discipline she represented. Tonight it was the turn of 'Terpsichore' – the muse of dance – and after more incantations had been uttered, the girl stood up. Instruments which had been brought were now played; a slow, rhythmic and melodious refrain started proceedings, to which Terpsichore began to dance in time, her movements both fluid and natural. As the music's tempo increased, so did her movements, until the point where the music and dance became as one, interchangeable as the dancer began to sing Sapphic poems while she danced. The musicians, along with the rest of the girls, now joined in, dancing wildly as they played. The performance had reached such an intoxicating state that the girls shed their night-dresses so as to feel the empowering moonlight fully on their pale-white and exposed skin and to experience completely the liberation from dancing naked in the open air.

While the scenes of wild abandon continued, Elsa, who had remained with her cloak covering her body throughout the whole ceremony, moved forward and taking Anne by the arm, manoeuvred her across to the altar and then up onto it, on her back, once more. Elsa let her cloak slip onto the ground and now, also naked, climbed onto the altar and then on top of Anne. She began to move her body up and down the other girl. As the movement became ever more rapid, Elsa began another invocation.

'Oh, Aphrodite, we honour you in the name of Sappho, the high priestess of love, poetess of the senses, seducer of the innocent; by engaging in the veneration of the flesh, I call on you, oh Goddess of love, beauty and sexuality, to witness this act in your name and that through the coming together of these two bodies, in physical union, we pay the ultimate tribute to you.'

As Elsa's movements became ever more rapid her feet began to push Anne's legs apart. The supine girl did not offer any resistance as she lay entranced and motionless, as she had been throughout the evening. The girl on top of her, however, had begun to thrust her body back and forth and on one of these movements, Anne's body jerked and she let out a moan, as if entered.

'We pay tribute to you, Sappho,' exclaimed Elsa, as she continued thrusting, 'and your tradition of physical love between women.'

One of the other girls stopped dancing and looked over to the altar. Shocked by what she now saw, she stormed angrily across towards it.

'What you are doing is not part of the ceremony,' she shouted. 'You are making a mockery of our sacred meetings.'

Before she could reach the altar, Gretchen stepped in her way and grabbed her. The girls wrestled with each other momentarily before a blow to the face from Gretchen sent the objecting girl to the ground. The other girls stopped to watch, equally horrified at what they were witnessing. By now Elsa was cloaked again and stood by the altar. She looked contemptuously at the assembled girls.

'Do not look so appalled,' she said. 'You are all my *hetaira* and I will say what happens or not within this Circle. And if any of you do not like it, or thinks they might tell someone about our meetings, I suggest you do not, as the consequences will be too terrible to comprehend. Miss Leigh was naïve in her ways, as there is so much more we can achieve through these gatherings.'

The girls stood in a huddle, confused and in shock. All they knew was that the Circle of Sappho had now been broken and would never be the same again.

CHAPTER NINE

For as long as Bridges could remember, George had possessed an eye for the women. He trusted his companion with his life, but not with any female he was friendly with. They had grown up roaming the streets together, although he did not know how long ago this was. He remembered though when George came to live with him. It was the year they built the row of houses opposite where Mr Swann was shot at by the man in the carriage. As young boys they watched as the walls slowly rose up and earned a little money by doing small jobs for the workers, as well as warning them when their boss was coming so they could stop playing cards and get back to work.

It was the day the builders had added the windows to the houses that George had found his mother dead. He returned home and there she was, sitting in her chair as though asleep. With no father, brothers or sisters to look after him, he ended up on the streets, sleeping wherever he could find.

When Bridges told his own mother about George, his family had taken him in. It was hard to feed another mouth at first, but after a short while George paid his way. George always protected Bridges as they grew up and they developed a language between the pair of them, even before Bridges' mother taught George to 'finger-speak'; Bridges' father was also deaf and so his mother had learnt how to communicate with him. She had taught her son as well. Bridges' vocal chords were intact, or so she once told him, as he could laugh and make noises, but as he could not hear language being spoken, he had no idea how to pronounce it. Bridges and George still used their 'secret' language when they did not want anyone knowing what they were saying; this was usually when they found themselves in a spot of trouble.

There was an older brother in the family but he had died. All Bridges could remember was that it had been sunny the day he last saw him. Bridges was down by the river, with George, when his brother came along and gave him a wooden knife he had just made. That was the last time Bridges saw him. It later became common knowledge that he had been killed by a local gang and his body thrown into the river, but even though he and George looked, they had never found any sign of it.

George had taken over as his protector full time, but it did not take long for Bridges to toughen up himself and together they became a match for the other children who tried to intimidate them. Looking back, it was always like that; George and Bridges against everyone else.

They had become thief-takers because of a magistrate. They had grabbed a man and held onto him as he came out of a building, after someone had shouted for them to do so. The gentleman who shouted, and whose house had been broken into, turned out to be the magistrate. He asked them if they wanted to become thief-takers. They were not quite sure what this entailed, but when he told them how much money they could make they said yes straight away. They soon began to get a reputation as a couple of hard men and on several occasions were asked to join one gang or another; but they always preferred to work alone.

Although they had earned good money, their financial situation had still been tough until Mr Swann arrived the previous year. Before his arrival, they had only been paid when they caught someone. Mr Swann, however, paid them regularly, whether they were successful or not. They had learned from the time they were children not to trust people with lots of money, but there was something different about Mr Swann, something they had both acknowledged from the moment they had seen him in the Duke of York asking about Wicks.

They were now in the Fountain Inn, waiting to meet Mr Swann and they had information which was sure to please him. It was the previous evening when the man Swann was asking about had been seen by the stallholder. The man was with Wicks. They were going into the Duke of York when the stallholder had noticed them. He had been certain it was him, but even more so after being shown the portrait they had been given by Mr Swann. Hopefully this information would put Mr Swann in a generous mood and they would get a little extra money. Everything was going well for them, Bridges thought, it was just a shame his thoughts were so troubled.

'The 'trouble' was a woman called Rosie, or rather the situation she now found herself in. Bridges had met her one evening at the Fountain; she had been with a group of women while he had been alone, as George was off in another part of town with a married woman. One of the women in the group could finger-speak, although not deaf herself, and she had 'spoken' for him when it became obvious he and Rosie had eyes for each other. The woman had also accompanied them the first few times they had gone out together – George had made up a foursome although lost interest after the second outing – but they had been on their own after that, as Rosie had learnt enough to finger-speak with Bridges.

Rosie lived in nearby Peter Street, although her landlord now wanted her out and had recently increased the rent several times, to the point where she could no longer afford to pay it. Bridges had given her what money he could and, added to her wages from her job at the factory, it had been enough for a while. However, with the latest increase it was no longer enough. Bridges had gone to confront the landlord but the meeting developed into a fight, resulting in Bridges' black eye. The landlord now told Rosie she had to leave by the end of the week or she would be forcibly removed. That was in five days' time.

When Bridges told George about it, he had refused to help. Rosie had met with Mr Swann to tell him about knowing Thomas Malone back in Ireland and, later that evening, after Mr Swann had left, George had made a crude pass at Rosie while Bridges was out the back of the inn. On his return he found George gone, his lifelong friend bearing a grudge against Rosie, to the point that he would not even discuss Bridges' suggestion of letting her stay with them until she found somewhere else. Rosie was making the best of it. She had laughingly told Bridges she would pawn her most treasured possession, a beloved violin – which she had had in her possession since childhood – and buy a mansion, but Bridges was worried for her and did not know what to do. He only hoped something would turn up and that it would be soon.

CHAPTER TEN

After Swann had finished at the abbey, he had returned to the house in Great Pulteney Street and had spent the next couple of hours checking his manuscript to make sure the information he had verified was correct. Once finished, he had left and headed towards the Avon Street district. He was to meet George and Bridges later that evening, but first had to change into a disguise.

When Swann had engaged the artist to create a portrait of the Scarred Man the previous autumn, he had inadvertently led Wicks straight to him. He had even been followed once when he was in disguise, or so he believed, and had therefore decided to take more precautions.

The warehouse Swann had subsequently rented for his more covert activities was in the Avon Street district, near the river. Its rear entrance was located at the end of several long and narrow passageways; ideal for observing if anyone was following behind. It was also ideal for keeping his promise to Mary of not bringing his 'work' home. Once at the warehouse he would choose a disguise; the space that the large building afforded meant he could keep a complete wardrobe of clothes, make-up, wigs and other assorted items there, much more than he would have been able to do at either the house in Great Pulteney Street or his consulting rooms at No.40 Gay Street. Once changed, he would then simply leave via one of the passageways and quickly lose himself among the throng of people always around in the area. From there he would be free to continue on to his destination, which tonight entailed meeting the pair of thief-takers, George and Bridges, at the Fountain Inn.

Swann sat at the writing desk he had set up in the library of the house in Great Pulteney Street. Light from the full moon came shining through the nearby window and he had no need of a candle to be able to see. He opened a bottle of '98 Lafite, poured himself a glass of the red wine and began to write his journal. He always tried to write an entry each day, recollecting his thoughts and any main developments in the cases he was working on.

He had not long arrived back from his meeting with George and Bridges, but the events of the whole day now invaded his mind, all wishing to be recorded as he opened his journal to the last entry and began to write.

Bath, Monday 26th March, 1804

Am I forever to be cursed to live my present life entwined with the ghosts of past ones? The day has presented a number of surprises and, at the same time, memories of an earlier existence have been resurrected and brought to consciousness once more.

The book Miss Jennings mentioned was so familiar to me, even after all this time, it was all I could do to stop myself calling out my beloved's name; that sweet sound I used to savour each time it emanated from my lips. But then why should it not be so, 'The Adventures of Telemachus' was her favourite work of literature and she used to read it to me when we were together to try and convert me to become one of its many admirers.

But I must stop there, for if I continue down this path of recollection I shall find the way too painful to bear. I know one day that I shall record it within these pages and spare no agonising detail, but now is not the time; there are other matters from the past that call for my attention.

The Scarred Man represents my life's work, or rather the work I have dedicated my life to; that of bringing those who killed my father to justice. I was perhaps one step closer to realising it for a while today. The confirmation of his presence in Bath, by George and Bridges at our meeting this evening, was swiftly made obsolete by the further news, delivered by the landlord of the Fountain Inn, that the Scarred Man had left the city that morning. My instinct in the White Hart, to search the streets to find him, was therefore correct. I may well have sighted him if I had done so, but now he is gone from my grasp once more.

One positive aspect to this episode is that I realise I felt his presence while in the city. The feeling that he was near came on late yesterday afternoon and was similar to when I encountered Malone at the fair all those years ago.

As disappointed as I am at this turn of events, I am not wholly downhearted for two good reasons. First, this sensing of him means I may now know when he is in close proximity and I intend, therefore, to follow my instincts next time. And second, I fully believe this will be sometime soon. Why am I so certain? Given that Thomas Malone was Wicks' predecessor in the city, and a connection has now been established between the Scarred Man and the two of them, it can be assumed there exists an association between the criminal element in Bath and that of London. And given the Scarred Man's former link with Thomas Malone, it can only be assumed he also has a connection with his brother, even after all these years. Also, on leaving the city, he headed out on the Bristol

Road, not the London Road, which means he may surely pass through Bath on his return to the capital.

Why Thomas Malone was murdered remains a mystery. Since being in Bath I have learnt that Wicks was responsible for the killing, but why did he perpetrate it? Probably to assume control of the city by usurping Malone; but did Wicks know of his connection to the London underworld (and who he was related to) when he killed him? What is strange is that the London connection seemed unconcerned by the murder, and merely continued with Wicks in charge as they had done previously with Malone's brother; business as usual. But this does not ring true in my mind and I believe that Wicks knew exactly who Thomas Malone was associated with in London and, likewise, that his brother knew exactly what was going to happen in Bath and did not stand in the way. Whether the London Malone ordered his own brother's death or merely allowed it to take place, the question remains as to what Thomas Malone had done to warrant his murder.

If it were not for the case I have undertaken for Lady Harriet, I would leave for Bristol this very moment and search the streets until I found him. But where would I even begin to look? As well as I may believe that I know the intricacies of Bath's criminal world and its streets, passages and alleyways, it would be like starting again in Bristol. I could send George and Bridges there again, but to what end? What could they find out in that city which could not be gathered in this one. Given the Scarred Man was heading in the direction of Bristol, it can be assumed, perhaps, that this city is also part of Malone's criminal web. I am certain that the Scarred Man will come back through Bath on his return to London, whenever that is, and this is my best chance of coming face-to-face with him. Failing that, I need to find out as much as I can about Wicks' operation in Bath and its connection to London. I will find George and Bridges tomorrow and ask them to make enquires and ascertain if any disgruntled members of Wicks' gang are willing to disclose the information I require.

In the meantime, I will attempt to solve the case undertaken for Lady Harriet, although the more I think about it the more I fail to understand why she requires my services at all, given her connection with the government's network of secret agents.

I cannot believe the conspiracy angle Lady Harriet mentioned though; that of Napoleon, through his secret network, having killed the girl and her teacher. If there is a murderer, then I believe either he or she to reside within the school grounds. I intend to learn more when I return there tomorrow.

At least I am not involved in Fitzpatrick's blackmail case. As much as I am sorry to disappoint my friend, it is one problem I am pleased not to have to concern myself with.

While I have been writing this entry one thought has come to mind: is it more than coincidence I was otherwise engaged with this potentially nonsensical case for Lady Harriet while the Scarred Man was in the city? Only time will tell.

CHAPTER ELEVEN

Early on Tuesday morning Swann hired a chaise and drove out to the school at Grove Park, where the deaths had taken place two days previously. The morning was dry and a slight breeze added to the pleasantness of the journey. The lone horse, harnessed to the chaise, made fair speed as it trotted up one of the northern hills out of the city and onto the flat expanse that was Lansdown.

The main building, Grove House, named after its original owner and where the majority of classrooms and dormitories of the school were now located, had been built in the late fourteenth century. It had once stood in the middle of grounds twice as large as they were today, but even so, the land that still surrounded it was generous. The estate had remained in the Grove family for one hundred and fifty years before being sold to a wealthy, self-made gentleman, who it was said had acquired his fortune by mysterious means. The new owner immediately set about altering the estate to his own design. He enlarged the gardens, covered the grounds with Classical statues and dammed the main stream that ran through the estate, so creating an island surrounded by a lake. Meanwhile, inside the main house, it was rumoured that major alterations had been undertaken in great secrecy.

False panelling and underground tunnels were said to have been installed, but these were, for the most part, merely the idle musings of the local clientele who frequented the nearby inn.

It was also suggested that all this work, both internal and external, had been for the mistress of the house, who held clandestine meetings with her female friends and where obscene rituals were performed naked. Whether this was true or not, nobody knew for certain. But what was known, however, was that after she died her husband abandoned the estate and moved abroad. The house and grounds was auctioned off in lots, with the main buildings and immediate land bought by an anonymous bidder. This person had subsequently become the main benefactor of the school that Miss Jennings opened.

Swann arrived at the gates to Grove Park and immediately noticed the absence of the protestors, which may have been, he surmised, due to the early hour. On being announced, he spoke briefly to Miss Jennings, who had arranged for him to interview the girls who had shared a dormitory with the dead girl. Before this, however, he requested permission to speak to Mr Bolton – the girl's 'protector' and temporary French master. Miss Jennings agreed and said she would assemble the first girl in thirty minutes' time, in her office. Swann thanked her and left.

Swann found John Bolton outside, standing on the lawn near the house. The other man was obviously expecting Swann as he did not seem surprised when he came up beside him. Swann was not sure whether the man knew the truth of the incident, whether Lady Harriet had enlightened him, or if he was still under the impression the two women had been killed in a boating accident. He therefore kept his questioning vague enough not to reveal the true circumstances if Bolton was unaware.

'I would like to ask you to describe to me your movements yesterday morning,' said Swann. And then, almost as an afterthought, added: 'Your name seems a familiar one to me, have we met before?'

'Not that I am aware,' replied the other man. 'As for my movements yesterday, I have told everything to Lady Montague.'

'Well,' said Swann with more than a little annoyance in his tone, 'I am asking you to repeat it for me, as my services have been engaged to discover exactly how the girl you were meant to be protecting came to be killed.' This seemed to convince the man and once he had cleared his throat, he began to speak.

'After the early meal and when the others had left for church, I accompanied Miss Templeton to the dormitory. She said she wished to complete the packing of her clothes.'

'And what happened when you reached the dormitory?'

'She went inside, while I remained outside.'

'Is this what normally happened?'

'This type of occurrence rarely arose, but yes; especially as there were no other doors in the dormitory.

'Then what happened?'

'I stood outside the dormitory for about ten minutes, maybe fifteen, as there was no hurry for her to be ready, because the carriage hired to take her home was not due for around two hours. After that I knocked on the door to check on her, but there was no reply.'

'Why did you knock then, when you said there was no need for expedience?'

'I cannot say for certain. Only, perhaps, that there was no sound from the room, which one might expect if a person is gathering their belongings together.'

'And then what did you do?'

'I knocked on the door again, but Miss Templeton still did not reply. This time I opened the door, or rather pushed it open, as a chair had been leant against the back of it.'

'Miss Templeton had not locked the door?'

'No. There is a rule in the school that there are no locks on the girls' rooms.'

'What did you see when you entered the dormitory?'

'It was empty. Miss Templeton's trunk was next to her bed, but she was not in the room. I walked over to one of the windows that faces the lake and found the latch undone and the frame slightly open.'

'Was it that window there,' asked Swann, pointing up at the building.

Bolton nodded. As he looked up his expression changed to one of surprise; a small balustrade ran along the building wall underneath the window, and from where the ground could be easily reached or another floor accessed. Swann noted Bolton's reaction.

'It seems you were unaware of the balustrade as a means of exit, or entrance?' said Swann.

It was obvious from Bolton's expression this had been the case.

'And then what did you do?'

'I came down the main staircase and out into the grounds to search for her,' replied Bolton.

'You searched for her on your own?'

'For a while I was aided by the gardener, but yes, for the majority of the time I searched alone.'

'So why do you think Miss Templeton left the dormitory without you?'

'I have no idea,' said Bolton.

'And where were you when her body was found?'

'I was with the coachman, who had by now arrived to collect Miss Templeton.'

'Thank you, Mr Bolton, those are all the questions I wish to ask for now.'

Despite his story, John Bolton was a key suspect. On his own admission there was no one else with him for most of the time Grace was 'missing', though one aspect in his favour was that he was still here at the school. If he had killed Grace, along with Miss Leigh, then surely he would have left the scene of the crime as quickly as possible?

These thoughts would have to wait, however, as Swann still had the girls to talk to, along with the gardener, Tom. He thanked Bolton for his assistance then headed into the main house and Catherine Jennings' office on the first floor.

Seven girls had shared the dormitory with Grace, but by the time Swann began to question the fourth of them, a pattern had emerged. It was not that they were deliberately colluding with their uniform answers, but rather, Swann surmised, they did not have much to say; especially as they were still under the assumption both their classmate and teacher had met their demise as a result of an accident. It became apparent, however, that Grace and Miss Leigh had been very much liked by all in the school and nothing unusual had happened in the time leading up to the tragedy.

The fifth interviewee was a girl called Anne. She had been, according to Miss Jennings, Grace's best friend, but her monosyllabic responses and vacant expression shed no real light on their relationship or gave any insight into what may have happened that morning. She was either ill, or had taken a substance, possibly for her grief, that had left her less than lucid.

Swann finished his questioning and Anne stood up to leave. As she did so she tripped and stumbled forward into him. He helped her stand upright again and she was then escorted from the room by Elsa, the head girl, who was sitting in on the interviews at Miss Jennings's request, given how upset they all were over the deaths.

By the time Swann had finished the interviews he was feeling quite frustrated and hoped Tom would be more forthcoming in his answers; he knew the truth surrounding the deaths and had actually been the one to discover the bodies. As he approached Tom's thatched cottage, Swann saw the middle-aged gardener bent over a flower bed near the doorway. Standing to greet him, Swann saw that he was around the same height as him, but the years of garden work had curved his back and he walked with a stoop.

Once the formalities had been dispensed with, Swann asked Tom to repeat the story he had briefly recounted the previous day. Swann claimed that he did not remember all the details, as he had not written them down, but it was a device to get suspects – and Tom had to be considered one – to repeat their 'story' so that any discrepancies could be investigated.

'Do you mind if we sit down,' said Tom. 'My back is a little sore.'

Swann nodded in agreement and the gardener briefly went into his cottage and brought out two wooden chairs. Once the men were seated Tom began to talk.

'On Sunday morning Miss Jennings had told me Miss Templeton would be leaving that afternoon and so I might see her about the grounds.'

'And did you see her in the grounds during the morning?'

'No, I didn't. The first time I saw her that day was when I found her body.'

'I understand,' said Swann. 'Did you see anyone else in the grounds or did anything strange or out of the ordinary happen?'

'I saw that gentleman who is staying here.'

'Mr Bolton?'

Tom nodded. 'He wanted to know if I had seen Miss Templeton, which I had not, and then asked if I would help him look for her. I did so for a while, but then went back to my bed of sweet peas. They have to be planted in late March or...'

'Is it that bed there?' interrupted Swann, pointing in the direction of a newly turned flower bed.

'Yes, that's it.'

'And you were working on that bed all morning.'

'The majority of it, I suppose.'

Swann noted that from Tom's cottage he could see straight across the lake to the island.

'But you did not see either Miss Leigh or Miss Templeton row across the lake?'

Tom shook his head.

'Where is the boat normally moored, when it is on this side?'

'Over there,' replied Tom, gesturing towards the water, 'behind those bushes.'

It was the same spot where Swann had stepped into it himself the day before, to be taken across to the island.

'At exactly what time did Mr Bolton approach you to help him search for Miss Templeton?'

'I couldn't say, but I know it must have been near twelve o'clock.'

'Why do you say that?'

'Well, because not long after, Miss Jennings returned with the rest of the girls.'

'And how did Mr Bolton act when you were both searching?'

'What do you mean, sir?' said Tom.

'Well, did Mr Bolton seem anxious, nervous, or calm perhaps?'

'Possibly a little agitated.'

'Why do you say that?'

'He was muttering to himself.'

'What did he say?' enquired Swann.

'I don't know. It was mumbled and also in a different language.'

'A different language? Was it French?'

'I don't know what language it was, only that I did not understand it.'

Swann nodded. 'So when you were searching the grounds, it did not occur to you to go across to the island?'

'No. It is forbidden to go there without permission from Miss Jennings.'

'Did you check to see if the boat was still at its mooring this side?'

Tom shook his head. 'There was no need as far as I was concerned.'

'Then what happened?'

'As I said, I went back to the flower bed and my sweet peas.'

'And you were there until Miss Jennings told you to go across to the island.'

'Yes,' nodded Tom.

'But when you got to the mooring the boat was not there?'

'That's right. So I swam across on the instructions of Miss Jennings.'

'Can you tell me exactly what you found when you arrived on the island?'

'As you saw for yourself, there is only one way onto the island and that is on the jetty on the other side. As soon as rounded the island I saw the boat moored, so I knew someone was there. I reached the jetty and pulled myself up; the banks around the rest of the island are too steep to find a grip. Once I was on the island I began to search it. I began with the temple, which is where I saw them.'

'What did you do, then?'

Tom did not answer.

'Is something wrong?' asked Swann.

'It is hard, Mr Swann, to think back on seeing them inside the temple. You must catch whoever did this.'

'Why do you think someone else caused their deaths, Tom?'

'After seeing their faces, I cannot imagine them doing that to themselves.'

Swann nodded.

'How well did you know Miss Leigh and Miss Templeton? Did you talk to them often?'

There was a moment's hesitation before Tom answered.

'Uh, no, occasionally the girl, Grace, I mean Miss Templeton, might stop and talk with me when I was out tending to the flowers.'

'What did you converse about?'

'Flowers mainly, she said how much she loved them.'

'And Miss Leigh, did you ever talk with her?'

'No.'

'You seem very certain.'

'I would say if I had.'

Swann accepted this for now.

'When you were in the temple, did you notice anything else? Perhaps something that may have been written.'

'There was nothing.'

'Perhaps a note or such-like?'

'Are you saying I'm lying?'

'Goodness no, I am not saying that at all. I am merely attempting to establish the facts surrounding these deaths.'

'There was nothing else in the temple,' said Tom, a little calmer.

'And then what did you do?'

'I swam back across the lake as quickly as I could.'

'Why did you not take the boat back?'

Tom thought for a moment and scratched his forehead. 'I don't rightly know,' he said. 'It must have been the shock at finding them.'

'So once you reached this side of the lake again, you told Miss Jennings.'

Tom nodded.

'And what did she do?'

'She gave instructions that all the girls were to be kept in the dormitories, which face away from the lake. Then she told me to swim across the lake again and bring back the boat. She said not to touch the bodies.'

'And did you?'

'No I didn't, not this time.'

'So are you saying you touched the bodies when you were there the first time?'

'I er, no, I mean, if I did, it was only to check to see if they were still alive.'

Swann nodded.

'And then what happened when you retrieved the boat?'

'I rowed Miss Jennings across to the island. When we reached it, she told me to stay in the boat while she went to the temple.'

'How long was she in there?'

'Around five minutes, maybe ten, I can't remember exactly.'

'Then she came back to the boat?'

'Yes. On her return she asked me to retrieve the bodies and bring them to the boat. After I had loaded them in, I rowed Miss Jennings across. I then took the bodies, one at a time, to the chapel.'

'Did Miss Jennings say anything while you were in the boat?'

'Only to give me instructions and then to say if anyone were to ask what had happened, to tell them it had been a boating accident.'

'Has anyone asked you?'

Tom shook his head.

'Thank you Tom, that is all for now.'

Swann stood up to leave, but then paused.

'Actually Tom, there is one more question I would like to ask. When you went into the temple the second time, after Miss Jennings had been in there alone, did you notice if anything was different?'

'Different?'

'Was there anything that looked as if it might have been moved or taken?'

'Not that I know. It all looked the same.'

Swann nodded and turned back toward the main house. As he did so he glimpsed a figure looking out at him from one of the dormitory windows. Before he could see who it was, they were gone.

CHAPTER TWELVE

Harriet Charlotte Montague was born in 1744 on the outskirts of Bath, in the village of Swainswick. She grew up in the small parish with her sister, Cassandra Jane, until the age of twenty, when Harriet married and moved away.

Although Swainswick was steeped in history – it not only laid claim to being the place where Bladud, the founder of Bath, and his herd of pigs were cured of leprosy, but nearby Little Solsbury Hill was purportedly the site of the Battle of Badon, one of King Arthur's greatest victories against the Saxons – such things meant little to Harriet. That is not to say she lacked interest in acquiring knowledge, as her voracious reading of her father's library proved. But the volumes she preferred to digest were the travel books he had accumulated and which from an early age put notions of adventure in her mind. As soon as circumstances and opportunity allowed, she had left the tiny hamlet of her birth for good; only returning for the funeral of her sister.

She had met her future husband, Lord Henry Smithson, when introduced at a supper party in Bath, given by a mutual friend. Although financially independent, he had recently been engaged in work of a sensitive nature for the government. He had come to the spa city to take its famous medicinal waters for a recurrent attack of gout. On his own admission, he had not been the most handsome man in the room that evening, but there was something about his rugged features and quietly spoken nature that made Harriet immediately fall in love with him. By the end of the evening, it was reciprocated. They were married later that year, 1764, at St Swithin's Church, in the parish of Walcot, and Harriet added the title of Lady to her name.

The newlyweds spent their honeymoon on the Grand Tour. They had chosen the shortest route across the Channel, from Dover to Calais, undertaking a night crossing which saw them approach the French coast at dawn. Although in sight of shore, a contrary wind had forced the couple into a small rowing boat in order to complete their journey. They had spent the following night at the Hotel Dessein, a charming old hotel in Calais, before heading south to Paris, passing through the towns of Boulogne, Abbeville, Amiens and Chantilly on the way. They had made good time, as the roads were in good condition, stopping only twice; once to stay a night at an inn and again to see the acclaimed treasures at the Abbey of Saint-Denis.

In the French capital they had visited such sights as the Louvre, Tuileries, the Luxembourg and the Observatory, along with pilgrimages to the churches of Val-de-Grâce, St Sulpice and Notre Dame; while in Italy they had marvelled at the Coliseum in Rome, been captivated by Florence's art and attended the Real Teatro di San Carlo in Naples.

Although her husband had initially resisted pressure from the government to continue his work with them while on honeymoon, by the time they left Italy for Switzerland he had capitulated. It was, as far as the government was concerned, the perfect cover; a newly married couple on their honeymoon travelling through Europe and being able to come and go as they pleased. For a while Lord Henry combined duty and pleasure, but before long he became increasingly busy and preoccupied.

The end of their Grand Tour came in Greece. They had intended to stay in Athens only long enough to visit the Acropolis and enjoy the view from Mount Lycabettus, but with someone of her husband's particular skills required there in the long term, they had ended up staying eighteen months. As part of his remit, Lord Henry had made several journeys to Crete, reluctantly leaving his wife to amuse herself with the other diplomatic wives. Lady Harriet's closest companion from this circle had been Esperanza, wife of the Spanish Ambassador, and they would often accompany each other, along with assorted bodyguards, into the Turkish quarter, located on the north-east slope of the Acropolis and famed for its labyrinthine streets full of market stalls and bazaars.

In 1770 they finally left Athens for Constantinople, where Lord Henry was to undertake work for the British envoy to Turkey. No sooner had they arrived, however, than he was required in Crete on an urgent matter. This time Lady Harriet insisted she accompany him. Having arrived on Crete and accommodation been secured, her husband immediately left for a clandestine rendezvous. On his way to this meeting, he was tragically killed in a fall from a mountain path. Harriet was informed of her husband's death by two British Government officials, who arrived at the mansion where she was staying.

The following day, as she was about to take the officials' advice and leave for England, she learned the truth surrounding Lord Henry's death; that it had not been an accident but murder. Keeping this knowledge to herself, but determined to find out who was behind it, she returned to Constantinople and volunteered herself to the British

Government, in order to carry on with her husband's work. They were initially sceptical but nevertheless gave her a number of tasks of a lowly nature to begin with, in order to assess her abilities. Having adequately proved herself with these, they began to realise what a valuable asset she could be; a financially independent, titled widow able to travel freely around the courts and embassies of Europe. For all intents and purpose she was the perfect spy. No foreign government suspected her and even if they did, by this time she had assembled a formidable book of contacts that could whisk her out of the country at a moment's notice.

In the thirty-four years which had passed, her role and responsibility had increased substantially and she had been involved in some of the most important and prestigious coups engineered by the British intelligence community.

In 1793 she had become unofficially attached to the newly formed Alien Office. The organisation had been created in the wake of the Aliens Act, which had been passed earlier that same year to help control the ever-increasing influx of French refugees and suspected revolutionaries entering England in the aftermath of the French Revolution. Although under the control of the Home Office in reality its remit was much wider, including the surveillance of foreign persons of interest, home and abroad, and general intelligence gathering.

The first department head, or Superintendent, of the Alien Office was William Huskisson, who, prior to assuming this position, had been private secretary to Lord Gower. Although unprepossessing in appearance, Harriet warmed to him, having found this former member of the 1789 club to be highly intelligent, fluent in French and a true gentleman who always showed her the proper *politesse*. In July 1794, however, he was succeeded by William Wickham, who immediately created controversy by flouting the rules regarding employment of foreign nationals and indulging in nepotism by employing many of his wife's relations. Nevertheless, during his tenure the organisation completely outgrew its original remit and expanded into what amounted to a fully fledged intelligence-gathering agency, complete with a vast network of agents, controllers and informers spread throughout the continent and beyond. But these developments only reflected the nature of the period. These were dangerous times, as not only was the threat of invasion by Napoleon a constant fear, so was the possibility of an Irish rebellion. Spurred on by the successes in America and France, the Irish wanted their own revolution in order to achieve independence from the British Government, and were prepared to take up arms to achieve it.

In recent years the Irish had attempted an uprising twice, but on both occasions fortuitous circumstances had conspired to foil their attempts. The most recent, a plot by a group of United Irishmen in Dublin under the leadership of Robert Emmet, the previous year had been quelled, mainly by the emergence not long beforehand of an informant. As well as providing valuable information regarding numbers of men, arms and other details, he had been instrumental in helping them blow up one of Emmet's arms depots a week before the arranged uprising. Emmet had stood trial and been executed later that year, although not before he had made a stirring speech in the dock. Lady Harriet had been against his death sentence and voiced her opinion as such, knowing his death would more than likely arouse sympathy for the Irish cause and make Emmet a martyr.

By the time of these events though, Wickham was no longer Superintendent of the Alien Office and although Harriet had no real opinion of his successor, she had come to dislike the new department head. He was a former military officer who did not suffer fools gladly. Although she was not beholden to him, or the organisation in general, she was nevertheless engaged in work of national importance and wished to be treated with the respect she felt her experience and position deserved. She had requested a meeting with him at the Avon Street office, but at the last moment the venue was changed and Lady Harriet found herself in a carriage being taken out of Bath. She was taken to a large mansion house located on the city's southern outskirts and escorted into one of the large rooms. Here she was requested to sit down. A few moments later, a door opened and in walked the man she knew only by his codename: Janus.

'So what is it so important that you wanted me to reroute my journey to London through Bath?'

'There have been certain developments here,' replied Lady Harriet, 'in regard to the Irish situation.'

'Not another informant murdered?'

'No! That was unforeseeable. His identity was unwittingly revealed. I am still trying to find out how it happened.'

'So what are these "developments"?'

'It is Lockhart.'

Janus sighed heavily. 'Go on,' he said.

'He has established a romantic attachment to my niece, Mary.'

'Yes, I know that, but I thought you had the situation under control.'

'I did, but it seems he has now developed a conscience and no longer wants to be of service to us, at least not in regard to any part which might jeopardise his relationship with my niece.'

'This is outrageous. He cannot be allowed to dictate what he does or does not want to do for us. You were the one who convinced me of his importance in this operation.'

'Do you think I am not fully aware of that?'

'I should never have agreed to the reprieving of his execution. He should have swung just like Emmet. I warned you he was unreliable. If anything goes wrong, it is my career at stake. You assured me his co-operation would not be in doubt.'

'I still believe it to be true.'

'From what you have said, it is clearly not. So what have you told him?'

'I informed him that he must continue to be part of our operation until October. By then we will know if the Irish have planned anything for the anniversary of Emmet's death and if they have, we will have dealt with it. After that, I have said he is free to marry my niece, but they must move abroad.'

'I always said you were skating on thin ice employing that jumped-up little philanderer. I do not like this situation in the slightest.'

'He has assured me the attachment is genuine.'

'And you believe him?'

'No, but I want him to believe that I do.'

'So what is your plan?'

'When October arrives, and any revolt has been suppressed, I will deal with him in my own way. I just need your approval.'

'Gladly, but remember, if anything goes wrong not only can we say goodbye to our jobs and reputation, but our liberty as well.'

Harriet nodded.

'We have enough trouble on our plate with the French. I am sure I do not have to remind you of the importance of Bath remaining in our hands in the event of an Irish rebellion. A recent official report states at least two reasons why it is probably the most strategic city in England, outside London, for the Irish. You have read the report I assume?'

'I originated it and there are three reasons: the percentage of Irish in the city willing to rise up to support any rebellion represents a tangible threat; it is a strategic location between Bristol and London; and the fact Malone has sent his right-hand man here on so many occasions, including giving him responsibility for employing Wicks to murder our previous informant, Malone's own brother, points to the fact that he realises the importance of Bath and no doubt has something big planned for it.'

'So where are you regarding finding a replacement for the informant?'

'We are currently targeting the right-hand man, the Scarred Man. There are several facts in our favour. He is English and he is also wanted for murder …'

'What did you call him?'

'The Scarred Man. At least that is what my nephew has named him. As we do not know his real name I thought it was as suitable as any other.'

'Your nephew? What has he to do with this matter?'

'He was the one who commissioned the portrait, you may remember, which the office has duplicated for our agents in the field.'

'Remind me why he did that?'

'The Scarred Man was one of those responsible for his father's murder twenty years ago. He is trying to track him down and bring him to justice.'

'So is your nephew a threat to this operation?'

'I am doing all I can to make certain he is not. As the Scarred Man is now in the area, I have engaged my nephew to investigate a straightforward murder-of-passion case, although he has been led to believe it is French retribution for our failed attempt on Bonaparte.'

'Do not even mention that fiasco. First Moreau, Georges and Pigrau all arrested and now the Duke of Enghien murdered.'

'What?' exclaimed Lady Harriet.

'Have you not heard? The Duke of Enghien was arrested last week and before anything could be done he was executed on the orders of Napoleon himself.'

'He cannot do that. The duke is a member of the reigning House of Bourbon and a legitimate heir to the French throne.'

'Well, as shocking as it is, he has done it, so there can be no more failures. Bring this Lockhart to heel. Anyone who threatens the success of this operation must be removed. Anyone! And if you are unable or unwilling to do so, then I will engage the service of someone who will.'

CHAPTER THIRTEEN

At seven forty-five Swann left the house in Great Pulteney Street and made his way towards the city centre. He was on his way to meet Fitzpatrick at the club where the magistrate was a member.

On Swann's return to his consulting rooms in Gay Street that afternoon, there had been a message waiting for him. It was from Fitzpatrick, requesting to see him on a certain urgent matter. After walking the short distance between their two buildings and entering Fitzpatrick's office, he had been invited to the club. The reason for the invitation concerned the nephew of Fitzpatrick's acquaintance, who was also a member, and the night before had cajoled the magistrate into extending an invitation to Swann. The prospective Member of Parliament wanted the opportunity to personally persuade Swann to take on his case.

Swann had been invited to the club several times before, although for his own reasons had always declined. But this time, as Fitzpatrick intimated it would be doing him a great service, as he would feel he had at least discharged his obligation to his acquaintance even if he still refused the case, Swann agreed.

They had arranged to meet outside the club entrance at eight o'clock and Fitzpatrick had given Swann a card with the address on it. He had then returned home for an evening meal with Mary, before she left for the theatre with Lockhart. Swann had spent the intervening period making notes on the case he was involved in for Lady Harriet. He had to admit, however, he was no closer to finding out who the murderer might be than he was yesterday morning, when he accepted the assignment. His gut instinct told him that neither Tom the gardener nor Bolton, the girl's 'protector', were guilty and unless there was someone else, not yet identified, it may have been, after all, a tragic *crime passionnel*.

As Swann walked across Pulteney Bridge he slipped his hand inside one of his pockets to retrieve the card with the club's address. Instead, he brought out a torn piece of paper. On it he saw the scribbled words 'Circle of Sappho'. In the top right-hand corner was a date, printed, as one would see in a diary or journal. It was yesterday's date; 26th March. He turned over the paper, but there was nothing else on it. The jagged edge down the left side, however, suggested it had been hastily ripped from a diary. Instinctively he turned around, as if expecting to see someone, but there was no one, or at least no one that had been close enough to put a note on his person.

As Swann continued on his way he recalled the events of the day. And then he remembered. Of course! He now thought back to the girl at the school who had fallen into him. What was her name … Anne? Yes, that was it. She had been the best friend of the dead girl. But what was the Circle of Sappho, was it an organisation the victims belonged to? There certainly had to be some connection, he thought, as the girl and the teacher both had a copy of the Greek poetess' poetry in their possession.

By now Swann had arrived at the club and saw Fitzpatrick waiting outside for him. He would see what more information he could find regarding Sappho on his return home that evening and would also enquire about it the following day, when he spoke to the dead teacher's sister on his visit to Frome.

'Thank you once again for accepting my invitation,' said Fitzpatrick on seeing Swann. 'The person we discussed is already here and was pleased when I told him you had agreed to come tonight.'

Fitzpatrick knocked on the door of the exclusive club, in a manner presumed by Swann to be a secret code, and after the magistrate's identity had been verified by a man looking out from behind a small peep-hole embedded in the door, it opened and the two men entered.

'There are several rooms,' said Fitzpatrick as they stepped into the main foyer, 'dependent on how one likes to spend their evening; whether that is cards, dice, political discussion or drinking.'

They ascended a staircase leading to one of the bars, and on reaching the top a familiar face appeared from a doorway beside them. It was the magistrate Kirby.

'Fitzpatrick, it is unusual to see you here two nights in a row and it is of course unusual to see your companion here at any time, given he is not a member!'

'Swann has every right to be here tonight, he is my guest,' replied Fitzpatrick.

'Do not act so defensive my friend,' said Kirby, good-spiritedly. 'I was merely enacting some humour, although granted it was at your expense. Anyway, I am now off to the faro table, gentlemen. I would invite you to join me but I would not wish to lead our Mr Swann into temptation.'

Fitzpatrick and Swann watched Kirby as he strolled purposefully down one of the corridors which lead off from the stairs. Halfway along he stopped and opened a door. A cloud of cigar smoke emerged from the room and Kirby vanished into it. Swann frowned at Kirby's 'temptation' remark. Was it just a chance remark or did he know about Swann's history? Either way, he had no time to contemplate it as an unfamiliar gentleman was now standing next to him with his hand extended.

'Swann, this is Charles Moorhouse, the gentleman I have mentioned to you.'

'Ah, yes,' replied Swann, as he gripped the man's hand and shook it. 'Pleased to make your acquaintance.'

The aspiring Member of Parliament stood six feet five inches tall, had soft, young-looking features, which belied his age, being as he was half a dozen years or so younger than Swann.

'Thank you for coming tonight,' said Charles. 'I have reserved a quiet room where we can discuss the matter in private.' He turned to Fitzpatrick. 'I hope you will not be offended, Fitzpatrick, if I request Mr Swann's presence alone.'

'Not at all,' replied the magistrate, 'if Swann is agreeable to it?'

Swann nodded to confirm that he was.

'Splendid,' said Charles. At that, he ushered Swann along one of the corridors and followed after him. Fitzpatrick turned and headed towards the bar.

They entered the room put aside for them. Inside were several Chesterfield armchairs and two four-seat sofas, upholstered in dark-red leather. Two of the armchairs were placed opposite one another, either side of a crackling fireplace. The politician gestured for Swann to sit down in one of them, then walked over to a cabinet and opened its glass door.

'Fitzpatrick informs me you are a wine connoisseur, Mr Swann.'

'I would not venture to call myself that, only …'

'Indeed, indeed. There is an appealing '87 Château d'Yquem, if that would be agreeable?'

'Most agreeable,' replied Swann.

Charles brought two crystal glasses back with him, along with the bottle, and poured a substantial measure into each. He offered a glass to Swann and put the other on the table between them. He then seated himself opposite.

'If you do not mind, Mr Swann, I will come straight to the point as to why I requested your presence here. How much do you know of my predicament?'

'Fitzpatrick has prevailed upon me the briefest of details. I understand that you are at present the victim of blackmail.'

Charles looked suitably forlorn.

'I will not try to condone my behaviour, or deny my indiscretion, Mr Swann. I know I have acted wrongly, but there is more at stake than my own reputation and career. If permissible, I wish to outline the reasons by which I feel you should reconsider your decision not to take on this case.'

Swann gestured for Charles to continue.

'This country of ours, England, is, I fear, standing on the precipice of disaster and faces one of the greatest challenges in its history. The last thirty years have seen monumental events – America's independence, the French Revolution and subsequent Reign of Terror, the ascendancy to power of Napoleon and the Irish uprisings – which have all severely chipped away at the very foundations of our nation. Everywhere one looks there is unrest, instability and potential conflict. Why, at this very moment Napoleon sits across the Channel waiting for spring to arrive, so he can 'jump the ditch', as he refers to it, and eradicate this island's freedom for ever. Whilst on our other coast, the Irish are across their own sea, waiting for any opportunity to exact revenge on us for what they perceive as unjust rule. And all the while these unsavoury and menacing forces gather themselves together and grow stronger on a daily basis, we have, for want of a better phrase, a dithering prime minister who refuses to embrace the need to equip ourselves realistically to rise up to face this challenge.'

Charles stopped talking momentarily in order to gauge Swann's reaction thus far. He raised his glass to his lips and swallowed a mouthful of the d'Yquem.

'Perhaps I am being too passionate but I believe in this country, Mr Swann, and I believe in its continued right to be free. I also firmly believe in the duty of government to serve the people and I believe this is not happening at present. Addington needs to be replaced as soon as possible and the only man suitable for the job is Pitt. With the King suffering another bout of illness, we have to be as secure as possible.'

'Why not Grenville or Fox to replace the prime minister?' asked Swann.

'They have too many personal issues between them to be able to ever lead this country. And besides, Fox is an advocate of peace on any terms. He has been against this war with France since Napoleon assumed power. "Is peace a rash system?" are his very words. "Must the bowels of Great Britain be torn out – her best blood be spilt – her treasure wasted?" We need war, Mr Swann, and our party can deliver it, but not with Addington at its head. We need Pitt to lead the country once more and behind him a strong, supportive government. This is where I believe I can make a contribution. As Fitzpatrick may have informed you, my intention is to become a Member of Parliament in a forthcoming by-election. Are you a supporter of the Conservative Party, Mr Swann? No, do not answer. I do not wish to know another man's leanings, especially when they may be in direct opposition to my own. I am a Tory, Mr Swann, as my father and his father before him. I believe I have a substantial career in politics in front of me and I know I can offer much to this country and her people. The fact of the matter is, Mr Swann, there are people depending on me to achieve certain goals in my political ambitions and this disagreeable matter might put an end to them.'

'So what exactly do the blackmailers hold against you?'

'A number of letters, Mr Swann, composed while infatuated with a girl at a certain establishment in the city and coerced by the recipient into writing them.'

'The contents of which, if made public, would I assume be most damaging?' said Swann.

'Exactly,' replied Charles. 'I have surely paid the price for my indiscretions, Mr Swann, not only in monetary terms but also in anguish and distress. Putting my own political aspirations aside for a moment though, I can only guess what this would do to my devoted wife and young son if these letters were published. I feel that I have so much to offer and it hurts me to even think of its potential loss. I can almost taste success. Pitt is gradually being brought around and coming to his senses. He has to be convinced to seize control from this amateur, to put his own personal promises aside and take power back, it is the only way to defeat Napoleon. And when the day comes, which I believe will be soon, I would like to think I will form part of that government which will help to secure victory for England.'

'If I understand you correctly, Mr Moorhouse, you are saying that you may be part of the next government, if you are successful in the city's by-election?'

'The by-election is not in Bath, Mr Swann. Goodness no. If I were to pit myself against such stalwarts as Thynne and Palmer I would never stand a chance. No, this is up in Knaresborough. One of the incumbent MPs has unfortunately passed away and his seat is therefore vacant.'

'I do not believe I have heard of this place; it is nearby?'

'No, it is in West Riding, in Yorkshire. It is a burgage borough.'

'Is that similar to a rotten one?'

'Only in so much as any form of democracy is absent within both. Whereas the electorate of a rotten borough are "guided", let us say, by a certain party or parties with a vested interest as to which way to vote, the main landowner in a burgage borough appoints the MP himself. In the case of Knaresborough this is the Duke of Devonshire. Up until now it has been staunchly Whig, but my supporters believe his allegiance can be swung.'

'Which MP was it that died?'

'James Hare.'

'I remember reading his obituary now,' said Swann. 'Was it about a week ago?'

'Ten days to be exact, and I take it as an auspicious sign that it was here in Bath that he expired.'

'He did not reside in Yorkshire, then?'

'Lord no! One does not have to live among the people one represents; merely speak on their behalf in the Commons. Although having said that, from what I understand Hare was not a great orator. A fine wit though. To answer your question about a governmental position, Mr Swann, this would probably not be achieved immediately, but if Pitt does assume position of prime minister, I am certain there would be a reshuffle soon afterwards, a culling of dead wood so to speak, and I believe there would indeed be a place for me in that government. So you see, Mr Swann, it is imperative that this matter of blackmail is resolved satisfactorily and as soon as possible. If this was to continue, then either the scandal would destroy my career or …'

'… or the blackmailers would have something more powerful in their grasp than money,' finished Swann, 'political influence.'

Charles nodded, gloomily.

'And do you think your blackmailers know this?'

'I can only hope they do not, but if I am successful at this by-election they would surely soon find out.'

Swann thought for a few moments.

'My reason for declining your case, when Fitzpatrick asked me yesterday, was that I have seen far too many of them, with most ending tragically. I cannot say I will be able to resolve this to your satisfaction but I will certainly give it some thought in the next day or so and if I feel I can do anything to help, be assured that I will do so.'

Charles smiled and rose out of his seat to shake Swann's hand.

'Thank you Mr Swann, that is as much as I could have hoped for.'

'Please tell me exactly how the handing over of the money is carried out. Would I be correct in assuming you give it directly to them or is there a third party?'

'I hand it over directly. I receive a message early in the morning, which tells me where and when to meet that evening and the amount of money I should bring. It has been a different location each time.'

'And when is the next meeting?'

'I have not been contacted yet, although I expect it to be any day soon. Lately it has been every other week and it will be two weeks tomorrow since the last time.'

'Well, as soon as you find out please inform Fitzpatrick, so that he can tell me. I will be there when you hand over the payment. Do not worry, though, as I will not compromise your situation. I shall not be seen and will only be there in an observertory capacity'

The two men left the room and headed back along the corridor to the top of the stairs. As they did so, Swann noticed an older gentleman gesturing in an attempt to catch the politician's attention.

'Thank you once again, Mr Swann,' said Charles.

'You are welcome, Mr Moorhouse. I will not detain you any longer, as I believe there is someone who wishes to speak with you.'

Charles looked across at the gesturing gentleman.

'Ah yes. Well, if you will excuse me, Mr Swann.'

Swann watched as the politician walked over to meet the other man, no doubt, he thought, in order to tell him the outcome of the meeting. Swann went through to the bar, although there was no sign of Fitzpatrick. He had only been in there but a few moments when a gentleman approached him. The man leant forward and spoke discreetly to Swann.

'Good evening, sir, I do not believe I have seen you here before. Are you a member of this club?'

'No,' replied Swann. 'I am a guest of Henry Fitzpatrick, although I do not seem to be able to locate him at present.'

'Ah, very good, sir,' replied the gentleman. 'I believe Mr Fitzpatrick in is the Faro room, sir.'

'Thank you.'

Swann made his way out of the bar and along the corridor, to the room Kirby had entered earlier. As soon as Swann went in he observed Fitzpatrick, albeit through a dense cloud of cigar smoke. He was sitting at a card table. Swann hesitated, but then went and sat down in the vacant chair next to the magistrate.

'Ah, Swann, there you are. I decided to try my luck at Faro.'

Across the table came the familiar voice of Kirby. 'Will you join us Swann? I have the bank.'

'I do not play,' said Swann.

'Each to their own, I suppose,' said Kirby. 'Henry, another round?'

Fitzpatrick nodded and Kirby dealt the hand. There were four other players gathered around the oval-shaped table. The game was easy to learn and had become popular due to its fast action and odds of winning. Players would participate by placing bets on cards pasted on a board, which had one complete suit – usually spades – on it. A deck of cards would be shuffled and the top card would be discarded. The next two cards were then dealt out by the dealer, the first card drawn being called the 'banker's card', the next, the 'players' card'. Any player who had placed a bet on a card pasted on the board and whose denomination matched that of the 'banker's card', lost their money. Anyone who had placed a bet matching the denomination to the 'player's card', however, won and received back double their bet. Two more cards would then be dealt by the banker and the game would continue, with the rest of the rules mostly being picked up as the players went along.

The game of Faro was, however, as Swann knew only too well, one of the card games where cheating was almost compulsory. Any man could cheat if he knew the game well, though the banker, who also dealt, would normally hold court above all. It was little wonder, he thought, that Kirby was in the banker's seat. As Swann watched for several hands, he noticed that Fitzpatrick and the other players had their share of luck but that the banker naturally had more. By the time they played a fifth hand, Swann could tell Kirby was cheating and by the seventh hand was able to observe how he was doing it. It was an old trick and Swann reprimanded himself for not noticing it sooner, though he had not been in a card room for at least five years. Although he knew Kirby was cheating, the way in which he was doing it meant that he could easily deny it and Swann would not be able to prove it. At the same time, he did not wish to cause disruption in the club, as he was, after all, a guest of Fitzpatrick. He would wait for the right opportunity.

'Count me out,' said the man two seats to the right of Fitzpatrick, after Kirby had enjoyed a run of six consecutive wins.

'Better luck next time,' said Kirby, shuffling the pack once more.

'I will take his place, if that is agreeable Kirby?' said Swann.

'Excellent,' said Kirby. There was, however, a slight expression of surprise in his eyes, which Swann immediately noticed.

The top card was once again discarded and the following two laid face up, one either side of Kirby. The banker immediately began to lose and the other players started to win a little of their money back. Swann himself won the first three games. Kirby laughed at Swann's 'beginners luck', as he called it, after he won the next two hands as well, but soon realised the other man was also cheating.

'Something wrong, Kirby?' asked Swann innocently.

'You seem to be enjoying an awfully good streak of luck, Swann; perhaps too good one might be inclined to say,' replied Kirby.

'Nothing you did not enjoy yourself before I joined the game, I am sure.'

Their exchange brought the room to silence.

'Then let us increase the stakes and see who has the better continuation of it. I suggest ten guineas per game.'

At this increase several players signalled their departure from the game. After a few seconds Fitzpatrick also gestured his retirement. This left just Kirby and Swann.

'It is time to change the deck, if you have no objection Mr Swann. Perhaps it might put us on an even level.'

'Of course,' said Swann.

Despite this move, which Kirby had orchestrated to give him the upper hand, Swann won the first three games. The other players had stayed on to watch and there were murmurings of admiration from several of them. Kirby looked visibly shocked. Nevertheless, after the next hand, which he also lost, he picked up a handful of coins and said: 'Let's play one hand for five hundred guineas.'

'You are being ridiculous, sir, there is surely a limit,' said one of the gentleman watching.

'As banker, I set the limit. If Mr Swann does not want to play for these stakes, he can simply leave the table and let a real gambler sit down.'

Swann smiled and remained seated. He then placed his bet on the knave card on the pasted board.

'The knave turns fool that runs away,' said Kirby, smiling.

'"When a wise man gives thee better counsel, give me mine again. I would have none but knaves follow it since a fool gives it." *King Lear*, Act II, Scene IV,' said Swann, finishing the quote.

'You know your Shakespeare, Swann, I will grant you that.'

Kirby then dealt the two cards and placed them face down onto the table. He turned the 'player's card' first. It was the nine of hearts. There were gasps from those watching, the room now swelled by members who had been told of the enormous wager. Kirby now picked up the 'banker's card' and gradually turned it over to reveal the Knave of Spades. He placed it down with a malevolent smile on his face.

'It seems your winning streak has just ended, Swann.'

Swann stared in disbelief at the card, knowing he had been taken by a truly accomplished cheat. He did not wish to cause a disruption by accusing Kirby of cheating, especially as he had been doing the same, so instead he simply congratulated Kirby on his win, settled the wager and stood up, ready to leave the room with his host.

'Truly bad luck Swann,' replied Kirby, 'but then you know what they say: like father, like son.'

Swann stopped and turned back towards Kirby.

'What did you say?'

'I was just commiserating with you over your loss.'

'You mentioned my father. Why?'

'Well, from what I have heard, before he died he was a terrible gambler and never knew when to stop. It seems you have inherited that part of him.'

Before anyone else could react, Swann had moved around the table and struck Kirby in the face, sending him sprawling backwards against the wall.

'You can say what you like about me but never insult my father's name again, or I will end your life!'

Kirby rose slowly to his feet, helped by two other members.

'Then I will offer you the chance. Bathampton Down at dawn on Sunday. I assume you will be Swann's second, Fitzpatrick?'

Fitzpatrick nodded solemnly.

'I will send my second to finalise details with you. Now, I suggest you escort your guest out of this club.'

Swann turned and left the room, followed by Fitzpatrick. Behind them Kirby wiped the blood from the side of his mouth, but there was a smile upon it.

CHAPTER FOURTEEN

Bath, Tuesday 27th March, 1804

What a fool I am! Falling for the oldest play in the book. Why did I not see what Kirby was doing? He was playing the long game, reeling me in with each separate win I achieved until, blinded by arrogance, I allowed myself to be beaten on the final hand. But then this is how these Machiavellian schemers operate; ensnaring their victim, pretending to unintentionally lose, again and again, when in fact they are merely biding their time for when the stakes are high enough to spring their trap.

But what could I do? I know there is a sickness in me, which takes hold whenever a game of probability offers its chance of exhilaration; an opportunity to pit one's skill against that of another and lady luck herself. At the same time, there is Fitzpatrick. I was his guest tonight but behaved abominably. I shall seek out his forgiveness tomorrow and offer to send a formal written apology to the club. No, wait! I am away from Bath all day and will not return until late. I will send a note to him in absentia and inform him I will endeavour to meet him personally the following day.

As to the challenge Kirby has set down, I can simply refuse to take part in the duel and if my honour becomes sullied as a result, then so be it. A misheard word, an unintentional gesture, a wrongly interpreted expression; all these things I have witnessed as being the reason for a duel and in each case one of the participants was subsequently killed.

I am angry that the magistrate insulted my father's memory but I will not take a life over it, not even Kirby's, however much I may dislike him. At the same time, I do not wish to put my own life at risk. To what purpose would either of our deaths serve? If I were to kill Kirby, what would I have achieved? I will have the blood of a magistrate on my hands and, given the illegal nature of the duel, there is every possibility I might end up in prison and would then not be able to continue my pursuit of justice for my father's death. Of course, if I myself was to be killed, this would naturally conclude that quest as well.

What demands to be answered though is why Kirby made the remarks he did? Where did he obtain his information? How did he find out about my past and why insinuate that my father was also a gambler? Did Kirby know about my time in France, when I recklessly gambled away my allowance twice over? It was only the disappointed expression on my adoptive father's face on my return to England which brought this addiction to its end. Or was it the time in London, with my lawyer, when I once more allowed myself to be taken over for a short period, at the expense of several thousand pounds?

My father was fond of watching other people play and learning about the various con games – his particular favourite being the three cups – but my father had been a responsible man and not one to frivolously gamble his money away.

It was in my father's memory and his fondness for confidence tricks and the men who perpetrated them that I learned as much about it as I could. That is why I can easily mark a man out who is cheating. But, it means nothing if one is not playing in an honest game; there is always someone who will be a better cheat than you, as tonight proved, especially if they hold both bank and cards. I allowed my heart to rule my head because I wanted to teach Kirby a lesson. Yet it was Kirby who taught me one and I have learnt it well.

Unlike before, I can now afford to lose five hundred guineas, although I resent the fact that it was won by a man whom I have come to find so disagreeable. But more than that, I am ashamed of my behaviour when I think of men such as George and Bridges, and others in the Avon Street district, who struggle every day to feed and clothe themselves and keep a roof over their heads. George confided to me at the Fountain that Bridges' companion Rosie, the woman who confirmed Thomas Malone's identity to me last October, is about to lose her lodgings through an inability to pay her ever-increasing rent. I do not know exactly how much it is, but it can only be the most trifling figure in comparison with the sum that I lost tonight on one turn of a card. In fact, between the three of them – George, Bridges and Rosie – I doubt they will ever accumulate five hundred guineas, even if all the money they possess in their lifetimes were added together.

The events of this evening have therefore given me a sense of perspective. Tonight has also made me reflect on what might have happened if my life had been different, if my father had not been murdered and I had not been adopted by the Gardiners. What would my position in life have been today? Would I be living a meagre existence 'on the street' like George and Bridges? Or would I have somehow still risen above my station, or at least that of my father's, and achieved wealth in another way? I would have learned to read and write, as my father would still have been alive to teach me, but what of education? Would I have had one? It seems most unlikely. And what of my career, my occupation; would I have been destined to follow in my father's footsteps and become a servant, to live a life in service? Of course, the key question that has to be asked is would I have gambled so much if I did not know there was money to recompense my debts? These are all passageways of conjecture my mind could wander endlessly the entire night, but the simple truth is this is my life and I am who I am.

In writing this entry my earlier heightened emotion at the evening's events has been dampened. I do not feel in an appropriate state *to undertake any reading on Sappho, especially at this late hour, so shall do so on returning from Lady Harriet's residence tomorrow evening, or rather this evening, given the clock has just signified the beginning of a new day.*

CHAPTER FIFTEEN

The carriage had left Mary at Lady Harriet's manor house in Beckington and then continued its journey to Frome with Swann as its sole passenger. He gazed out of the window and tried to put the events of the previous evening from his mind. A long day lay ahead of him and he needed to stay alert and focussed. With the note he had found in his pocket mentioning the 'Circle of Sappho', and the fact he was on his way to meet the victim's sister, he felt confident the case was moving forward and might achieve a breakthrough soon.

Swann was initially to meet Thomas Bunn, a widowed solicitor, who would act as his guide around Frome. He had never practiced law commercially, choosing instead to spend his time and inherited wealth on helping the poor and needy of the town, while at the same time trying to persuade council leaders to implement his building plans for its improvement. Up until this point, he had made more progress with the former than the latter.

The small market town of Frome was located at the eastern end of the Mendip Hills in Somerset, close to its neighbouring county Wiltshire, and had been founded at the end of the seventh century. The town had really come to prominence, however, in the sixteenth century. The large number of sheep grazing in the area, along with an already established market in the town, meant it became a centre of the woollen industry in East Somerset. For a period of time, as Thomas Bunn liked to remind anyone who would listen, it had also been bigger, in terms of population, and wealthier than Bath. At the same time it had attracted much praise from travellers, including the author Daniel Defoe, who, on a visit in 1720, had stated that were its growth to continue in the same manner over the following few years, it would very likely become 'one of the greatest and wealthiest inland towns in England.'

The carriage descended into North Parade, a long stretch of road that was the main route into Frome, and passed through the tollgate into the marketplace; the heart and centre of the town.

Unfortunately for Frome, Defoe's prediction was not realised and although at its height the town had been sending the equivalent of a waggon-load of cloth to London each day, the local industry was now in slow decline. This was, in part, due to the reluctance of the town's clothiers to embrace new technology and also because a great deal of its end product had been exported to France; which the war had immediately curtailed. There had been some who had profiteered from the war, making military uniforms, but for the most part work-forces had been reduced, buildings had become disused and a sense of gloom had descended on this once prosperous town.

As soon as the carriage entered the town and Swann began to observe the townsfolk, he could see the same world-weary expressions on many of the men, women and children that he saw regularly in the Avon Street district in Bath (and before that, in many areas of London). There were, of course, those in the town still prospering – several of the clothiers, tradesmen and other local craftsmen – but for the most part, the overall impression of the people of Frome was that they were no strangers to poverty.

The carriage turned right onto Cork Street. It was along this street that Thomas Bunn resided. He lived at Monmouth House, the building he had inherited, along with his financial wealth, from his father following his death. The house had been built by Bunn's father, a doctor, around thirty years beforehand. It stood adjunct to Monmouth Chambers, a property which, by the time Dr Bunn had purchased it from linen draper Joseph Pritchard, stretched all along Cork Street to the bottom of what was known as Stony Street.

The buildings, Monmouth Chambers and Monmouth House, were said to have been named after the rebellious duke who stayed briefly in the town in 1685. It was not a productive visit though, as during the two days he was in Frome two thousand of his men deserted the cause; that of assuming the monarchy from the recently crowned James II. The population itself was indifferent and the duke received neither support nor encouragement from them (although equally they did not hand him over to the Loyalist forces a mere ten miles away). The Duke of Monmouth left Frome on 30th of June and within a week had been defeated at the Battle of Sedgemoor and, within a month, had been found guilty of treason and beheaded at Tower Hill in London.

The carriage now stopped outside Monmouth House and Swann alighted. The driver waited until he saw his passenger was safely on the pavement and then cracked his whip. The pair of horses trotted off and the carriage went along the street for a few more yards, turned around at a suitable place and then headed back to the end of Cork Street and on into the marketplace once more. The carriage passed Swann as he stood outside the building, waiting for his knock to be answered. Presently the door was opened by a male servant and Swann was admitted inside. He was escorted into the library and the servant then retired from the room, informing Swann he would make his master aware of his guest's presence there. While he waited, Swann walked over to one of the several bookcases that lined the room and began to peruse the volumes on its shelves.

'I hope you are finding some books of interest?' said a voice behind him. 'I have what I believe might be called an eclectic collection.'

Swann turned around as a man crossed the room to greet him.

'Mr Swann, it is good to meet you. I am Thomas Bunn.'

The two men shook hands.

'Please forgive me,' said Swann, gesturing in the direction of the shelves, 'but I cannot help but look at any bookshelf I find myself near. I am fascinated as to what volumes other people may have acquired.'

'Then we share a fascination, Mr Swann. Now, Lady Harriet has told me of the purpose of your trip to our wonderful town today, and we shall indeed endeavour to go and see Mrs Grant in due course. Before I do so, however, can I offer you a drink?'

'I will decline, Mr Bunn, as I am eager to speak to Mrs Grant as soon as possible.'

'I completely understand. We shall leave without delay, Mr Swann, although I would like it very much if we walked up to the house; it is not too far, so I can show you something of our town.'

'That sounds most agreeable,' replied Swann, having already sensed the pride this gentleman held for the place in which he resided.

As the two men made their way to the main door, Swann spoke again.

'Mr Bunn, I feel I must warn you that when I arrived I noticed a group of rough-looking men loitering on the street a little way along from your house. They may cause us trouble, so we had best be on our guard. Do not worry though, as I am armed.'

Bunn opened his front door and smiled. 'Those men mean us no harm,' he said, gathering a handful of coins from a large box in the hallway and putting them in his pockets. He then gestured for Swann to go through the front door.

No sooner had they left the house, as Swann had expected, the men saw them and started to follow. Instinctively, and despite what his companion had said, Swann reached inside his jacket.

'You really do not need to worry, Mr Swann. Please believe me.'

Thomas Bunn retrieved the coins from his pockets and put his hands behind his back. As they made their way along Cork Street, Swann heard the money falling onto the pavement behind them. He briefly glanced around and saw the trail of coins rapidly being picked up by the men.

'I prefer to do it this way, Mr Swann,' said Bunn, as they turned left at the end of Cork Street, 'so I do not see their faces and they retain at least some modicum of dignity.'

The squabbling over the remaining few coins now taking place behind them did not seem dignified to Swann, though he said nothing.

'I understand from Lady Harriet you reside in Bath, Mr Swann?' said Bunn.

'Yes. I have a property in London but have been in Bath for about six months.'

They walked across the marketplace and into a narrow thoroughfare called Cheap Street, which had a watercourse running down its middle.

'This is charming,' said Swann as they walked up alongside it.

'Yes, its source is high up the hill and at one time descended under King Street. It is believed the water was diverted a century or two ago to make this wonderful attraction.'

'We have a Cheap Street in Bath as well,' said Swann. 'Although I can imagine what the reaction might be if the Corporation decided to divert a watercourse along its length!'

'Ah, I know it,' said Bunn. 'Did you know the name comes from the old English meaning "market"? Until the end of the fourteenth century, if I remember correctly, your street was actually called Souter Street, meaning Shoemakers Street.'

'You know Bath well, Mr Bunn?'

'Quite well, I went to school in the city for a short while. My father died when I was eight years old and afterwards guardians were appointed to oversee my education. I first went to Kilmersdon and then Wells, but at the age of twelve I was sent to the Broad Street School in Bath. Do you know it Mr Swann?'

'I have passed the building a few times; it looks a reputable school.'

'It was a respectable enough Classical school, let us say, run by Reverend Morgan.' Bunn smiled fondly as he remembered the man. 'As well as Greek and Latin, I took French and Geography. I even learnt to dance, ride and draw. Not that I do much of those last three subjects these days. He was a wise man though, Reverend Morgan. He only punished when absolutely necessary to uphold the direction and efficiency of the school. It was a most enlightening time in my life, Mr Swann, especially being surrounded by such magnificence in the architecture of the city. I also subscribed to a reading library, where I read works by only the most distinguished of writers. I had, of course, read Homer as part of my studies, but I find Greek and Latin to be nothing more than dead languages. *The Iliad* and *The Odyssey* are the most wonderful of books, but I do find they are in the language of scholars and do not represent the everyday people I find myself surrounded by in Frome, or for that matter, when I was in Bath. I remember going once to a different part of the city, near the river, it is many years ago now, and the poverty and degradation I encountered there changed my view of the world for good. I think it was at that moment I decided I would do all I could to help the poor and needy.'

'I believe you refer to the Avon Street district in Bath. I know it only too well.'

'Ah, is that what it is called? I was in Bath for two years before it was decided I should train as a legal professional and was dispensed to Chard. I have retained a fondness for Bath ever since, Mr Swann, and would like to see Frome emulate its magnificent architecture and thus enjoy a similar reputation. With the money I inherited from my father I do all I can to bring this about. If there is time later, I would be grateful if you may indulge me in showing you locations for my plans.'

'Of course,' replied Swann. 'I am sorry to hear that you lost your father so young. I was twelve years old when my own died.'

'Oh?' said Bunn, looking across at Swann. 'Without wishing to appear rude, Mr Swann, I was under the impression from Lady Harriet that her brother-in-law, your father, had died within only the last few years.'

'You are correct in thinking that Mr Gardiner died within the last few years, but he was not my real father. I was adopted by the Gardiners after my real father was killed. And like you, I was then sent to boarding school not long thereafter.'

'Then we were in the same position. We are both self-made men, Mr Swann, and we should therefore be proud of ourselves.'

'I had not looked at it that way before,' replied Swann.

The two men now reached the top of Gentle Street, named after the person that once owned the land and not due to the incline, which was anything but. Behind them was the Waggon and Horses Inn. It was from here the cloth-laden waggons had left for London.

Thomas Bunn stopped by a piece of ground.

'If you would be so kind as to indulge me, Mr Swann, I will briefly tell you about one of the plans I have designed for this town. I have a vision of a great thoroughfare running all the way to marketplace. As you yourself experienced, the outward route heading south leaves a lot to be desired. I have proposed to the local authority that it begins over there,' Bunn pointed to the left of where they now stood, 'and will sweep majestically down the valley to the centre. Once finished, it would completely revitalise the town. With all the coming and going of waggons from the woollen industry it is completely unsuitable for traffic as it is. And I do not want to stop there, Mr Swann. I also have planned a crescent, to match those you have in Bath, or even, dare I say it, to surpass them. Forgive me if I have gone on too much, but I am passionate about this town of mine.'

'Do not concern yourself, Mr Bunn. You are certainly a man of grand designs and your enthusiasm for Frome is visible for all to see.'

They continued upwards and on into an area known as Keyford. It had been founded as a separate settlement, but now the boundaries of its larger neighbour were encroaching to the point that it might soon form part of that community.

Partway along the main road, which ran all the way through the parish and on towards the grand estate of nearby Longleat, they turned off into a narrow passageway. They continued along it for a little while until they reached a small rundown cottage at the end of a terraced row. Thomas Bunn stopped and knocked on the door. They had arrived.

CHAPTER SIXTEEN

'The Life of Elizabeth Singer', by Mary Gardiner

It has been written by an eminently more competent writer than this particular tyro that if a woman does not want her life to be judged too harshly after death, then she must conduct her affairs, private and public, in a manner which will assure her reputation remains intact; not for her own satisfaction, however, but rather for the future generations of women for whom her life may be held up as an example to which to aspire and emulate.

A problem arises when only certain aspects are selected after death and instead of a well-rounded life being presented, and whose purpose is to uplift, educate and inspire our sex, those aspects are used instead to subjugate, repress and stifle. A prime example of this malpractice has been with the poet and author Elizabeth Singer Rowe whose life, if one is to believe the host of male writers, critics and commentators that have celebrated her since her death in 1737, was one of virtue, piety and reverence. In 1783, for instance, it was written that 'the conduct and behaviour of Mrs Rowe might put some of the present race of females to the blush, who rake the town for infamous adventures to amuse the public,' while only within these past twelve months has an anonymous writer alluded to 'virtue and her genuine beauty [that should] recommend her to the choice and admiration of a rising generation.' As accurate a portrait as this might be for describing several female poets and authors over the centuries, and this writer would certainly not deny this as being so, in the case of Elizabeth Singer Rowe, however, this is simply not true. Yes, she no doubt embodied all these qualities throughout her lifetime, but to concentrate solely on these attributes is to give her character a limited rendering, because hand-in-hand with her virtuousness and reverence there was also vitality and rebellion, and where her nature exhibited piety it simultaneously exuded predilection.

This biographical sketch, therefore, intends to expand on the circumscribed depiction we have been given of this remarkable woman and to redress the circumvention bestowed upon her, so as to present a more complete and balanced representation which will seek not to decrease or diminish her appeal but rather to enhance it, so that we finally have a true likeness of a woman we can all aspire to within our daily lives.

Elizabeth Singer was born into an environment of nonconformity, with the religious beliefs of her parents and those of their friends and associates in direct opposition to that of the reigning King. In 1674, the year of her birth, Charles II had been on the throne of England for fourteen years, following the restoration of the monarchy, and during this period a concerted effort had been made to secure the return of Anglican dominance in the Church of England and to eradicate any religious deviation. To achieve this, several laws had been passed, including the Corporation Act of 1661, the Act of Uniformity the following year, the Conventicle Act two years later and the Five Mile Act, which became enshrined in 1665; collectively, these pieces of legislation becoming known as the Clarendon Code.

These authoritarian attempts, supported by Royal approval, were merely the latest in a series of changes, clashes and conflicts within the English religious landscape that had begun 150 years earlier, with the Act of Supremacy and the breaking away of the Church of England – at Henry VIII's insistence – from Papal authority in Rome. In doing so, this split ushered in a century and a half of discrimination, persecution and intolerance of religious groups in direct opposition to that which was followed by the sovereignty, although through successive monarchs and their shifting theological allegiances, those undertaking the persecuting often found themselves suddenly becoming the persecuted. In the wake of this spiritual turmoil, however, various religious movements that were deemed as not 'conforming' came into existence or merged, which included the Baptists, Quakers, Wesleyan, Congregationalists and Presbyterians.

William Singer, Elizabeth's father, was a Presbyterian minister in Ilchester, Somerset, also his daughter's birthplace, but was thrown into gaol for his beliefs. After his release he moved his family north-eastward to the thriving market town of Frome, where he gave up ministerial duties and became a clothier. His business prospered and he grew wealthy, but his nonconformist beliefs remained and he supported a dissenting congregation in the town.

Although spending a period of time at boarding school, Elizabeth's poem 'To one that would persuade me to leave the Muses' leaves the reader in no doubt as to her opinion of conventional female education at the time, her real 'education' was undertaken within the social environment she experienced once back in Frome and the intellectually enlightened men who inhabited it, most, if not all, being acquaintances of her father and the influential circles he moved in. The primary influence was, of course, her father, who encouraged her interests in music, painting and, above all, literature, and although she became accomplished both artistically and musically, it was towards the discipline of prose and poetry she was focused; writing her first verse at the age of twelve.

Other significant men who influenced her education throughout her formative years included Henry Thynne, son of Lord Weymouth and heir to the nearby family residence of Longleat, who taught her French and Italian, and Bishop Thomas Ken, who further encouraged her forays into poetry. On reaching womanhood she began to attract the attention of further important gentlemen, several of whom, as well as perhaps wishing a romantic attachment, also became her literary champions. These included Matthew Prior, Dr Isaac Watts and John Dunton, the latter being the owner of the 'Athenian Mercury' and who published several of Elizabeth's poems in the periodical, albeit anonymously.

In 1709 she met her future husband, Thomas Rowe, himself a child of a dissenting minister and a scholar in his own right. By now Elizabeth was a published poet, having seen her first collection of poetry in print thirteen years previously. They met in Bath and married the following year, after which they moved to London. Despite the difference in ages – she was thirty-six, he was twenty-three – by all accounts their hearts and minds were equal and they shared a happy and stimulating life together. Tragically their union lasted a mere five years, Thomas dying of consumption in 1715. Elizabeth returned to Frome, naturally heartbroken – 'since that fatal moment, my soul has never known a joy that has been sincere' she would write – and became somewhat of a recluse.

Following her father's death four years later, in 1719, she became financially independent for the rest of her life and devoted herself to writing prose and poetry that reflected her melancholic existence: 'I look backward, and recall nothing but tormenting scenes of pleasures that have taken their everlasting flight, and forward, every prospect is wild and gloomy.'

Thus she lived out the remaining eighteen years of her life in this way…'

'Very good, very good indeed,' remarked Lady Harriet, as she laid her niece's manuscript onto a small table beside which she had been standing. 'Perhaps a little verbose at times, but that can be edited down. The main thing to remember, however, is that as reclusive as Elizabeth may have been, she enjoyed a voluminous correspondence with friends, including the Countess of Hertford, the daughter of Henry Thynne, the man she learnt French and Italian from when younger. It has a very strong opening though; you take us straight into the heart of the subject.'

'Thank you, Aunt Harriet,' replied Mary. 'I am especially satisfied, even if I say it myself, with the opening.'

'Quite my dear, you should be pleased with it. Have you finished your tea?'

Mary nodded.

'Then I suggest we head into Frome so we can visit Elizabeth's house.' As they were about to leave, Harriet looked at the handwritten pages again. 'Yes, this is excellent. I feel you have really captured her personality. It will be a worthy addition to the series.'

The carriage, which had earlier dropped Swann off at Thomas Bunn's house, now conveyed Harriet and Mary along the same route towards the centre of Frome. They had arranged to meet the current resident of Rook Lane House, the property where Elizabeth Singer Rowe had spent the majority of her time in Frome, at midday. They had taken the opportunity of having breakfast together, whence Harriet had read the opening pages of Mary's manuscript. Although she was slightly hurt by the 'verbose' remark, Mary was nevertheless overjoyed that her aunt seemed pleased with what she had read so far.

Over breakfast Harriet had subtly questioned Mary as to Swann, and whether he had mentioned the case he was working on for her. It seemed that he had kept his word and not said anything to her about it. He also seemed to have no idea that the Scarred Man had been in the city, or at least if he did, had not mentioned this to his sister either. The weekly letters Mary sent were, for the most part, full of interesting observation but no real information Lady Harriet could use in her official capacity, so it was good to be able to question her niece personally.

Mary's love for Lockhart seemed genuine and, from what she had said, she truly believed his was for her as well. Harriet wished she could tell Mary the truth of Lockhart's past, but her hands were tied. There were issues of national security at stake, the very freedom of the country, and although she would do everything in her power to prevent it, she knew what was coming and that it spelt unhappiness for her niece. All she could do was to follow the plan she had devised and be there to pick up the emotional pieces when it came to fruition.

The carriage travelled down North Parade and into the centre of Frome once more. Harriet wanted Mary to gain a perspective on what she was writing; to see the actual places Elizabeth Singer Rowe had experienced while in Frome, as well as visiting the house she had lived in and the chapel where she had worshipped. This would provide a sense of place and perhaps help Mary with any rewriting, if she required stimulation. Harriet had been slightly apprehensive that Mary's prose might be stilted and the chapter stiff, but her niece seemed to have found inspiration from somewhere and had produced a very readable and inspirational piece of work.

The driver made his way up from the marketplace, but instead of turning right into Cork Street this time continued up Stony Street. Reflecting its name, the journey up was bumpy and uncomfortable for the passengers, who were rocked around inside the interior of the coach as they made their way up the steep incline. The roads had been widened and improved but Frome remained a narrow lane-strewn conurbation. As if reinforcing this point, literally, the carriage hit a large stone and the occupants were thrown against their respective sides of the carriage.

'Are you hurt, my dear?' asked the older woman as they righted themselves.

'I am fine, thank you Aunt Harriet.'

'Sorry, Lady Harriet,' shouted the driver from his position up front. 'I care there has been no damage to your persons?'

'We are both fine, thank you Johnson, but we would be most grateful if further altercations with stones could be avoided.'

'Very good, Lady Harriet,' the driver replied.

If North Parade was a relatively straight and smooth ride, the journey out of the town southward was a different matter. There were two routes leading up out of the marketplace, each with their advantages and disadvantages. Whichever course one chose, however, a short but uneven journey up Stony Street was required. From here, Catherine Hill branched off to the right and took travellers westward, whilst those desiring to carry their journey on southwards, turned left, briefly east, and then along Palmer Street towards St John's Church. Once here, there were two options available; both upwards and equally hazardous for pedestrians and carriages alike. The first of these, Gentle Street, was the route Thomas Bunn had travelled with Swann earlier that morning. Knowing the topography, Bunn had wisely decided they should ascend on foot. The second way, and the one the carriage driver had been directed to take by Lady Harriet, was Rook Lane. They climbed out of the valley and up a steep hill to an area known as Behind Town. It was here that Rook Lane House, the one-time residence of Elizabeth Singer Rowe, was located. The carriage halted outside the building and Mary and Harriett then alighted.

CHAPTER SEVENTEEN

'Mr Leach, this is Mr Swann,' said Thomas Bunn.

Standing in the doorway of the cottage was a big, burly-looking man: brother-in-law of Miss Leigh, the deceased teacher. He acknowledged Swann and then stood aside to let them in.

'My wife is expecting you, Mr Bunn.'

'Thank you,' said Bunn, as he and Swann made their way inside.

The cottage interior was cramped and immediately Swann felt an atmosphere of oppression. Although the husband's welcome had been cordial enough, it had lacked warmth and Swann sensed the man possessed a cold nature.

'I understand you are to begin your employ at the Asylum soon, Mr Leach,' asked Mr Bunn.

'My wife says it was you we have to thank for securing it. We are in your debt once more,' said Leach in somewhat of a begrudging tone. Bunn seemed not to notice though and merely raised his hand in a dismissive gesture.

'It was nothing, Mr Leach, given I am a trustee of the place. Wherever I can help families rise above their situation I am more than happy to oblige.'

As Leach went off to see if his wife was ready to receive them, Bunn turned to Swann.

'The Asylum is nearby, here in Keyford. It was completed last year and is soon to have its first intake of young girls destined for service. I have had the task of selecting them myself. There will also be several elderly men accommodated there as well, all of whom are, how is one to put this, past their labour. They will be given bed and board.'

'That sounds an unusual combination, if I may so,' replied Swann. 'Young girls and old men?'

Bunn smiled. 'Yes, the town is unique in that way, I believe,' he said, fondly. 'We also have a place in the town centre housing young boys and old women.'

Mr Leach returned and then led them into the back room of the dimly lit house. His wife had been in the process of breastfeeding their first child, but had now put the baby in a small basket beside her. As the men entered the room she went to stand, but Bunn gestured for her to remain seated.

'Please do not get up on our account, Mrs Leach. This is Mr Swann, the man who I mentioned yesterday. He is here to ask some questions about your sister.'

Mrs Leach nodded respectfully towards Swann.

'First, let me say how sorry I am about your sister's death,' said Swann.

'I will be out back, I have wood to chop,' said her husband and he left abruptly.

Swann looked across at Bunn. 'I would prefer it if Mrs Leach's husband remained,' he said.

Bunn looked across at Mrs Leach, who nodded. She stood up and went outside. There was a brief exchange and a moment later they both returned. Leach sat down on a chair beside his wife.

'I appreciate your return Mr Leach,' said Swann. 'I hope this will not take too long, but it is essential I learn everything I can. As you may or may not know, it is not only your sister-in-law's death I am investigating, but that of a pupil from the school as well.'

Swann turned to Mrs Leach.

'Did your sister have any enemies that you know of, Mrs Leach, anyone who might wish to cause her harm?'

'Her sort always attracted trouble and rightly so,' interjected Mr Leach. 'It was disgusting the way she behaved.'

'Frank, please,' said Mrs Leach.

'Well, it's selfish what she did. We have no money to bury her.'

'Do not worry yourself about that, Mr Leach,' said Bunn. 'I am certain it is something which can be arranged'.

'Mrs Leach, were you close to your sister?' continued Swann.

'Not really, I'm afraid to say. We never had been, even when we were growing up. She was always closer to our brother, although he died several years ago. She then moved away and I lost contact. Any news about her usually came to us from people in the area. She worked away for a while, I believe, looking after the children of a well-to-do family.'

'Do you know where this was?' asked Swann.

'No, only that it was abroad. She came back to live in this country and visited us once, but …' she paused.

'Please go on, Mrs Leach,' said Swann. 'You said she came here.'

'Yes,' said Mrs Leach, hesitantly.

'When was this, Mrs Leach?'

'At New Year, she'd heard I'd given birth and wanted to see her nephew.'

'And this was the last time you saw her?'

The woman nodded.

'How did she seem to you when she visited?'

'Well, it is hard to say; she did not stay long.'

'Oh, and why was that?' asked Swann.

Mrs Leach was silent.

'Because I told her to go,' said Mr Leach. 'I didn't want her kind in this house.'

'Frank!'

'Her kind, Mr Leach?' said Swann. 'What do you mean?'

'It was shameful how she behaved and I told her so.'

Mr Leach now looked at Bunn.

'Mr Bunn, I'm grateful to you for my employ, but I'll not sit here a minute longer to discuss that wretched woman. She's already brought enough shame on my wife and this family. If it means the loss of my job, then so be it!'

With that he stood and left the room, this time going out the front door.

'Frank! Come back!'

The door slammed shut and he was gone.

The baby had woken from the noise and begun to cry. Mrs Leach picked it up and rocked it in her arms.

'I am sorry for my husband's behaviour sirs, but he has been under a lot of stress lately. His sister has not been well and until Mr Bunn kindly secured this job, Frank has not been employed for a good eighteen months. Please don't tell him, Mr Bunn, but if the truth is known, he is scared of going back to work.'

This was acknowledged by both men.

'So, these "rumours" your husband mentioned, what exactly were they about?'

Mrs Leach hesitated. 'From what I understand, the rumours were that my sister preferred women to men.'

'Thank you, Mrs Leach. One last question, if I may,' said Swann. 'Does the name "Sappho" mean anything to you?'

Mrs Leach shook her head.

'Thank you for your time Mrs Leach,' said Swann. 'We will let ourselves out.'

'Do not worry about your husband, Mrs Leach,' added Bunn. 'I will make sure he settles in with his job. I will call on you both again soon.'

'Thank you Mr Bunn,' replied Mrs Leach, 'and I hope I have been of some help, Mr Swann.'

'You have indeed, and once again I am sorry about your sister's death.'

The two men left the cottage and retraced their steps towards Gore Hedge, so-called, according to tradition, because during the English Civil War several heads had been put on spikes there.

'I am sorry about Mr Leach,' said Bunn, 'most regrettable. They are both good people.'

'Do not concern yourself, Mr Bunn. I believe I have all the information I was seeking.'

'I was intrigued to hear you mention the name Sappho, Mr Swann.'

'Oh, you have heard of her?'

'Indeed, and I have read a few of her poems, or at least what fragments remain of them. May I enquire as to her connection with Miss Leigh's death?'

'I believe Miss Leigh was connected with a group who has that name in its title.'

'That would make sense,' said Bunn.

'How so?' asked Swann.

'It is said Sappho preferred her own sex's company to that of men. She ran a school on the island of Lesbos, in Greece, where she taught the daughters of rich families, but it is said that she also engaged in certain extra-curricular activities with many of them, if you understand my meaning.'

'I see,' said Swann.

'She is known as the tenth muse,' added Bunn, 'and one can understand why if you read her poetry. As for Miss Leigh, it is thought she became what is known as a female-husband. This was before she secured employment with the family Mrs Leach mentioned. I understand it was Switzerland where they stayed last summer. They wished to employ a tutor and governess for their four daughters.'

'So how did Miss Leigh become educated?'

'Self-taught, I believe. She became friends with several influential women in the town and it was through them she had access to books and teaching materials. I helped her in regard to a legal matter once, although I cannot remember the exact details.'

'And after her job as governess, she returned to Frome?'

'Only briefly; the story I heard is that she had lost her position after becoming too involved with one of the young girls under her charge. She then set herself up as a private tutor.'

'Was this in Frome?'

'No. By then she had moved to Bath and it was around that time she came to the notice of Lady Harriet. It was Her Ladyship who arranged her employment with the school. I am sure you know that though.'

'Yes,' Swann lied.

The two men had now reached Behind Town and stood near Rook Lane House.

'Ah, if I am not mistaken I believe that is your aunt's carriage ahead of us.'

CHAPTER EIGHTEEN

'I understand from Lady Harriet that you have this very day paid homage at the former home of the illustrious Mrs Rowe, Miss Gardiner?'

'You are right, Mr Huntley,' replied Mary, 'and I also visited the chapel where she worshipped and beneath which she is buried. Do you know her work well?'

'If I am honest, I do not have much time for her, although I reserve admiration for her later work, especially her more pious and reverential writings. I believe they represent her true nature.'

Mary was slightly bemused by these remarks.

'Forgive me Mr Huntley, but my brother has spoken of your keen literary acumen and perception. I do think though, in light of your evaluation of Mrs Rowe, he may have been mistaken.'

'Touché, Miss Gardiner, and please forgive me, my dear, as I could not help indulge in a little amusement at your expense. I chanced upon your biographical sketch of Mrs Rowe on Lady Harriet's table this afternoon, after my arrival, and I would not remain in business as a literary agent for long if I did not peruse, however fleetingly, any unpublished manuscript that happens to cross my path.'

The other guests around Lady Harriet's dinner table, except Swann, laughed nervously; many relieved the verbal sparring between Huntley and Mary had been based on nothing more than a fabrication, at least on Huntley's part.

'In fact, Miss Gardiner,' continued Huntley, 'I consider Mrs Rowe to be one of our most esteemed authoresses and poets, as well as a well-rounded woman, in terms of her attributes, which your essay has fully appreciated. You have a style about your prose which is, in turn, praiseworthy and enviable. Possibly a little verbose and didactic in places, if I may venture such an opinion, but overall I feel you have captured her essence and brought the subject to life in a manner which the great artists achieve on canvas. But then, of course, having seen your work, I know you are an accomplished portrait artist, as well.'

'I believe your statement regarding having seen my niece's work to be erroneous, Mr Huntley,' said Lady Harriet, in a measured but light-hearted manner, 'given the fact you have not previously met my niece, at least not to my knowledge, and therefore have had no opportunity to view her artistic endeavours.'

Swann instinctively knew he had to assist his good friend in extricating himself from a potentially troublesome situation.

'On the contrary, Lady Harriet,' he interjected. 'Huntley met Mary in Bath last autumn, at the Luchini exhibition. As Mr Luchini was Mary's art teacher at the time, I am naturally inclined to suppose I mentioned to him, in passing, my sister's accomplishments in portraiture, but can only assume my descriptions were so vivid, Huntley here believes he has actually viewed several of them!'

'Yes, that sounds like me,' said Huntley laughing, although visibly relieved at Swann's intervention. 'I do remember the exhibition well, but obviously had forgotten our conversation, Swann. By the way, how is your piece on Bath Abbey coming along?'

'It is as good as completed,' replied Swann, 'and will be with you by Sunday.'

'Good. I would not want *you* dying on me as well, before it was finished. Although, obviously I would not wish you dead after its completion, either!' Richard Huntley was the kind of person who would throw in a remark and then retire quietly to observe the verbal melee that ensued. On this occasion, however, he had been brought to account by Lady Harriet, herself known for her well-aimed comments. He had taken an instant dislike to her from their first meeting, but as they both worked for the same section within the Aliens Office, he knew he had to tread cautiously. As for Swann, Huntley was grateful for his intervention. It had been chance that brought them together in a London bookshop a few years previously, when a passing remark by Swann to the bookseller about an author Huntley represented had opened a literary conversation that had since led to friendship. When he later learnt that Swann was related to Lady Harriet, it seemed like provenance that the encounter had occurred.

It had been an eventful week for Lady Harriet. The murder of a diplomat's daughter and an employee of a close friend had been a bad way to start the week. This had been followed by the unwillingness of one of her agents to carry on the work he had been spared the gallows in order to undertake; a struggle to distract her nephew from the pursuit of a man he sought over his father's murder; and what had amounted to a dressing down from a man who, if not her direct boss, could easily cause a lot of trouble for her. And now there was this; a potential breech of security caused by Huntley's carelessness that could bring all of her carefully orchestrated plans crashing down, through the mere utterance of one untimely remark. She had thought at the time, when the Scarred Man portrait was being duplicated from Mary's original rendering, for agents in the field, that Huntley did not have a high enough level of clearance to warrant receiving a copy – but she had been overruled. Her instinct had been vindicated. The transgression was diffused now though, through the intervention of Swann and the fortuitous meeting at that exhibition the previous autumn. Now to return to the business in hand; this evening's gathering.

Alongside Lady Harriet were eight guests seated around the dinner table and each one had been invited by Lady Harriet for a different, specific reason known to her alone. Along with Swann, Mary and Huntley, was Lockhart, Catherine Jennings, Mrs Forsyth, a near-neighbour of Harriet's, and Colonel Braithwaite and his 'daughter' (a successful subterfuge carried out in regard to everyone else seated around the table, except for Harriet, who knew the truth about their relationship, and Swann, who had concluded it through his observations of them throughout the evening).

A ninth guest, John Bolton, the deceased girl's chaperone, had been invited but had not yet arrived. Whether he would now appear was open to conjecture, especially as the second course was about to be brought in.

As one group of servants cleared away the remains of the first course from the table, so another group began to bring in the dishes of the next; placing them on the table in accordance with prearranged instructions. Where there had been dishes of petit patties, Soup de Santé, haricos of mutton, chicken, turkey, tongue, sheep's rump and sweetbreads-à-la-daub, there were now scalloped oysters, apple puffs, prawns, Fowl à la Braise, rib of lamb, broccoli and Pompadore cream.

Not long after this course had been served, and with everyone replete with their fill of food and feeling the effects of the alcohol, a half-full wine glass was tapped several times. The various conversations taking place ended and all eyes focussed on the instigator of the sound.

'Thank you for your attention, ladies and gentlemen,' said Lockhart, standing up. 'I have an announcement to make. As many of you may know, Miss Gardiner and I are engaged to be married.' Lockhart glanced down at Mary, seated next to him, and she smiled. 'Until this evening, however, we had not yet finalised a date. Having had a most agreeable conversation with Lady Harriet, the aunt of my betrothed, I am pleased to announce that the wedding is to take place at the end of October.'

Mrs Forsyth and Catherine Jennings, along with Colonel Braithwaite and his 'daughter', immediately offered their congratulations to the happy couple, while Swann, Lady Harriet and Huntley used the distraction to gather their thoughts regarding the announcement.

'Lady Harriet has also kindly agreed to host the service and celebrations here in the grounds of her house, as well as providing accommodation for those guests travelling a great distance,' continued Lockhart. 'This obviously all depends on whether Lady Harriet's builders have finished their work, of course.' This last sentence was delivered sardonically.

The congratulating guests all laughed. Mrs Forsyth turned to Lady Harriet.

'Is there any news when your builders may actually conclude?' she enquired.

'They have assured me they will be finished by the end of the summer,' replied Harriet.

'Yes, but have they told you which year?' quipped the colonel, rather red-faced from his over-indulgence of alcohol that evening. Miss Jennings and Mrs Forsyth, along with Mary and Lockhart, all laughed at the colonel's witticism, and even

Huntley managed the briefest of smiles. When the colonel proposed a toast to the couple, they all lifted their glasses in unison and wished Mary and Lockhart the very best for the future.

As far as Harriet was concerned, the evening had gone from bad to worse. For the second time tonight one of her guests, with whom she had close working ties, had spoken out of turn. The agreement to an October wedding was only provisional, she had told Lockhart when they had met before dinner, and would depend on what happened in the intervening months. To announce it 'officially' in front of witnesses was beyond disobedience. If she wanted the Office's secret operation to be successful, however, she would just have to stand back and do nothing for the time being. She needed Lockhart as much as he needed her and he knew it!

Swann was inwardly furious he had not been consulted about the wedding date and would confront Lady Harriet at the earliest opportunity over it. As for Huntley, the announcement meant that his earlier faux pas regarding Mary's portrait had now been well and truly annulled. If his had been no more than a skirmish, then Harriet's agreement to a wedding date was tantamount to a declaration of war. He still could not believe, given what he knew of her relationship with Lockhart and the man's notorious past, that she could not only arrange a date for him to be married but the bride was to be her own flesh and blood!

Catherine Jennings, although outwardly congratulatory, pondered the sense of a woman wanting to subjugate herself to a man. Had she not said as much last year, during a talk in this very building? She wholeheartedly believed the responsibility of a woman remaining true to herself within marriage lay solely with the woman, she had told the packed room. She should therefore ensure that the man she is going to marry will not stand in her way of continuing personal development. Miss Jennings had recognised Mary from that talk, and now wondered how much of her speech had been retained.

Mrs Forsyth, on the other hand, could not imagine a woman not being married to a man. She had enjoyed nearly forty years of married bliss and the secret, if anyone ever ventured to ask her, was that they were spent with several different husbands. It seemed no sooner had the passion begin to wane from one of her marriages, the husband would 'fortuitously' pass away and she would find another, sooner rather than later, to take his place and so rekindle the fervour.

Lockhart's announcement reminded Colonel Braithwaite of his own marriage and how much he regretted undertaking it. This thought, however, was tempered by the fact his wife was many miles away, holidaying with friends in Brighton, and he was able to spend the night in the company of his 'daughter' and enjoy Harriet's hospitality of the guest room. As for this 'daughter', she wanted only to be married to the wealthy and elderly colonel, yet at this present moment she also wished herself in the opposite seat to where she was now, in that of the bride-to-be, having taken a fancy to the man who had made the announcement.

As for Lockhart himself, he was overjoyed that he had found the courage to announce it tonight, as it meant Lady Harriet could not indulge in any delaying tactics given as it was now in the public domain. He knew it was a gamble to have done so, as there were certain risks involved, but then had he not always been so lucky. The fact he had met someone of Mary's calibre, after everything he had gone through, surely meant something. And long may it carry on, he thought to himself. He would just have to figure out a way to keep all the plates spinning until October. He could do it. He would just have to convince Kirby to let him continue working for the organisation but not to escort the women. If Swann found out about it, he would surely tell his sister and there was every good chance that she would believe him and bring an end to their engagement. It was now almost seven months since he had met Mary and he still felt the same way about her. No, if anything, his feelings were even stronger.

The meal ended not long after the toast had been made and as much as Harriet would have liked to have said good-night to the guests there and then, she offered her assembled visitors the opportunity to play cards; hazard being the game of choice.

In the time it took everyone to walk from Harriet's dining table to the nearby room where several card tables had been set up, Swann had become engaged in two furtive conversations. The first was with his sister. 'Are you happy for me, Jack?' Swann thought for a moment before he answered.

'I do not believe he is the right man for you, Mary,' he had replied honestly, 'but if it is your desire to marry him and you are truly happy, then I am happy for you.'

Mary went through to the other room, content at her brother's answer. As Swann moved forward, he felt an arm grab him and hold him back. It was Huntley.

'Jack,' he whispered. 'I cannot tell you how I know, but the man with the scar you seek will be in Bath sometime on Saturday night and will be in the city for no more than a day. I implore you not to seek him though, as your life will be in great danger. If you do, however, you must know that you are, at present, being played as that of a pawn in a game of chess. That is all I can say for now.' He put a finger to his lips in a 'silence' gesture. And with that he was gone.

CHAPTER NINETEEN

After numerous games of cards, the party of guests at Harriet's residence had started to go their separate ways. A drunken Colonel Braithwaite had retired with his 'daughter' to his host's guest bedroom, replete with the four-poster bed that awaited them, while Huntley had made his farewells and left the estate completely.

Swann had been walking up and down the corridors, looking for Harriet and determined to confront her over the matter of the wedding. He had left Mary and Lockhart in the card room conversing with Mrs Forsyth, who had been in the process of giving them advice on what constituted a successful marriage.

The door to the library was ajar and there was a light inside. He knocked on the door and entered.

'Forgive me, Lady Harriet, I did not realise you were with company.'

'Do not worry Swann,' replied Harriet. 'Catherine was about to retire for the evening.'

'Yes, Harriet has kindly offered me a guest room for the night. The hour has become later than I would wish to return to the school.'

'I was just updating Catherine on your progress into the deaths at her school.'

'I am afraid I have not made much,' replied Swann, addressing Miss Jennings. 'I wonder though whether you will be at the school sometime tomorrow?'

'My carriage will be returning Catherine in the morning,' replied Lady Harriet.

'Good,' said Swann. 'I would be grateful if you could arrange it so I can talk to Anne again. She was one of the girls that shared a dormitory with Grace and I have a couple more questions for her.'

Swann had not mentioned to Lady Harriet or Miss Jennings about the Circle of Sappho yet, as he was not certain whether either of the two women in his presence now were involved in it.

'Will ten o'clock be agreeable, Mr Swann? I shall be at the school by then.'

'That will be most agreeable, Miss Jennings,' replied Swann.

Miss Jennings said her goodnights to Harriet and Swann and made her way out of the library.

'I thought we had an agreement to make certain the marriage did not happen,' said Swann to Harriet, as soon as Miss Jennings was out of sight.

'And so we did,' replied Lady Harriet.

'Then why have you arranged a date for the wedding behind my back?'

'I have my reasons,' said Harriet quietly, as she crossed to the library door to close it. 'Our agreement has not changed. It is just that certain developments have occurred which necessitated me being seen to be arranging the wedding.'

'I do not understand. All I know is that something I thought we were both supposedly against is now taking place with seemingly your full agreement and co-operation.'

'Swann, listen to me. There are things you do not understand; there are powers at work which are greater than us. I cannot divulge details; I only ask that you trust me in this matter. Believe me, I do not want this marriage any more than you do and I have no intention of allowing it to proceed.'

'What about Mary?'

'That is where I need you, Swann. You will have to be there for her when the time comes to terminate the engagement.'

'Terminate?'

Lady Harriet was silent.

'Is Mary in danger?'

'Swann, this is not the time or place to —'

'Damn it Lady Harriet! I believe it is. I will never willingly let any harm come to Mary and if it does, I can assure you that I will not stop in my pursuit to bring anyone remotely responsible to justice.'

'Are you threatening me, Swann?'

'No, and I apologise for my outburst, but you talk about country, service, government. What are these things compared to family?'

'You are not the only one who has lost someone dear and seek justice for them.'

'What do you mean?'

'As you know, I was widowed far too soon.'

'Yes, I know, your husband died in an accident, he fell from a mountain path.'

'It was no accident,' whispered Harriet. 'He was murdered.'

'I am sorry, Lady Harriet,' replied Swann, his voice quiet. 'I had no idea. What happened?'

'He was betrayed by those he worked for and I have made it my life's work, just like you with your father, to avenge his death.'

Harriet gestured for Swann to sit down in one of the armchairs near the fire, reminiscent of his meeting with Moorhouse only the night before at Fitzpatrick's club.

'What I am about to tell you I have never told anyone else,' said Harriet, sitting down opposite Swann, 'and you must swear to keep it to yourself.'

'Why are you telling *me*?'

'I want you to know you can trust me and that in many ways we are alike in what we seek. My husband, as you may be aware, was financially independent but worked for the government, in the same capacity as I do at the moment. We had not long arrived in Constantinople when my husband announced he had to go to the island of Crete on an urgent matter. He had been there several times before, while we were living in Athens, but always on his own. This time I told him I wanted to go with him. He was reluctant at first, but I convinced him to take me and so we went. No sooner had we arrived at our hotel than he left for a meeting from which he never returned. I was told that on the way there, he had accidentally fallen from a goat path somewhere in the mountains and broken his neck. The two British Government officials who told me the news advised that I should leave for England. Once I agreed, they made arrangements for my departure the following day.

'Early the next morning, however, an envelope was pushed under my door. I picked it up and went outside to see who had delivered it, but the hallway was empty. Inside the envelope I found a note. It said that my husband had been murdered and if I wished to know more, I should go to the address written below. I was obviously shocked by this news, as well as being grief-stricken by Henry's death, but I kept my wits about me. Was it true? Had my husband been murdered, or was it a plot to lure me somewhere so I could be killed as well. I decided that I owed it to my husband to go. The address turned out to be a building in a narrow alleyway, a little way from the main market square. I did as the note had instructed and made sure I was not followed. I was scared, but found an inner strength. All I cared about at that moment was being true to my husband's memory.

'I knocked on the large wooden door, in the manner I had been instructed. A small flap in the entrance was lifted and I saw a pair of eyes peer out. It was then closed and after a few seconds the door opened and I was ushered in. It was a type of estaminet, with an uneven stone floor and chairs and tables haphazardly placed around the dimly lit room. There was no one around except for the man who had let me in and another man who now appeared from behind a curtain. They were both foreign, although when the second man spoke it was in relatively good English. "Please do follow me," he said. I did as he had instructed and ducked under the curtain after him. This led out into the rear alleyway, where the man now stood, holding the reins of a donkey. He gestured for me to climb up on its back and I did so. Once I was upright on the beast, he slapped its backside and we headed off through the backstreets of the city until we came to a small doorway halfway along a particularly long passageway. He stopped, knocked several times in the way I had done earlier at the estaminet and then, without a word, helped me off the donkey, tapped its backside again and away he went. By the time I looked back at the door it was ajar, and a fierce-looking, dark-skinned man gestured me in. Inside, the room was dimly lit and sparse. There were boxes stacked here and there and I had the feeling it was a type of small warehouse or office; a table and two chairs – one of which was occupied – were the only furniture in the room. As I stood there, the man in the chair rose and came towards me. As he neared me, I saw he had a kind face but it was troubled. His accent was foreign but when he spoke it was in perfect English.

"'My name is Yorgos. I am sorry for your loss; your husband was a good man. He was also a friend to me. I cannot believe he is gone."

'He gestured for me to sit down and once I had done so resumed his own chair. He then offered me a drink but I declined. I was thirsty but I wanted more to hear what he had to say.

"'Your husband was murdered," Yorgos stated. "He was carrying a message the people who killed him did not want delivered. It was no accident he fell from the mountain path. He was deliberately pushed by one of the men who were meant to be guiding him."

"'How do you know?" I whispered.

"'One of the men in an organisation I belong to saw what happened. He was trailing them in case they ran into the Pasha's troops. The Pasha is the man who rules Crete. So what will you do now, return to England?"

"'Eventually, I am sure, but I owe it to my husband to find answers. Do you know who the man was that pushed my husband?"

"'I would strongly advise you do not stay," he said, in a firm but gentle manner. "These are dangerous times for anyone on the island who is not Turkish, but especially for an English woman alone. Do not waste your time searching. The man who pushed your husband is already dead, as are the other two men with him."

"'But how? Why? Who would do that?"

"'The 'how' is that their throats were slit. Their bodies were discovered at the bottom of a ravine. The 'why' is because the person who ordered your husband's murder did not want any witnesses to the crime; and as for the 'who', that we do not know, although I would suggest you look to your own government for an answer."

'He looked across at me.

"'I can see in your eyes what it is you intend to do, but if you start out on the road of revenge your life will be over."

"'Without my husband it feels as if my life is over anyway. What I want to do is return to Constantinople, to continue his work."

'Yorgos thought for a few moments, shook his head, and then looked across the table at me.

"'I can see you are a strong-willed lady and although I strongly advise you to go back to England, if you are that determined to stay, I shall help you in any way I can. For now, though, return to your hotel and await my instructions.'"

'I did as I was told and made my way back to the hotel. The two government officials were not happy when they found out I was staying, but there was nothing they could do about it. I was a financially independent woman who had no ties to the embassy or government. I stayed in Crete for about a week prior to my passage back to Constantinople. Before I left, Yorgos gave me several names and addresses of contacts, many of which my husband had known.

'In time I learnt more about the circumstances surrounding my husband's death and put the pieces of the jigsaw together. It seemed he was given information regarding a rebellion that was to take place on Crete. He had gone to the island to relay this information to the leader of the uprising and was on his way to meet him at his mountain base when he was murdered.

'This was in 1770, of course, and by then the Cretans had been under Ottoman rule for more than a century. By this time most of the population had become Muslim. It was not that they believed in that particular religion, but more to escape the restrictions Christianity brought on them. Although the Christian faith was more or less tolerated by the Turks, the island's Christian traders had an immense tax burden placed upon them. As well as taxes on their businesses they also had them on their houses, although the most hated of all these taxes was the *kharatch*. This was a type of tax that was, in effect, a protection racket. By 1770 discontent had become, perhaps unsurprisingly, rife among Christians in Crete, as on other Greek islands and parts of the mainland, and so when the opportunity to rise up against their oppressors was offered, it was taken with both hands, especially as their ally would be one of the Great Powers: Russia.

'The rebellion on Crete was to be led by a wealthy merchant and ship owner called Ioannis Vlahos. He had been educated abroad – in Italy – and while there was given the nickname Daskaloyiannis, meaning 'teacher'. On his return he had become a successful businessman and accumulated a lot of money. In the course of conducting his business he often travelled to the Black Sea. On one occasion, while there, he met the Orlov brothers: Aleksey and Grigory. Both were Russian agents working for Catherine the Great's network of spies. They were thought to have been key conspirators in bringing her to the Russian throne by overthrowing her husband, Peter III, eight years earlier. The Emperor had then died shortly after the palace coup, in mysterious circumstances, and it was believed that Aleksey murdered him.

'By the time Daskaloyiannis met Aleksey and his brother he was commander of the Russian naval forces. The brothers' remit was to stir up as much trouble in the Ottoman Empire as they could. The Russians were the Turks' sworn enemy and had been fighting them for the past two years.

As well as Daskaloyiannis on Crete, the Orlov brothers also contacted leaders in the Peloponnese, on the Greek mainland (this area being chosen by the brothers as they believed it had the strongest military force at the time). Their plan was simple. There would be uprisings on the mainland and Crete, supported by the Russian navy, and this would lead to a nationwide revolt and rebellion against the Turks. The initial uprising on the mainland went ahead and when the Russian fleet appeared in nearby waters, it seemed success was at hand. Daskaloyiannis brought his forces down from the mountains into the cities on Crete, but unfortunately for him the Russians had never had any intention of sending reinforcements to help, merely to use his rebellion as a distraction from their main focus of the Peloponnese. Although Daskaloyiannis was initially victorious, without the promised Russian fleet to support them, his forces were quickly and brutally suppressed by the Turks and Daskaloyiannis himself was flayed to death in a square in Heraklion.

'Through his several visits to Crete, my husband had become acquainted with Daskaloyiannis and they had become friends. When my husband found out that the Russian fleet were never intending to come to Crete to support his friend, he immediately set sail for the island to inform him. He could not entrust such vital information to anyone else and so had carried out the journey into the mountains himself, to deliver the message. This information cost him his life.'

'So was it actually the Russians who killed him?' asked Swann.

'No, or at least if they were involved, it was not directly. They benefited from my husband's death, of course, as the planned uprising in Crete went ahead and created the diversion they were hoping for to carry out their attack on the Greek mainland. The person who actually pushed my husband off that path was a local, a Cretan who had been bribed. Although he did not live long enough to benefit from his own pieces of silver, as he was one of those found in a gorge with his throat slit the following day. No, ultimately the order for my husband to be killed came from someone in the British camp. It was in their interests that the rebellion should take place and Daskaloyiannis, the leader of the rebellion, seen to have been betrayed, as it gave them leverage in any future negotiations with leaders that might have formerly conducted business with Russia. The British could say, therefore, that the Russians could not be trusted. Any conflict is good for government dealings, if it adds to your cause, which this one did: this is why my husband was betrayed and killed by his own countrymen.'

'So do you know who gave the order?'

Harriet nodded. 'I believe so.'

'So why are you still alive?' asked Swann.

'The person does not know I am aware of their role in my husband's death. As you point out, if they did, I would be dead.'

'Who is it?'

Harriet smiled.

'My dear Swann, I am not about to disclose the person's identity. For a start, I do not want to endanger your life unnecessarily.'

'I would suggest the fact you have even told me this story, Lady Harriet, is enough to do that.'

'You are right and I am sorry. Only two other people knew the truth and they are both dead. I am the only one left. And now, of course, you Swann. It would therefore be better for both of us if you did not breathe a word of this to anyone.'

'Your secret is safe with me, Lady Harriet. But can I ask you a question? If you know who was behind your husband's murder, why do you not seek to kill him now?'

Harriet looked into the fire and prodded some dying embers with a poker.

'I have only recently discovered this person's identity and I do not believe it would be appropriate to kill them at this time,' she replied. 'At least not in the present climate. As I said earlier, there are greater issues at stake than seeking revenge for a death so many years ago. Do not be mistaken, there is not a day goes by when I do not think of my husband, mourn his loss and wish to seek retribution for what was done to him: having to live these past thirty-four years without the one true love of my life has been a kind of hell. But we are all mere players in a greater game, and to have this knowledge is enough. I will bide my time and one day will exact my vengeance. It is the same with your quest, Swann, I am certain. There are wider consequences to be considered in both our cases.'

'What do you mean? Do you have information about my father's killers?'

'If I knew anything, and I do not, I could not divulge it to you even if I wanted to. There are things you cannot possibly be aware of and it is in your best interests that it stays that way.'

'What if you die before this man?'

'That is a good point, but I have prepared for that eventuality.'

Harriet stood up and went over to a bookshelf. Here she retrieved a key which was hidden inside a panel and then moved across to a small table near a far wall. She unlocked a drawer in the table, removed an envelope, and then returned to again sit opposite Swann. She held up the envelope.

'All the evidence I have discovered over the years is gathered together in a folder and deposited in the vault of my legal representatives in London. Their name and address is written on a sheet of paper in this envelope, along with special instructions that will allow the folder to be handed over to the possessor of this envelope in the event of my death.'

'What is to stop anyone finding this envelope and retrieving the folder now?'

'My legal firm have been given strict instructions that the folder is only to be given to the person with this envelope after they have definite confirmation of my death. So, in the event of my death, you know where the envelope is, if you so wish to retrieve it.'

Swann nodded.

'Consider it done, Lady Harriet.'

'Thank you, Swann. This is partly why I have told you the story. I was hoping to find someone I could rely on and the opportunity presented itself tonight.'

'One thing I do not understand though …' began Swann but before he could continue there was a loud knocking on the library door. Lady Harriet stood up and went over to open it; outside stood one of her male servants.

'I am sorry to trouble you Lady Harriet, but I believe you would wish to know the news immediately. We have been informed that one of your dinner guests has been killed.'

CHAPTER TWENTY

Bath, Wednesday 28th March, 1804

The events of tonight have left me as shaken as those of yesterday evening and the encounter with Kirby, perhaps even more so; the announcement of a wedding date for Mary and Lockhart, the conversation with Huntley, Harriet's story surrounding her husband's death and, of course, another murder. I have a strong feeling that everything that happened tonight is in some way connected.

I will focus on Huntley and his unguarded comment first. He talked with authority at having seen Mary's portraiture work and yet to my knowledge has not met her before tonight – despite what I said at the dinner to Harriet, I did not actually introduce them at the exhibition – and there is no feasible way he would have visited our house to view her sketchbook. I can only think, therefore, that it is the portrait of the Scarred Man that he has seen as this is the only portrait Mary has completed which is in the 'public domain'. But where and when?

Given this is the case then, where would he have seen it? Possibly when George and Bridges were showing it around, as part of my investigation. But then how would he link it to Mary? Even if he was told the portrait had been given to them by me, he has never met her or seen any of her other work. It must be assumed therefore that Huntley has seen the portrait of the Scarred Man elsewhere: but how? I have never shown the original to anyone and the only copy Mary made of it is the one I gave to George and Bridges.

The most likely answer is very disagreeable though, as it can only be assumed that Mary, at some time, made a second copy and gave it to a third party – a person she trusted and who also knows Huntley. Given Harriet's reaction to Huntley's unguarded comment, I am inclined to think that she is this person. But why would Mary do this? One can only surmise that Harriet requested it, but then how did she know about the portrait in the first place? Did Mary tell her, or did she somehow discover it through her network of spies on the city streets, in the same way that Wicks found out about it? Whatever the truth is, and given what I have deduced, I will assume there exists another copy of the portrait of which Harriet is in possession.

But to what end would Harriet request a copy of the Scarred Man's portrait? Given what she said this evening about the search for my father's killers – 'It is the same with your quest, Swann. There are wider consequences to be considered in both our cases,' – it must be assumed she was lying when she said she did not know anything. And given this, it can be assumed that Harriet knows the whereabouts of the Scarred Man and that he therefore must be under surveillance. But why? Is he somehow involved in issues of national security? And after what Huntley whispered to me as we were about to go into the card room, it seems likely that, along with Harriet, Huntley is also working for the Alien Office, or is somehow otherwise connected to my aunt's network of spies.

I do not intend to ask Mary about the second copy of the portrait immediately. Instead I will act on Huntley's information regarding the Scarred Man and will search the back streets of the Avon Street district for him on Saturday night and all of Sunday, if necessary. I will also inform George and Bridges so they can report back with any relevant information.

At this point I have to ask where Lockhart fits in to all this? From what I understand from Harriet, the wedding date has been set because of 'something greater'; but can I trust Harriet when she says her intention is to stop the wedding going ahead? If she has lied to me about not knowing anything with regard to my father's killers and has requested a copy of the Scarred Man's portrait from Mary behind my back, then I have to tread carefully in any future dealings with her. And the story she told me about her husband's death, is this true? Was someone connected to the British Government ultimately responsible for his death? And what of the envelope she showed me, did it really contain her legal firm's address?

I realise that I have not even thought of the school deaths and the latest developments in the case. I am also aware I still have to conduct my research into Sappho before my visit with Anne tomorrow. With regard to my visit to Frome, it was good to meet Thomas Bunn and I have learnt several things about the town that I did not know beforehand, but Miss Leigh's sister did not have much to offer in terms of information relating to the case; if anything, it was her husband who contributed the greater share; implying Miss Leigh was attracted to her own sex. I will bear this revelation in mind when I am at the school tomorrow, although given the latest death this evening – that of John Bolton – the reason for going there again may now be obsolete. If Bolton was the murderer, then the case is closed. Am I supposed to believe that it was by sheer coincidence that he was attacked and killed by highwaymen on his way to Harriet's dinner party tonight? But still, there is something about him which plays on my mind, a familiarity to his name, although I am certain I have not met him previously. If the Sappho research does not take too much of my time, I will look back through my notebooks to see if there is anything in them that will shed light on the mystery of John Bolton.

The events of this evening, however, have thankfully distracted me from Kirby's challenge and my unacceptable behaviour yesterday night. I hope Fitzpatrick received my informal apology and I intend to pass by his office tomorrow to do so in person.

CHAPTER TWENTY-ONE

Swann stepped into the small wooden boat and pushed off from its mooring. He began rowing himself across the lake towards the island, his mind trying to make sense of the events of the previous few days.

He had returned to the school with the intention of talking to Anne, the pupil he believed had surreptitiously placed the 'Circle of Sappho' message inside his pocket. On reaching the school, however, he had been informed by a rather shaken Miss Jennings that the girl was dead; having committed suicide by jumping off the roof of the main building, not less than thirty minutes before Swann had arrived. The body had now been removed to the chapel – where the bodies of Miss Leigh and Grace had been laid out only a few days earlier – and the girls allowed back out of their dormitories. Swann had been shown the roof by Miss Jennings and head girl Elsa – the key to which Anne had somehow acquired – and then her dormitory, where Swann had been only a few days previously searching for clues regarding Grace's murder. There was nothing in her belongings that was of any use to Swann's investigation, although a disturbance of the ground up on the roof suggested the possibility of a struggle.

Swann spoke briefly with Miss Jennings afterwards and she informed him of the events leading up to his arrival. 'I arrived at the school in Lady Harriet's carriage this morning, at approximately eight-thirty,' she told him. 'After I had spoken to my deputy, to find out if anything eventful had happened in my absence – nothing had – I went to locate Anne. She was with the rest of her year, along with a few of the older girls, so I beckoned to her. I told her you wished to talk to her and that she should make herself available in the common room at ten o'clock. Not twenty minutes later there was screaming from outside and on looking out from my window, I saw her body on the ground.'

Anne had not appeared anxious about talking to Swann, or so Miss Jennings said. If anything, she seemed happy about his imminent arrival, which made her subsequent action even more mysterious. Swann had then requested to go across to the island, this time by himself, to which Miss Jennings had agreed.

So, if the first two deaths had been at the hands of a third party, then the murderer had struck again, which ruled out Bolton as the killer, given that he himself had been killed the night before. Having checked his case notes, Swann had discovered why his name was familiar. During an investigation a few months earlier, he had chanced upon a discussion concerning Napoleon and his extensive network of agents in this country. Someone had mentioned the aliases French agents assumed while in England and how they differed from county to county. He was not sure of them all, this person said, but knew several of them. In the home counties, for instance, the name 'John Brown' was used, in Devon and Cornwall it was 'John Smith' and 'John Thomas' respectively, and in Somerset, that of 'John Bolton'.

In Swann's list of suspects this now left Tom, the gardener. There was definitely something that he was not telling him, something he was hiding, but was it that he was the murderer? The fact that Tom had swum to the island to find the bodies meant he could have swum over earlier, perhaps after discovering the boat was gone.

Swann was heading to the island with one purpose, to retrieve what he believed to be the diary from which the note about the Circle of Sappho had been torn. As he had not found anything in the girl's belongings, his instinct told him it was on the island. Once retrieved, the diary would hopefully provide the answers to this mystery.

The sky was overcast and threatened rain as Swann rowed across. He reached the jetty and tied the rope to the mooring post. He stepped onto the island and began the short walk to the stone temple. The sound of a branch snapping alerted him to the fact he might not be alone on the island and for a moment, up ahead, Swann thought he saw movement.

Taking the pistol from his jacket pocket Swann swiftly made his way to the temple entrance and cautiously went in. He looked around the gloomy interior but no one was evident. Had it been a figment of his imagination? No, he had definitely seen someone. He examined the walls of the temple to see if there was another way out, a secret passageway perhaps, but Swann could discern nothing that would allow someone to leave other than via the opening he had just entered. There was the inscription he had noticed the first time, above the opening. He read it once more: *Procul, o procul este, profani* – 'Be gone, be gone you who are uninitiated'. In Virgil's *Aeneid*, the hero of the book, Aeneas, encounters this Latin inscription on the threshold to the underworld. He nevertheless enters and encounters his father's spirit, who gives a prophetic vision of his future.

As well as above the entrance, Swann now saw the same inscription written into the far wall. His instinct told him the walls of the temple hid another way out, but for now he could do nothing further here. He turned and went back outside.

When the island had originally been created, it had been planted with broad-leaved trees – sycamores, beeches, oaks, maples – whose all-encompassing foliage would hide the activities of the island from prying eyes on the main grounds and house. Even in winter, when the leaves had fallen, the density of the trees easily hid any activity, especially that taking place in the small clearing Swann had now discovered within the island's groves.

As far as Swann could discern, there was a design to the way in which the island was laid out, with small trails and paths leading around it. All the paths, however, eventually found their way to the middle of the island and the small clearing where Swann stood. Within the clearing was an outdoor temple, replete with the statue of a female figure atop a stone plinth, which Swann recognised as Aphrodite. If he remembered his Classical education correctly, the Greek goddess had been the result of a liaison between Zeus and the Titan goddess Dionë. She had grown to be a beautiful woman and was worshipped by the ancient Greeks as the goddess of love, beauty and fertility.

In the clearing there was a stone circle. Was this the Circle of Sappho? There had been nine muses, so he had read the previous evening, with Sappho being the tenth muse. The geography of the seating certainly reflected this, with the nine stone seats in a circle and a tenth, a little way outside the circle, but still having command of the others. A pit near the stone altar, in the middle of the seats, showed signs of a recent fire, as well as several sets of footprints in the clearing.

Swann's attention was drawn towards a clump of trees to his left. On the ground lay a makeshift wooden shovel, hurriedly abandoned it seemed, beside the beginnings of a freshly dug hole. From the footprints in the soil nearby it looked like there had been two people here who, possibly, had been disturbed by Swann when he came ashore.

Swann picked up the shovel and began to dig. About two feet down the shovel hit a solid object. Swann uncovered the earth and found a small brown wooden box, basic in design. The hinges were not rusted and the exterior did not feel damp. Swann opened the lid. Inside was a piece of dark green material, wrapped around an object. Swann carefully unwrapped the material and found what he was looking for inside: a diary. He turned to a particular date and matched the missing page to that of the piece of paper he had been given. If there had been any doubt before, then there was none now. If Anne had indeed given Swann the note, then the diary either belonged to her or else had recently been in her possession. He lifted the front cover and realised it had been the latter. The name written inside was that of Grace Templeton, the girl who had been killed alongside Miss Leigh, and who had shared a dormitory with Anne. Had Anne taken the diary for safekeeping, after her friend's death, and had come across to the island to bury it?

Swann began to read the first page but realised this was not the time or place to puruse it. He would read it at home. He decided not to mention the diary to either Miss Jennings or Lady Harriet, but rather pursue this particular line of enquiry himself. Within these pages, he hoped, lay the truth behind the murders at the school, and the truth about the Circle of Sappho as well.

Swann secured the diary on his person, wrapped inside the dark green material once more, and put the now empty box back into the ground. He made one final circuit of the island and then briefly went back inside the temple. He concluded that this interior was where initiations into the Circle of Sappho occurred and afterwards they would pass through the entrance, under the inscription, and out on to the island to take part in their rituals and ceremonies. But there was a problem with this hypothesis and that was the question of how they had entered the temple in the first place? For now he did not have the answer to that particular conundrum and so decided to return across the lake. He felt his jacket as he reached the jetty to ascertain the diary was still safe, and then stepped into the wooden craft. As he rowed back across the water he had the distinct feeling he was being watched again by someone on the island.

CHAPTER TWENTY-TWO

On arriving back in Bath from his visit to the school Swann immediately went to Fitzpatrick's office. The magistrate was at his desk, reviewing a recent case of manslaughter.

'There is no need to apologise,' said Fitzpatrick kindly as Swann explained the reason for his visit. 'The events of Tuesday evening are already forgotten.'

'That is very magnanimous of you, Henry.'

'Think nothing of it.'

'I was intending to send a formal letter of apology to your club, as well.'

Fitzpatrick responded to this proposal with a dismissive gesture of his hand. 'There really is no need,' he said. 'I have been into the club since and it has been resolved agreeably. Besides, Kirby is just as responsible in this affair. I would not wish for this to go outside of the room, but I think his behaviour was ungentlemanly and verging on scandalous. Have you informed Mary regarding the duel yet?'

'No and I do not intend to, as I have decided—'

'Do you not think she deserves to beware of this? If you were to be killed … I mean if anything was to happen to … I am concerned for your safety, Swann, especially as I believe Kirby to be a fine shot.'

'That is most laudable of you Henry and I appreciate your concern, but you do not have to worry as I will not be taking part in the duel.'

'What? Has Kirby withdrawn his challenge? That would at least explain why his second has not yet been to see me.'

'No, Kirby has not withdrawn his challenge; I am no longer going to accept it. I am going to visit him when I leave here to inform him. There will be no duel.'

'Kirby will not agree to it.'

'He will have no choice. Despite his insult to my father I have no intention of killing him, and I also do not wish to risk my own life in the process.'

'Swann, I do not think you fully understand. It is not that simple. For a start, if you do not take part your reputation will be sullied.'

'A reputable name, I believe, is not required to continue my line of work.'

'If you do withdraw, Kirby will insist that someone takes your place.'

'Then I will simply not venture the name of anyone.'

'If that happens it becomes the responsibility of the withdrawn participant's second to fulfil the arrangement.'

'What does that mean?' said Swann.

'It means that I will have to fight Kirby.'

'Henry, I do not wish you to do that.'

'I will have no choice. There are witnesses to my agreeing to be your second. If your place is not taken and your obligation in regard to this challenge fulfilled, then as your second my own reputation will be ruined. I shall no longer be able to hold my present magisterial position, as my authority will be undermined.'

'Do not be so rash, Fitzpatrick, the act of duelling is illegal let us not forget. If we are caught, will your reputation not be ruined anyway?'

'We magistrates are normally lenient on duels, even where one of the participants has died.'

'Surely there is something that can be done?'

'Only that the duel is carried out to the satisfaction of the challenger, Kirby.'

'Did you say Kirby's second has not been to see you?'

Fitzpatrick nodded.

'Then perhaps we are worrying over nothing,' said Swann. 'Perhaps Kirby has had second thoughts and wisely decided against going ahead with this madness.'

'Perhaps,' replied Fitzpatrick, unsurely.

The magistrate then remembered something.

'By the way, there has been a development with Charles Moorhouse; he has received another demand for money.'

'When?'

'This very morning, he came to tell me. Can I ask you something?'

Swann nodded.

'Why did you change your mind and take on his case? You seemed adamant you would not.'

'My instinct tells me that in the coming months we are going to need men like Moorhouse within government. I am not a complete advocate of his particular party's policies, but I do agree with him that Pitt is probably the only man for the job at this current time. At the same time, he will also need a strong set of ministers behind him if we are to defeat Napoleon. I have taken the case because if Moorhouse does obtain a governmental position, the blackmailers will have an even stronger hold over him and a politician within their grasp would be a very valuable commodity to have; that is something I would not wish to see happen, for all our sakes. Has he been given instructions as to where to take the money this evening?'

'Yes, the old East Gate, near the river. He has been told to be there thirty minutes after sunset.'

'Then I shall be there too.'

'You will be in disguise?'

Swann nodded again.

'I am worried about this.'

'Do not concern yourself, Henry, I will take precautions against being followed, trust me.'

As Swann walked down the stairs of Fitzpatrick's building he thought about George and Bridges, and the latter's friend, Rosie, and her present situation. Fitzpatrick's concern about Swann being recognised or followed had brought to his mind the warehouse, which he had subsequently rented after the artist had been murdered the previous year. His 'wardrobe' only took up the top floor of the building and the fact he only used it at irregular intervals meant it was empty for long periods of time; prone then to possible criminal elements – although he had secured it with the strongest locks he could purchase – or worse, vermin, who would eat away at his disguises. As he stepped out into the city's afternoon bustle an idea to benefit all had come to mind.

CHAPTER TWENTY-THREE

Leaving Fitzpatrick's office Swann headed up the road to his own, in No.40 Gay Street. Once there, he retrieved Grace Templeton's diary from about his person and undid the green material in which it had been wrapped. He placed the material on his desk and took the small black volume over to the window, where an armchair was situated. He sat down and opened the diary, which he hoped would contain clues to its owner's murder.

The first few entries, which were dated, related to the start of term. For the most part, however, they recorded only relatively mundane details, comprising the routine of the day: *Awoken at 6 o'clock. Prayers, breakfast, morning lessons, luncheon, afternoon lessons, walk, tea, preparation for following day's lessons, free time, supper, prayers, bed.*

There was an entry listing the weekly quota of lessons, which included *music three times a week, along with practising every day, drawing on Monday and Wednesday, and on Tuesday dancing.* A meal plan showed the type of food the pupils were given: *Roast beef on Monday; Tuesdays and Fridays roast shoulder of mutton; a round of beef on Wednesday; Thursdays boiled legs of mutton; and stewed beef with pickled walnuts on Saturday. Fast on Sunday. Two days a week 'choke dogs', dumplings with currants in them, while on other days rice or other puddings.*

The school's personnel were listed and brief observations written down. A very tall and stout but plain Miss Fleming, for example, was listed as having her own sedan chair. Swann observed Miss Leigh was recorded as being kind-hearted, amusing and knowledgeable.

Swann sighed, laid the diary down on his lap and gazed out of the window to the cityscape outside. It seemed as if this had been a false trail. What Swann had hoped for did not seem to be there. The diary had promised so much, yet in actuality it was no more than the musings of an adolescent girl and the recording of the minutiae of school life. Although some of the observations about her teachers had within them wit and sophistication beyond her years, the details themselves gave no clue as to the tragic ending that would befall their writer, or any reference to the Circle of Sappho.

Swann flicked through the next few dozen pages of the diary to satisfy himself as to its worthlessness. As he did so he could see that the later entries had changed. Although written in the same hand, the entries were not dated, were longer and contained, at a brief glance, more emotional content. Swann retraced the pages to the point where the entries changed and then continued to read. The first couple had been dated but then crossed through.

A wonderful turn of events this afternoon, which I find myself so excited about that my heart is beating faster even as I record the details. It was a normal lesson with Miss Leigh, we were discussing literature, but afterwards she asked me to stay behind. To start with I felt I must have done something wrong in class, but when the rest of the girls left and we were alone, Miss Leigh told me that she believes I show great promise and she wished to converse with me later. We arranged to meet in her room during free time. So, when the older girls were involved with their filigree and pasteboard and younger ones their dolls, I went across the corridor from my dormitory to Miss Leigh's room. On arriving she seemed somehow different, more relaxed perhaps. She immediately began to talk about the ancient Greeks and their myths and legends. She mentioned the nine muses and then asked me if I knew who Sappho was. When I said I did not, she told me about her. Sappho, she said, was also a teacher of girls, although she was more famously known for the poetry she wrote. She picked up a book that was on a table beside her and read a poem from it, which Miss Leigh said was by Sappho. She asked me what I thought of it. I did not know what I was meant to say, or if she wanted me to say something particular, so I just told her how it made me feel – how I felt the hairs on the back of my neck rise and how it gave me a funny feeling in the bottom of my stomach. I do not know whether this was the right answer, as she did not say anything in reply, but she seemed pleased and smiled, so I assume I had not said anything wrong. After a few moments, she asked me whether I would like to join a group she organises at the school, which re-enacts several of the ceremonies and rituals Sappho and the girls she taught used to perform. As Miss Leigh describes it, I will find 'a practical way into the Greek female mind', which was not that different from our own, if only we would recognise and develop it.

This is it, thought Swann, the Circle of Sappho. It had to be. It all made sense: Miss Leigh, the girls, the island, the temple and clearing with its circle of stones and altar. He quickly turned the page and continued reading.

I said that I would like to join and she told me that the circle meets twice a month, once at the time of the new moon and once when it is full. She then told me that the next meeting is to take place the following evening and that I am to leave the dormitory after dark and make my way down to the entrance to the library. She told me not to tell anyone about it and that she hoped I will find the meetings enlightening. She then leant forward and kissed me on the forehead, before placing a book in my hands. It is the book of poetry by Sappho and she said she had marked certain poems that I must read in preparation for tomorrow evening.

The entry ended. Swann immediately focussed on the next one, which began on a new page and was undated.

Tonight I am to meet the group. I do not know what to expect and in many ways I regret so eagerly accepting Miss Leigh's invitation. In class today she seemed distant; only a smile and a small nod as I was leaving showed me that she had not changed her mind and my invitation has not been revoked. While writing in class though, I did chance to look up one time and saw Miss Leigh staring in my direction as if in a kind of trance. The poems of Sappho I was asked to read by Miss Leigh make me feel strange, like nothing I have experienced before. The poems I have studied before have made me think, but these poems make me FEEL!! Whatever I may say, I am pleased to be going tonight, whatever awaits me. I trust Miss Leigh.

The following entry concerned her observations and feelings having attended the meeting.

This evening's events have left me exhausted but exhilarated. My only hope is that I can do justice in words to the sensations I experienced. I left the dormitory at the appointed hour and made my way downstairs to the library entrance. The corridors and main staircase were quiet and whereas there had been many girls around earlier, I now found myself alone. As I made my way down the stairs I thought I heard someone coming up, so I hid in a cupboard on one of the landings. Whether there was actually someone there I do not know, but after a little time all seemed quiet again and so I came out and resumed the journey downward. On reaching the library, I stepped inside, as instructed. It was completely dark, but I had been told to expect this. As soon as I closed the door behind me, a female voice spoke. 'Do not be alarmed,' she said, 'we are to take you to Miss Leigh, but you need to be blindfolded.' Miss Leigh had told me to do whatever I was told and so I willingly let them tie a piece of material around my head, covering my eyes. For a few moments I did wonder about the point of my being blindfolded in the pitch blackness, but then I felt the warmth of a flame near my face and realised a torch had been lit. I was then led across the room and I heard the sound of something opening. A rush of cold air made goosebumps appear on my arms and legs. I must have been taken through an opening and then we descended a set of steps. Although I had slippers on, I realised it was stone stairs, as the coldness penetrated up through the material and chilled my feet.

There were probably around twenty steps in all and when we reached the bottom I could smell dampness in the air, which itself felt stale and old. I lost my footing about halfway down the steps, but immediately two hands steadied me and I made the rest of the descent without assistance. We then went along a passageway which had an uneven stone floor. It became colder the farther along we went and I began to shiver in my cotton nightdress.

Eventually we reached what I later found out was the initiation chamber. Here I was helped down onto my knees. After a few moments I heard the sound of a familiar voice: Miss Leigh. 'Welcome both muses and novices alike to this gathering tonight. We are here to honour and worship Sappho and through her, the great goddess Aphrodite. The nine of you here tonight represent the nine muses; with three of you from each of the fourth, fifth and sixth years respectively. With the start of the autumn term, and with the three girls from last year's final cohort having now left, we invite three girls from the lower year to join, in this way bringing our number back to nine. Those of you who are blindfolded, and there are three of you, all from the fourth year, must never breathe a word about what you witness this evening and at future meetings. You will be initiated and purified before your blindfolds are taken off, but once that is done you will form part of the Circle of Sappho and complete it once more. I implore you not to resist the initiation rites, in the knowledge you are in safe hands and no harm will come to you; that I promise. I know it is cold but as we perform the ceremony, imagine your body on a warm summer's evening, on the slopes of Mount Parnassus, where the Greek mysteries used to be held.'

The girl next to me stood up and was led away. As I would soon discover, there was an altar in the room and I heard the girl being helped up onto it. Words were spoken and after a short while it became my turn. I was led towards the altar and then two hands stopped me. The straps of my nightdress were brought down, off my shoulders, and the garment fell to the floor. I now stood completely naked, except for my blindfold. Goosebumps appeared over my body once more as I was gently manoeuvred onto the altar; I was surprised to find the stone was in some way gently heated. Once I was on the altar, I heard Miss Leigh's voice once more. This time she said to me, 'Do not worry, what is about to happen is for purification purposes.' My body was then covered with oil and other sweet-smelling oint-ments. It was, I have to admit, a pleasant sensation.

Once the anointing was completed, a robe was put on me. Before my blindfold could be removed, however, the rest of the Circle had to acknowledge and welcome me. Once this had happened, my blind-fold was then taken off. It took a moment for my eyes to become accustomed to their surroundings, but then I saw Miss Leigh next to the altar, with two of the older girls. The other four girls knelt before me in a semi-circle; three of the girls I recognised from the year above, and the fourth girl I knew as the head girl, Elsa. I did not recognise the other two from the top year, who were standing near Miss Leigh.

The girl from my year that had been initiated first stood to my right. We smiled briefly at each other, in recognition we had been invited to the group, and then looked with united curiosity at the third initiate, who was now being led toward the altar by the two final year girls. We watched her anointment and welcome, and knew our lives at school would never be the same again.

CHAPTER TWENTY-FOUR

More than a quarter of a century after the last legal duel in Britain was fought between Viscount du Barry and Captain Rice in the autumn of 1778, Kirby stood on the site where that fatal encounter had taken place. Bathampton Down, a large expanse of land that formed part of the eastern slopes surrounding the city of Bath, was far enough away to afford the seclusion required for participation in this now-illegal activity.

Kirby was facing a life-size, hastily made figure secured against a tree, and was in the middle of shooting at it. He fired off his two pistols and was satisfied when he saw both bullets had reached their intended mark, striking at the point where the heart would have been in a real opponent. He began to reload. At that moment he was aware of movement to his right, off in the distance. Within moments he heard the unmistakable sound of a horse at full gallop. He finished reloading and as the rider approached he turned and aimed both of his primed pistols in the rider's direction.

'You are late,' Kirby told Lockhart, lowering his pistols.

'I was held up,' replied Lockhart, dismounting as he spoke.

He led the horse to a nearby tree, where Kirby's horse was already tethered, and tied his own mount's reins around it. He thought it best not to tell Kirby the truth; that he had been looking at wedding invitations at Mary's insistence.

'Your message said you wanted to see me here urgently?'

'Yes,' replied Kirby. 'You are to be my second on Sunday.'

'What?' cried Lockhart. 'I thought you already had someone?'

'He carelessly allowed himself to be killed last night in a drunken argument. So you will take his place.'

'I do not want to undertake it. I will not undertake it. If Swann is killed and Mary finds out I was in any way involved, it will jeopardise the wedding; it might be cancelled altogether.'

'Money accounts for a great deal, Lockhart, but it is not everything.'

'I have told you before, Kirby, I am not marrying Mary for her money.' Though it will, he thought, greatly enhance my standing and go some way to eradicating the financial predicament I find myself in.

'If you do not agree to be my second, your financial predicament is likely to get worse, as I shall withhold the latest payments due to you.'

Lockhart realised that he could not refuse, and nodded solemnly.

'Good, that is settled then,' said Kirby. 'Now, I want you to go to Henry Fitzpatrick's office this afternoon. He is to act as Swann's second at the duel on Sunday, so I want you to arrange the details with him. We shall use pistols, of course, and insist on fifteen paces but accept twelve; I have practised for both and either will suit my plan adequately. Confirm the hour as dawn and the duel is to be fought *pour la mort*.'

'To the death?' exclaimed Lockhart. 'Is it not a gamble, as Swann will fire first?'

'Not in the least. From what I understand of our Mr Swann, he believes himself an honourable gentleman,' said Kirby. 'Ha, the very thought of it! Did you know his father was a compulsive gambler? He lost all his money playing cards. And Swann has tendencies to do the same, given the opportunity.'

'No, I did not know that. Where did you hear this?'

'An investigation was carried out into Swann, so Wicks told me. His London connection hired someone to look into his past. Still, we digress. As you rightly stated Lockhart, as the challenged, Swann will have the right to fire first and no doubt he will aim somewhere here,' Kirby pointed a finger to his heart. 'Once he has discharged his pistol, I will then aim mine and kill him.'

'What if his aim is true?'

'Why do you think I must insist on there being only between twelve and fifteen paces, the last thing I want to happen is for him to miss my heart and wound me.'

'I do not understand,' said Lockhart, frowning.

'If Swann hits me here, I will not be harmed.' Kirby tapped his jacket at the point of his heart. 'It was my brother's jacket before he died of fever,' he said. 'He served in India and while there he learnt from their irregular cavalry a way to stop swords and even bullets from causing damage. They would quilt a number of cotton cloths together, or else use refuse silk from cocoons. This has numerous silk handkerchiefs bonded together. Anyway, I suggest you ride back into the city at once and make those arrangements with Fitzpatrick. Once you have completed that, I want you back at my office at six o'clock. I have another job for you this evening.'

'I am seeing Miss Gardiner this evening; we are to dine together.'

Kirby turned to face Lockhart.

'For your sake, Edmund, I hope you are not going weak on me. Wicks has a swift and easy way of dealing with those lacking the necessary fibre.' Kirby ran his finger across his throat, from ear to ear. The message was clear.

'I will be there,' said Lockhart reluctantly. 'What is the job?'

'I will inform you at six.'

Lockhart untied his horse and remounted it. As he was about to ride off, Kirby shouted across to him.

'And do not forget, the duel is to be *pour la mort.*'

Lockhart nodded and rode off with a heavy heart and a sense of impending doom.

CHAPTER TWENTY-FIVE

Swann checked the time. There was still an hour to go before he had to make his way down to the warehouse to change into his disguise. From there he would go to the Fountain Inn, to inform George and Bridges about the evening's undertaking. He turned the page of the diary to the next entry, and continued reading.

We are finding it hard not to speak of last evening during our lessons today but we have all taken Miss Leigh's caveat to heart; that we must not breathe a word about the Circle to anyone, not even each other while we are outside the sacred places. There is a difference about us, however, a blossoming in our beings that only we are privy to. It feels like torture, at times, to know that there are others who share my experience and yet I cannot speak to them of it. But I want to stay true to Miss Leigh and the Circle, and would not wish to endanger either in any way, so a covert exchange of glances within the classroom will have to suffice. I count the days to the next meeting, which will be at the time of the full moon.

The following entries contained much the same musings, including the ways in which the girls secretly communicated with each other. The next meeting arrived and some of the details had been written down.

Tonight we met at the library once more and entered the steps as before but this time with our blindfolds removed; as we were now initiated they were no longer needed. I had arranged with the other two girls in my dormitory that we would leave individually, so as not to arouse suspicion, and then meet up at the library. I was last. I went downstairs and into the book-lined room without event or hindrance, then swung the appropriate panel open and stepped inside. When I reached the bottom of the stone steps, the other two girls were waiting for me and we made our way along the corridor, to the ceremonial room, together. We were full of anticipation and excitement, having already seen the full moon through our dormitory window, but had to conduct this journey in silence, as part of the route the passage took was under the staff rooms and we did not want to alert anyone to our presence below.

We arrived at the initiation chamber and were finally allowed to talk as this area was, so Miss Leigh told us, underneath the lake.

We had remained inside the initiation chamber during the previous meeting, but tonight Miss Leigh said we were to go outside. I was not quite sure what this entailed, although all became clear soon enough. Miss Leigh stood up and beckoned for us all to follow. We waited by a curtained entrance, on the opposite side of the chamber, while Miss Leigh took a large golden key from her pocket and unlocked a wooden door. It was pulled open and we went through one by one and then carried on down another passageway. At the end of this was a series of stone steps leading upwards and we followed Miss Leigh to the top, where a large stone blocked our way. Several of the girls pushed it aside and moonlight flooded the passage. Passing the stone I found myself in a small temple. We waited until the final girl came through and then went out through the temple's entrance onto the island. We followed Miss Leigh along a path to a small clearing. Here a circle of stone seats awaited us, surrounding a stone altar. This is where the evening's ceremony was to take place.

Before the ceremony began, Miss Leigh announced that she wanted to talk to us about what she called 'reclaiming the night'. She told us that the night traditionally belonged to women; why it was our right as females to encompass and allow the night to open up and develop our intuition. It represented the magical, creative side in a woman, she said, and everything which is opposite to the customs and social mores that we, as girls, and then as women, have to adhere to if we wish to be fully accepted, and not exiled, by society. She told us of an incident that had happened when she had lived abroad as a governess to a family who had several daughters. It was a country where women had to be clothed from head to toe in heavy black robes whenever they went outside, and they were never under any circumstances allowed to unveil themselves to any man to whom they were not related. Miss Leigh told us that these women had a very strict home-life, where they had to obey their husbands and look after the man's home and his children, with no rights of their own.

One night though, she witnessed something which had stayed with her to this day. The family were staying at a house in a small town, in mid-summer, and the society in which she found herself seemed as heavy and claustrophobic as the weather. She had finished her duties for the day and was lying in bed, about to go to sleep, when a strange noise reached her ears. It was a mixture of metallic clashing and wailing voices, becoming increasingly louder. Curious, she got out of bed. As she watched from the window she saw, to her astonishment, a procession of women coming around the corner not too far away. Every one of them was without her veil; they had been discarded! And instead of robes they wore long dresses. Their hair was loose, flowing freely down their backs, and as they moved along the street the women wailed and sang, all the while banging drums, cymbals and other percussion instruments. To the rhythm of this noise they danced wildly, surrendering control of their bodies and minds to the full moon, which shone brightly in the night sky.

As they came closer she went out onto the balcony. From here she could see the whole street, able to observe but not be observed. Not that the women would have taken much notice of her, as they seemed lost within their own worlds. They passed beneath her window and she could see their faces, their expressions one of ecstasy and total abandonment. And yet wherever they were at that very moment, they were no longer separate but together in a place where women were free to express themselves. In this way, they had reclaimed the night as their own.

The following morning Miss Leigh had walked around the bazaar and there, once more, were the women going about their daily business, their veils across their faces and dressed in the dark attire which symbolised their suppression.

It was as if the night before had been only a dream, Miss Leigh said, yet she knew it had been real. These women, with their secret life, were walking among men who thought they were under their control, with no idea that they were actually beyond their control and at least once a month, at full moon, showed their real selves.

Miss Leigh explained that within every female there is a primitive, wild side and that we need to harness the powers of nature to help strengthen this naturalistic side. Using the night allows us to access those emotions and feelings which are dormant during the daytime. She said this was why she had begun the Circle of Sappho in the first place, so that through these meetings, and her teachings, we could learn to awaken this side of our nature and once it had been allowed to emerge, use it in a positive, powerful way. And it was very important this happened, she said, because if allowed to surface without any control, it could become dangerous not only for the individual but also for the society in which they lived.

Yet, these primitive emotions must be allowed to surface, said Miss Leigh, as to ignore them would only turn us into the daytime personification of those blacked-robed women; suppressed and arti-ficial. To be able to endure our future lives as 'dutiful wives', we would always have this other side of us which could not be taken away; something which we could call our own and that would allow us to be free when we needed to be.

In the same way as we had our duties and obligations to the school, lessons, prayers and routines, once a month, under the full moon, we could renew our powers through participation in the moon goddess ceremonies and worship of Aphrodite. This is what Sappho taught, she said, and this is what a previous inhabitant of the estate had understood. It was her notebook, Miss Leigh told us, which had first suggested the idea of starting the Circle, or rather continuing it, as it had originally been created by another woman. Miss Leigh had discovered this notebook when she had swum across the lake to explore the island. She had found it in a box, along with several other items relevant to performing the necessary ceremonies for empowerment. The box had been left inside the recess of a temple, which had been built on the island. From what Miss Leigh had learnt since, the woman's husband had encouraged her fully and indeed had built the island, temple and passageway that linked them with the main house. If and when we students were to marry, she said, this would be the desired state of union, the two people helping each other to reach their potential, not just as husband and wife, but as man and woman. Although some of our husbands might find the concept of mutual union abhorrent, if they were to find out the reality, she said, they would in fact benefit greatly from it. In this way we might help our husbands find their own empowerment in the years to come.

It seems both women and men have access to this 'night' power, although women normally benefit from it more, which is a way to allow fierce emotions that burn within them to be let out. As these were normally suppressed during the day, this nocturnal outlet allows it safely to be expressed. It is actually through women that *enlightened men – as Miss Leigh called them – might find their own outlet and connection to this power.*

She then warned us that we have a responsibility to ourselves, as women, and to our husbands, to retain access to this force and keep it alive within us. It is solely down to us because our very survival depends on our connection to our deeper instinct.

The entry finished. The ceremony itself had not been recorded. The next entry mentioned the fact that Grace had been invited to Miss Leigh's room that evening to discuss an important matter. Swann turned the page, but stopped. The entries were now unreadable, as they had been written in code. He looked at the clock; it was time to leave. He would return to the diary with the intention of deciphering its code and learning the secrets that must surely be hidden within it.

CHAPTER TWENTY-SIX

Swann left his office in Gay Street and headed towards his warehouse in the Avon Street district. As he crossed over Wood Street and into Barton Street he noticed Isabella Thorpe. Ever since his arrival in Bath, she had been trying to convince Mary to organise a dinner party so she could become 'better acquainted' with him; so far he had been successful in avoiding it. She was conversing with a friend a little way down Barton Street, so Swann quickly retraced his steps and headed along the southern side of Queen Square and then turned left into Princes Street and into the more notorious part of the city, where he had his warehouse.

About a month ago he had seen Isabella while he was in disguise. He was in his usual beggar's outfit, as he was on his way to see George and Bridges at the Fountain Inn, but upon seeing Isabella had thought for a moment of formally introducing himself to observe her reaction, but refrained as the consequences of 'breaking cover' could be calamitous, even fatal. He had walked past and as he did so, overheard her comment to a companion: 'People like that should not be allowed in this part of town.' Swann smiled to himself at the memory.

Once in his beggar's disguise again, Swann had made his way back to Avon Street itself and the Fountain Inn, where no one but George and Bridges knew his true identity. Inside, he found the two men already there. He bought three drinks at the bar and carried them across to where the thief-takers were sitting.

'Mr Swann, why that is very kind of you, sir,' said George, as the drinks were placed on the table in front of him.

'You can have this one as well, George,' said Swann, pointing to his own glass. 'I may need clarity tonight. Do you and Bridges know what to do?'

'Yes, Mr Swann. But where are we heading, you haven't told us yet?'

'Lansdown Crescent. It is in the Upper Town, do you know of it?'

George nodded and Swann told him the house number, the description of the gentleman they would be shadowing, and the exact spot where Swann would be hiding when the money was handed over. He had left instructions with Fitzpatrick earlier to inform Moorhouse that he would not be followed from his residence, but instead Swann would be concealed near the old East Gate – where the money was to be handed over – to observe the transaction. He wanted Moorhouse to believe there was nobody shadowing him as experience had taught Swann that he would most likely keep looking behind him, and thereby arouse suspicion if the blackmailer or his associates were watching. He wanted George and Bridges to follow this prospective Member of Parliament in case the location was suddenly changed or if Moorhouse became a victim of another crime, robbery, with the large amount of money he was carrying. If there was a change of plan, one of the thief-takers would remain with Moorhouse while the other would let Swann know.

'Once you arrive at the old East Gate,' continued Swann, 'find somewhere to wait out of sight but from where you can see me. If I raise my left arm it means there is trouble but to stay where you are. If I raise my right arm it means …'

'… there's trouble and to come right away,' finished George. 'Exactly.'

Swann realised Bridges had not signed a word or lip-read since he had entered the inn. His head was down and he looked miserable.

'What is wrong with Bridges?' he asked George.

'It's Rosie, sir. She is being thrown out of her home tomorrow.'

'I see. Well I may have a solution.'

Swann tapped Bridges' arm and he looked up.

'Do not worry, Bridges,' Swann signed. 'I know of a building in the area where Rosie can stay as long as she wants to.'

Bridges' expression did not change.

'I do not understand,' Swann said to George. 'I thought Bridges would be happy.'

'She lost her job yesterday and had to pawn her violin, but still cannot afford to stay anywhere for long.'

'I assume you have not had a change of heart regarding her staying with you?'

George looked sheepish but resolute.

Swann tapped Bridges' arm again. 'Perhaps I forgot to mention it, but this place is rent free. Rosie does not have to pay any money for as long as she stays there.'

At this news Bridges' grinned. He downed the contents of his glass and hugged Swann.

Twenty minutes later, after Swann had deliberately taken a long and convoluted route through the city's streets, he found himself at the old medieval East Gate. He was cautious, glancing around to observe who was in the vicinity, before settling back behind a large pile of rubbish in a dark alley-way. From here he could observe the transaction between Moorhouse and the blackmailer, but not be observed himself. The site chosen for the exchange was a suitably isolated one – even though it was right in the middle of the city centre – and at the same time strategically well-situated, as it had several means of escape heading off in many directions.

Swann felt secure knowing the two thief-takers would be nearby in the event of trouble. With blackmail, as any crime, the potential for violence was always present.

No one had passed his viewpoint for about ten minutes prior to the moment Swann spotted, out the corner of his eye, movement to his right. As the figure approached, he recognised it as Moorhouse. As he walked past the spot where Swann was hidden, another figure emerged from the shadows ahead, near to the East Gate. It was a woman. Swann had not expected that.

'Fancy a good time my love?' the woman asked Moorhouse.

Swann realised the danger; she was a prostitute, not a blackmailer, but could easily damage the whole rendezvous.

'No, thank you,' replied an anxious Moorhouse.

'I know how to please a man,' she cooed, unwilling to take no for an answer.

'Please go away. I am meeting someone here; they may see you.'

Angry at this rebuttal the woman strode off, muttering obscenities as she went. A few moments later another woman appeared, but she too was swiftly sent on her way.

'Who were those women?' a voice from the shadows demanded.

'Prostitutes, whores,' replied Moorhouse.

A bearded man stepped forward, emerging from the direc-tion of the river. Swann realised the man had been waiting in the alley.

'Do you have the payment?'

The man spoke with an Irish accent that sounded vaguely familiar to Swann. Moorhouse held aloft the bag in which the money was contained. The blackmailer gestured for it to be handed over, which it was. The exchange was brief and Moorhouse momentarily looked around, perhaps expecting something to happen, before turning and leaving. The bearded man himself then turned back towards the river and disappeared from view. Swann waited a few seconds then stood up. Damn! Swann suddenly realised if the blackmailer was heading to the river, he might have a boat to take him across to the other side. If this was the case, Swann would lose him. He had to act fast. He started to move from his spot but immediately squatted down once more as the blackmailer re-emerged from the alleyway. The river had been a ruse. The bearded man passed within a few feet of Swann, but remained ignorant of his presence. As soon as he thought it was safe to do so, Swann left his hiding place and began to follow. He could not see them, but he knew George and Bridges would be in attendance.

The blackmailer reached the outskirts of the Avon Street district. Swann was not surprised. He had wondered if Wicks was behind the blackmailing and this was his territory. He assumed the bearded man was one of Wicks' henchmen and was taking the moneybag straight to his boss. Suddenly three men emerged from a side alley and instantly set about the bearded man.

'Get 'im,' cried one of the robbers, as another struck the bearded man in the face which felled him to the ground.

This was surely not part of any plan, Swann thought as he ran forward, his right arm in the air. He dived into the trio of robbers, who were unaware of his presence until that moment, knocking two of them to the floor. Swann picked up the other man and punched him in the face, sending him sprawling against the wall, his head cracking as it collided with the stone.

As Swann turned his attention back to the other two robbers, he saw one with a pistol aimed at him. Before he could fire, however, he was knocked out by the foot-long iron bar Bridges always carried about his person.

The bearded man lay on the ground, groaning. What should Swann do? He could not leave the man here, but at the same time did not want to reveal that he had been following him. Swann thought about this dilemma for a short while and then gestured for George and Bridges to help the man up. They moved along the passageway, underneath the light from a nearby gas lamp. It could now be seen that the man had been wearing a false beard, which was hanging at an angle off his face. As the light caught the man's bloodied features, Swann gasped.

'Lockhart!' he said.

'Swann?'

'Where are you taking the blackmail money?' Swann growled. 'Wicks?'

'I do not know what you are talking about,' replied Lockhart, feeling his body where he had received several punches and as many kicks. 'I was just passing this way when I was attacked by those men.'

'Do not play me as a fool, Lockhart. I followed you here from the East Gate, where you collected money from Mr Moorhouse. I know you are involved in blackmail, but not who organised it.'

George tugged at Swann's shoulder. He whispered in his ear.

'Yes, George, I believe this is also the person you followed to Bristol. Is that not correct, Mr Mottram? I think that was the name you used while in that particular city. What is Mary is going to make of all this?'

'No, Swann, please do not tell her. She would disown me. Ask anything of me.'

'You admit then that you are part of this blackmail scheme.'

'Yes.'

'Who is behind it?'

'As you suspected, it is Wicks. I was on my way to him with the money.'

'So what do you suggest I should do?'

'Let me go, as if nothing happened.'

Swann laughed. 'Why would I do that?'

'If Wicks does not receive the money, I will be killed.'

'And why would I wish to prevent that?'

'Swann, there are things that you do not know.'

Swann smiled. 'That phrase is becoming rather familiar of late.'

'You have to let me go,' said Lockhart. 'I cannot say why, but you must if you have any thought for King and Country and if not for them, then for your sister.'

'How is Mary involved in these matters?'

'You would not want to deprive her of her bridegroom, would you?'

Swann did not respond, as Bridges was now signing that one of the robbers was beginning to gain consciousness. The small group moved out of the passageway and around the corner.

'I will let you go on one condition,' said Swann.

'What is it?'

'I want you to retrieve the letters that are being held over Mr Moorhouse's head.'

'But Kirby has them, if he ever found out …'

'So Kirby is involved as well. I cannot say it surprises me. You will have to make certain he does not discover who took them. It is your choice, Lockhart. I could rouse Fitzpatrick right now to arrest you and there would be nothing at all that Kirby could do about it. That would, of course, also end any wedding plans.'

Lockhart realised he had no real choice.

'Give me until Saturday. I have to be at Kirby's office in the afternoon and by then I will have figured out a way to obtain the letters.'

'You have until Saturday evening at this very time, eight-thirty. If you double-cross me you will live to regret it. In the meantime, I will take this as evidence.'

Swann picked up the moneybag.

'I need that,' protested Lockhart. 'I have to make sure Wicks receives it.'

Swann thought for a moment. If he was lying then Swann would have an irrefutable way to break off the attachment with Mary; she would certainly not want to be associated with a known member of a blackmail gang. If he was telling the truth, Swann realised Lockhart was probably the best chance he had of bringing this case to a satisfying resolution. He handed the moneybag back to Lockhart.

'We will escort you to where you have to go, to make sure you do not run into any more trouble.'

As good as his word, Swann and the thief-takers followed Lockhart to a nearby brothel, which was owned by Wicks and frequently visited by Kirby. As Lockhart stopped by the building, he looked either way and then entered.

Swann turned to his two erstwhile companions.

'A most satisfactory outcome to the evening, gentlemen,' said Swann. 'Now, let us repair to the Fountain for some well-deserved drinks.'

George and Bridges grinned.

CHAPTER TWENTY-SEVEN

Leaving George and Bridges at the Fountain Inn, Swann returned to his Gay Street office. He decided to go straight to his rooms rather than return to the warehouse to remove his disguise as he did not wish to receive unwanted attention which walking back through the Avon Street district at that time of night in gentleman's clothing would undoubtedly bring. He was not so foolhardy.

The developments of the evening had been dramatic; not only had Lockhart's involvement in the blackmail scheme been uncovered, but a thought had occurred to him in regard to the coded entries in the diary which had prevented him from reading any further that afternoon.

On reaching his office he sat down, opened the diary and immediately began to copy the page out on to a piece of paper. Grace had used what Swann knew as a mono-alphabetic substitution cipher, which, despite its highly convoluted-sounding title was, in fact, one of the more basic codes. The cipher simply required each letter in the alphabet to be replaced by another; these replacements had to remain consistent throughout all the text. Therefore 'N' might be replaced by 'X', 'A' by 'D' and so on. The objective for Swann was to find which letters appeared most frequently. This would allow him to 'break' the code and read the remaining diary entries. He began with the top five letters, in order of their most frequently occurring, which in the English alphabet were 'E', 'T', 'A', 'O' and 'I'. These letters would then become known as the 'first', 'second', 'third', 'fourth' and 'fifth'. After the equivalent letters, in terms of most frequency, had been found within the coded text, they could be substituted back – for example if 'D' had been substituted for 'A', then 'D' would have appeared as the third most frequently appearing letter in the coded text, therefore proving itself to be equivalent to 'A', the 'third' most frequently occurring letter in the English alphabet. A table containing all the equivalent letters and their respective counterparts could then begin to be assembled. Once this table was completed, the previously unreadable entries could then easily be reverted back to English.

It took Swann several diary pages and as many hours to complete this table of 'equivalents', but once finished, the entries became legible again. During the process he poured himself several glasses of red wine, all of Portuguese origin. He would have preferred to have finished the '98 Lafite he had opened the previous night, and of which half a bottle remained, but he would have to be content with what he had, as the Lafite was at the house in Great Pulteney Street and he did not want to return there in disguise. With the war still raging and the French ban on wine, the bottles from that country he did possess were kept in the wine cellar at the house. The Portuguese wine was kept at his office for any clients who required fortification or situations such as this one.

He decided he would read the diary entries at the office and then, at first light, return to the warehouse to remove his disguise. He had sent a message to Mary to say he would not be home that night, but would return the following morning in time to accompany her on the walk to Swainswick, to visit Mrs Gardiner's grave.

He lit another candle, poured another glass and brought his chair nearer to the table upon which the diary lay open, ready to divulge its secrets. The first entry described the evening after Grace's first ceremony, where she had been invited to Miss Leigh's room.

The room was cold. There was a single candle, which Miss Leigh had lit and put on a small table. It gave out light but no warmth, at least not where I was sitting on the edge of the bed. Miss Leigh saw I was shivering a little – this was partly from being cold but also from being alone in the room with her – and brought a bottle down from a shelf. She poured some of its contents into a glass and handed it to me.

'This will warm you,' she said.

I hesitated, but she gave me a reassuring smile. I drank it and it indeed warmed me.

Miss Leigh then talked about Sappho and her love for the girls at her school and how she prepared them for their future lives; not only through her teaching in the classroom but in the bedroom. I felt a little embarrassed at first, at such talk, but Miss Leigh poured another glass for me and I found myself listening intently to what she was saying. After I finished this second drink, Miss Leigh came over and sat on the bed next to me. She gently stroked my arms and, after a few moments, as if half-playing, pulled me in close and kissed my forehead. She told me what a wonderfully delicate forehead I had and then kissed it again. My head became hot from the sensation. She held me for a while, as she stroked my arms, and then slowly laid me back onto the bed. I gave no resistance.

I no longer felt cold. As I lay on the bed, Miss Leigh continued to rub me, but now other parts of my body as well: my shoulders, putting her fingers underneath the straps of my cotton nightdress;

my knees, at the spot the material of the garment ended; my ankles, where her thumbs massaged the hard part of the bone; and my feet, which she took great care over, gently squeezing each toe individually between her forefinger and thumb. As she did all this, I felt as if a thousand candles had been lit within me.

Her hands ran down the length of my legs and then back up again several times. On one occasion, however, as her hands travelled upwards they carried on, stopping at my chest. As Miss Leigh cupped her hands, I felt my cheeks start to burn but instinctively, involuntarily, those parts of my body under which her hands now rested, rose to meet them. After a while of this caressing, her focus moved back downwards and I admit I did cry out a little as she touched me more intimately. The next moment, my nightdress started to be slowly rolled up – I did nothing to stop it – with each roll exposing more of my body, until it was turned up all the way to my neck, becoming like a cotton necklace, as the rest of my body below lay exposed. As if wishing to preserve my modesty, Miss Leigh blew out the candle.

And then a strange feeling, I felt myself leave my body and rise upward to where I could look back down on the unfolding scene; my vision nocturnal, my awareness heightened. I saw myself laying there, my eyes closed and the cotton nightdress still around my neck. I saw my body exposed to the night, my chest, my stomach, my hips, my legs. And then I saw Miss Leigh, attentive, considerate and caring, seeing and experiencing what she was doing at one and the same time.

Believing I could feel no greater satisfaction, I suddenly found myself brought back into my body with a jolt. Something foreign, something unknown had entered me. I did not know what it was, but I did not want it gone. A feeling now began to build, unlike anything I had experienced before, an overwhelming sensation which began to make me shudder inside. I wanted to cry out in happiness, scream with delight, but knew I could not; I did not want to alert anyone nearby and I did not want to abandon myself so completely in front of Miss Leigh. Perhaps sensing what was happening, she

*clasped her hand over my mouth and gently whispered in my ear,
'Let yourself go, my love, everything will be fine.' That was all I
needed as I let out a long, guttural moan of pleasure.*

*I lay there exhausted but exhilarated, my feelings in turmoil, yet
with a great peace descending over me. Miss Leigh bent forward and
kissed my forehead once more. That is all I remember, as I must have
fallen into a deep and satisfying sleep.*

*When I awoke it was to the harsh cold of morning and Miss
Leigh shaking me.*

*'Wake up, you have to leave now.' She said it kindly but there
was urgency in her voice. 'You have to go back to your own bed. You
cannot be found here.'*

*I crossed the hallway to the dormitory and slipped between the
cold sheets trying to assimilate the previous night's experience. It must
have been around 5.30 a.m., as I was only in bed for about fifteen
minutes before Miss Leigh herself, on duty for our dormitory that
week, entered the room and announced it was time for us all to wake
up. The room was cast in semi-light and as the other girls began to get
up around me, I noticed Miss Leigh briefly glance at me, and at that
moment I longed for the time we might find ourselves alone again.*

Swann read for a further few pages, and as the relationship
between student and teacher developed, so too did the inti-
macy between them. Perhaps the deaths had been a *crime
passionelle* after all – with the teacher unable to relinquish
her charge, or perhaps an argument had ensued – but Swann
wanted to be certain. Something was not right, something
which did not make sense.

As he continued to read though, scanning the subsequent
entries, he felt his eyelids become heavy and begin to close.
He willed himself to stay awake, but after a few moments the
diary slipped from his hands and hit the floor, closing once
more on any secrets that might still lie within it.

CHAPTER TWENTY-EIGHT

'Jack? Jack, are you in there? Jack! It's Mary.'

Swann awoke suddenly, still in his disguise, in his office chair.

'What … hello? Mary?' It took a few seconds to gather his thoughts, but then he stood up and made his way across to his office door. He opened it and saw his sister, with another young woman behind her.

'Jack, you did not return home this morning, although dressed as you are now, perhaps it was just as well. You know Miss Austen? She will be accompanying us on the walk to Swainswick.'

'Good day Miss Austen,' said Swann. 'As you observe, I have been caught completely unprepared.'

'I assumed from your message that you would be here, when you did not return this morning,' said Mary.

'What is the time?' asked Swann

'It is a quarter to ten. We had intended to set off by ten, but Edmund has sent a communication this morning suggesting we make our start at eleven.'

'I will change and be with you within the hour, then,' said Swann.

'We shall meet you at Molland's tea shop. It is in Milsom Street.' She turned to her companion, 'If that is agreeable, Jane?'

'Most agreeable, Mary, their Marzipan is divine.'

The two women left and Swann set about the business of returning himself to an appropriate state of dress. As he did so, he thought back to the diary entries he had read the previous evening. He would aim to read the remaining pages that evening, but the likelihood there had not, after all, been another person on the island was becoming increasingly likely.

As is the generally accepted opinion when organising excursions such as a walk, the organiser has always to expect the unexpected or, at the very least, that the numerous details of the excursion are likely to change not once, but several times before its actual commencement. The walk to Swainswick had been no different; not only had the time of departure been changed, but also the number of actual walkers themselves had increased and decreased several times throughout the preceding few days. There had, at one particular moment, been a total of seven people intending to undertake the excursion, but one by one, for various reasons, the number gradually decreased to four: Fitzpatrick was unexpectedly required to preside over a court case, replacing another magistrate that had become too ill to adjudicate; Jane's sister, Cassandra, felt she had the makings of a cold and therefore did not wish to risk the physical exertion the walk would entail; and Isabella Thorpe, who had somehow learned about the outing and approached Mary in a shop in Bond Street to say how much she was looking forward to accompanying the party, suddenly had to render her apologies when she realised a new delivery of hats, at the aforementioned store, was taking place on the very same day.

Even two of the remaining four participants had been in danger of not being in attendance; Lockhart through his nocturnal activities, and Swann, through failing to wake up in time without the intervention of Mary. Nevertheless, at eleven o'clock precisely, after Swann had met the two ladies at the tea shop, the trio met Lockhart in the middle of the King's Circus. He had his back to them on their arrival, but as he turned to greet them, Mary let out an involuntary gasp.

'Edmund, whatever has happened to your face? It is all swollen and bruised!'

'I was set upon by robbers last evening, my dearest.'

'Where did this happened, Edmund, not in the Upper Town?'

'No, my business took me into a rather notorious area of the city I'm afraid. Thankfully, some passers-by lent their assistance and saw my attackers off.'

Lockhart acknowledged Swann with a furtive glance.

'Oh my love, perhaps you should be resting and not come on the walk.'

'My dear Mary, I would not miss it for the world.'

'Well, as long as you are certain.'

With Lockhart's presence confirmed, Mary introduced him to Miss Austen and, along with Swann, the small group headed out of the King's Circus and towards Lansdown Road; the walk having now officially begun.

The route which had been agreed upon saw the quartet make their way up the lower reaches of Lansdown to a junction that took them to the village of Charlcombe. Its church, a fine example of medieval construction, had been the location of author Henry Fielding's wedding seventy years earlier.

'Are you familiar with Mr Fielding's work, Mr Swann?' asked Miss Austen, as they left the church at Charlcombe.

'Yes, I very much enjoy his factual and theatrical output, but must confess I derive the most pleasure from his literary creations, especially Joseph Andrews, and, of course, Tom Jones.'

'It is so refreshing to find a gentleman who enjoys the novel form; I usually have to invent them.'

'Of course, Mary has told me you are a writer. And what do your fictitious gentlemen enjoy reading?'

'A great variety: Fielding, Johnson, Cowper, Richardson, and one character thoroughly enjoys the work of Mrs Radcliffe.'

'Ah yes, *The Mysteries of Udolpho*.'

'You know it?'

'And indeed have read it, Miss Austen, along with *The Italian* and another one, whose title escapes me at this moment. As we are discussing gothic novels, I have read all of Gregor-Smith's books.'

Miss Austen was silent.

'Is something wrong, Miss Austen?'

'It is the name you have mentioned. I would suggest a most impolite gentleman, irrespective of his skill as a writer.'

'Why do you say that?'

'Well, on the insistence of a mutual friend I posted a copy of the manuscript of a novel I had a written – a parody of the gothic form – to Mr Gregor-Smith for his comments. I never heard a word from him. Of course, he is now abroad and my manuscript has not been returned.'

'Was your manuscript entitled with a feminine name?'

'Yes – Susan. Why?'

'I had the opportunity of visiting him at his residence before he left England and I saw your novel on his table. He had read it and was meaning to return it; obviously he was unable to do so. If I remember, he was most impressed with it and commented on how you should continue writing, as you might have a great career.'

Miss Austen blushed slightly.

'Then it appears it was most presumptuous of me to condemn him without a proper trial.'

'You are not the first, Miss Austen, but are you working on something else at present?'

'Yes, another novel. I have yet to find a suitable title for it, but it concerns four daughters who find their world turned upside down on the death of their father. I have written about seventeen thousand words so far.'

Their conversation continued as they descended across fields and lanes to the lowest point of the valley, before ascending into the parish of Swainswick. It was in this hamlet that Mrs Gardiner, Mary's mother, had grown up alongside her sister Harriet. It had been her wish to be buried in the family vault at the stone church dedicated to St Mary the Virgin and, when she died, she had been reunited with her husband, who had agreed to be interned there as well.

After paying their respects, the party of walkers traversed the nearby fields to an ancient hill-fort known as Little Solsbury. The site was associated with King Arthur as it was here, or so it was said, that one of his greatest victories against the Saxons, the Battle of Badon, had taken place.

'What an incredible view,' said Lockhart as they reached the summit. 'What is this place called again, Solsbury Hill?'

'I am thankful my grandfather cannot hear you say that, my love,' smiled Mary. 'According to Mother, he took an instant dislike to anyone who did not call it by what he considered its "correct name"; that of Little Solsbury. But yes, it is a wonderful view and on a clear day you can see as far as Salisbury Plain.'

They made their way across the top of the hill to where a carriage had arrived with their picnic. The carriage driver, along with a male servant, had driven as far as they were able up the narrow track on the western slopes and then carried the hampers on foot up the remaining steep incline. When the party arrived, now famished from their exertions, the fare laid out on blankets was a welcome sight and they sat down immediately to eat.

After they had finished the picnic, Swann stood and walked over to the edge of the summit to admire the panoramic view. The other six hills which surrounded the city could be seen from this seventh; but it was towards one specific hill that Swann's attention was focussed. Bathampton Down, across the other side of the river, was where he would find himself in less than forty-eight hours and where his life might end.

As he stood watching, a bird of prey appeared in the sky. It circled nearby, in search of food. After several circuits it suddenly swooped to the ground and as it soared up again, Swann saw in amazement a snake dangling from its talons. As he continued to watch, the snake began to attack its captor and after several moments the bird let go its grip and the snake dropped to the ground.

'What an incredible sight,' remarked Lockhart, now standing next him and who had witnessed the spectacle as well.

'In ancient times they would have interpreted it as an important portent,' replied Swann.

They stood for a moment in silence before Lockhart turned to Swann.

'Swann,' he said. 'From what I understand, it seems you have not told Mary about the duel.'

'No and I do not intend to burden her with it.'

'But what if you are killed?'

'I do not think that is your business.'

'I would have to disagree with you there. As we are soon to be related and I care deeply for your sister, I believe it is my business.'

Swann sighed. 'I intend to leave written instructions for her provision and a personal letter to her.'

'Do you believe that is enough? Do you not wish to give Mary an opportunity to say her goodbye personally?'

'You seem quite certain of my imminent demise.'

'No, no, it is just …'

'I understand from Fitzpatrick that you are acting as Kirby's second?'

Lockhart nodded reluctantly.

'Please believe me, Swann. I know we are not as agreeably acquainted as I would wish, but I did not seek this position or indeed relish it now it is mine. But I am beholden to Kirby at present, so have little choice.'

'Either way,' said Swann, 'if anything does happen to me on Sunday, I am most concerned for Mary, given your involvement with such undesirable types.'

'I am aware my situation looks disagreeable but you must believe me when I say that by the time we marry in October, this part of my life will be over. If anything does happen to you in two days' time, and God willing it will not, you can be assured I will protect Mary with my life.'

'You can begin to prove your sincerity by obtaining the letters I requested, if you have not already done so.'

'I will be at Kirby's office tomorrow afternoon, undertaking final preparations for the duel, and intend to find an opportunity to procure them at that time.'

'Then we shall meet tomorrow evening, at eight-thirty precisely by the East Gate, so they can be returned to their rightful owner before I undertake the duel. Remember, if they are not in my possession by that time, I shall tell Mary everything.'

Lockhart nodded.

'Tell Mary what, Jack?' asked Mary as she and Jane walked towards the two men.

'It was nothing, my dear sister, only talk regarding business.'

Mary sighed resignedly.

'That is why I never allow two gentlemen the chance to engage in conversation alone in my fiction,' remarked Miss Austen. 'You can never be certain what they may discuss.'

The group laughed.

The party descended towards the waiting carriage. The route it took went straight down, bypassing the lower part of Swainswick village and into the neighbouring Lam Bridge – named for the nearby Lam Brook and the bridge that spanned it. The main residency in the area was the former manor house, Lark Hall, located at the bottom of the Lam Valley, which had been converted into a coaching inn due to its location on the main route out of the city for travellers and mail coaches heading north to Gloucester.

As they were passing the Larkhall Inn, a loud noise emanated from one of the carriage wheels. The next moment it had stopped and the driver appeared at one of the passenger windows.

'With all due apology,' he said, 'but one of the wheels has to be repaired; it should take no more than thirty minutes.'

There was the option of completing the journey into the city centre on foot, but the consensus from the travellers was that they had undertaken enough walking for that particular day and so decided to avail themselves of refreshments while they waited for the carriage to be repaired.

The Larkhall Inn was a hub of activity as the quartet walked in, with a clientele consisting of travellers enjoying a respite on their arduous journeys, a number of men associated with the coaching business itself and a few other local customers. Swann and the others quickly engaged in conversation, especially after it was discovered the landlady shared the same first name as one of the party: namely Miss Austen.

'We traversed up Solsbury Hill,' said Lockhart, on being asked where they had walked.

'Never heard of it,' said one of the locals.

'Forgive my fiancé,' said Mary, knowingly. 'He means Little Solsbury.'

There were nods of approval from the locals and the landlady.

'Ah, you're from around here, Miss …?'

'Gardiner, although my maternal family are the Montagues of Swainswick.'

There were more nods of approval.

'My father worked as a gardener for the Montague family years ago. Yes, they were a good family, so he said.' The speaker was a man who introduced himself as Mr Cornish. On the party's arrival, he had been in discussion with another man known in the inn as Thierry de Turffe, even though he was not French.

'We saw an eagle with a snake in its claws,' said Lockhart, trying to make up for his earlier faux pas, but to no avail.

'I do not think so,' remarked another man who, along with a companion, had been writing away furiously in a corner of the inn. 'More likely to have been a common buzzard, I would hazard a guess.'

'You have got about as much chance of seeing an eagle,' the companion added, 'as you have of seeing Bladud having taught his herd to fly.'

There was laughter around the inn.

'Get back to your scribbling,' Cornish said good-naturedly to the pair of resident authors. 'Don't mind them,' he said, turning to Lockhart. 'They sit in here and think they're Boswell and Johnson.'

Not long after, the driver appeared, to inform Swann and the others that the wheel had been fixed. They bid farewell to their temporary hosts and made their way out of the inn.

CHAPTER TWENTY-NINE

Bath, Friday 30th March, 1804

It seems almost a lifetime ago that I visited the school and found the diary and yet it was only yesterday. It has proved enlightening in terms of revealing that Miss Leigh and Grace had established a relationship, that subterranean passageways exist underneath the grounds of Grove House and, of course, it has proved the existence of the Circle of Sappho itself. What it has not done yet, however, is to reveal who else might have been involved in their deaths, and, I fear, may not do so.

The walk to Swainswick has certainly aroused emotion. I have become enamoured with Miss Austen, I realise; her wit and intelligent mind are most enlightening. It is unfortunate she is to leave the city for a few months, but assuming she will return by October, to attend the wedding, I shall venture to further our acquaintance. I will enlist Mary's help in this.

I am not, of course, forgetting the small matter of Sunday and the duel with Kirby. The thought of dying has put life in perspective and having shared such delightful conversation with Miss Austen today, I realise that at some time in the future, if I survive this duel, I could possibly venture to enjoy an intimate relationship again.

But what of Lockhart? I still cannot make him out, although after today's conversation I wonder if I have misjudged him. He seems genuine in his plea that he wants to shed the criminal activities he is currently engaged in. Perhaps the first step in discovering whether he is genuine or not will be his acquisition of Moorhouse's letters; if he does not produce them, as promised, then I shall indeed inform Mary of all I know.

Swann closed his journal for the night. He then opened the diary and began reading the remaining entries.

I am devastated. I have received news today to say I am to leave the school in two weeks' time and travel abroad with my parents for the foreseeable future. I have to find a way to tell Miss Leigh.

In a following entry Grace told Miss Leigh the news that she was to leave the school. Unsurprisingly, it was not taken well. The more Swann read, the more it seemed to be leading to the inevitable conclusion the teacher had, after all, killed Grace and then poisoned herself.

Swann then cast his mind to Anne. He did not believe that she had committed suicide. If she had been looking forward to his arrival, as the school principal had indicated, then why throw herself from the school roof? At the very least Swann owed it to the two dead girls, if not to Miss Leigh, to discover once and for all if someone else was involved. Two entries later and Swann read the first hint of what he was looking for.

She keeps it from me but I know something troubles her. I know my news has had an adverse effect on her, I can see it in her eyes when she looks at me, but there is something else, something unrelated to my news. She will not talk about it and for the first time I feel a tension between us. She smiles and says everything is fine but I know it is not fine, as our relationship is no longer the same: where there was union, there is now distance; where there was joy, there is now sadness.

Swann read on and soon discovered the answer to what was troubling Miss Leigh.

I have at last found out what is causing Miss Leigh to be so miserable. One of the girls in the Circle is threatening to reveal our secrets; of the Circle's existence itself. Miss Leigh will not tell me who it is, but I think I can guess; it can only be one of three after all.

No names were mentioned but, like Grace, Swann could guess who it was. From what he had learned from reading the diary, each year, at the start of the academic term, one of the three final year girls who belonged to the Circle would be chosen by Miss Leigh to be her 'special' companion – her 'Atthis'. They would then indulge in a physical relationship throughout the year, until the girl left the following spring. The next academic year the process would be repeated. With the appearance of Grace, however, she had become that 'special girl' instead. One of the three girls from the final year, it seemed, was not happy about this situation and was threatening to expose the relationship and the Circle itself.

If someone was threatening to expose the Circle and Miss Leigh then … it hit Swann like a thunderbolt. What if Miss Leigh and Grace had not taken the boat across to the island after all. What if they were already on the island, having used the secret passageway, and it was the murderer who had taken the boat? And if the murderer had rowed the boat across and left it there, it could possibly mean only one thing. Swann intended to put his theory into practise first thing in the morning. He read on to see if there was any more information which would support his theory and found it in the very last entry, written the night before the two women had died.

Now she knows I am leaving, she has said she wants to become the 'special girl', but Miss Leigh has refused. I am afraid for Miss Leigh, especially as she is prone to violent outbursts. Miss Leigh tells me it is because of a condition she has, but will not tell me what it is. I can tell Miss Leigh is scared of her, of what she might do, but she tries to hide it from me, so as not to worry me before I leave tomorrow. But I do not want to leave the school now; I do not want to leave Miss Leigh here alone …

CHAPTER THIRTY

Catherine Jennings addressed all the girls of the school in the main hall, after morning prayers had been completed. 'Mr Swann will be coming back to the school today and wishes to speak with you all. He has found out information regarding a group called the Circle of Sappho, which apparently exists illegitimately at the school.' Miss Jennings looked towards her head girl. 'Elsa, Mr Swann wants to talk to you first.'

'Why, Miss?'

'As I understand it, he thinks that as head girl you may have heard something about this Circle of Sappho. He also believes that Miss Leigh and the two girls who have died this week were somehow involved.'

'Yes, Miss Jennings,' Elsa replied coolly.

'Thank you girls, I am not certain when Mr Swann is due to arrive but please be prepared to talk to him when he does.'

The girls were dismissed and Miss Jennings made her way out of the main school building. Once outside she crossed the grounds to Tom's cottage. She knocked on his door and he answered.

'Tom, I want you to ready the boat for Mr Swann when he arrives. After he has spoken to the girls he wishes to be taken across to the island, as part of his investigation into the murders of Miss Leigh and Miss Templeton. He believes there is an item there which will confirm the murderer's identity.'

'Very good, Miss Jennings.'

'I will go back to my office and wait for him there.'

As Miss Jennings turned and made her way back to the main building, she passed Elsa hiding in the nearby undergrowth. The head girl had followed the school's head and had positioned herself, unseen, in order to overhear her conversation with Tom. Now that she had heard it, she realised there was not much time to discover what it was on the island that might expose her. She had to find it, whatever it was, and get back in time to talk to Mr Swann. She made certain the boat was moored on the house side, so proving there was no one already on the island, and after she watched Tom amble back inside his cottage, returned to the main house.

Once inside the school building, Elsa stopped briefly in the kitchen and then made her way to the library. There were two girls in there and after she told them to leave, they did. She closed the door and pushed the secret panel. Once through the gap, she pulled the bookcase closed behind her and descended the stone stairwell. She reached the bottom and made her way, in the dark, as quickly as she could along the passageway. Her heart was beating faster now, but there was no time to lose and no time to be afraid. Everything had happened so fast that she had not been able to find Gretchen. The last she had seen of her was back in the assembly hall, after prayers.

Elsa passed through the initiation chamber and the curtained wooden door, which she unlocked using the golden key she had taken from Miss Leigh. She left the door unlocked, as it would only slow her down on her return, and hurried along the passageway until she reached the stone steps which led up to the rear of the island temple. She ascended these and at the top pressed a lever to loosen the stone from its resting place. She put her shoulder against the cold rock and began to push with all her strength.

She now realised, as she felt resistance to her efforts, that this was the first time she had made the journey alone, at least in this direction. The other times had been either as a member of the Circle or with Gretchen, when they had come to look for the diary but had been disturbed in the process. In fact, they had only just managed to get back inside the temple and close the stone behind themselves before Swann had entered. When they had come back for the diary later, it had gone.

The one time she had previously made this journey on her own, of course, was after she had killed Miss Leigh and Grace, but then it had been in reverse. She had complained of period pain, while at church, and had been sent back to the school before everyone else. She knew Grace was leaving that day and wanted to confront Miss Leigh. After arriving back at the school, she found the boat moored on the house side. She then overheard the French master and gardener talking and found out Miss Leigh and Grace were missing. Knowing where they were most likely to be, she began the journey she had just undertaken. Having reached the wooden door, she found she could go no further. The door was locked to her. She banged on the wooden panels, but to no avail. So she had retraced her steps and when she saw the men searching elsewhere in the grounds, untied the boat and rowed herself across to the island.

Elsa had reached the island unnoticed and tied the boat up against the wooden post attached to the jetty. She then made her way towards the temple. As she neared the entrance she edged closer, so she could hear what the two occupants of the temple were saying.

'Do you think Sappho killed herself for Atthis?' she heard Grace say, her voice slightly slurred.

'Yes. It is said Sappho fell in love with Phaon, a boatman, but it was unrequited and after he sailed away to Sicily she killed herself.'

'Do you believe the story?'

'No, I believe it was invented by men as they could not endure the thought of a woman loving another so passionately. If she did take her own life, I like to think it was because of Atthis. In my mind, Sappho heard Atthis had died and, unable to bear the grief, threw herself off the cliffs at Lefaka. And in that way they were reunited in another place to enjoy their love eternally.'

The more she heard, the angrier Elsa felt. It should have been her in the temple with Miss Leigh; by rights it should be a final year girl who was chosen to be Miss Leigh's companion. She had waited her turn patiently, but had been cruelly rejected. She could not help the way she was; her body was how God had made her. There was no doubt this was why Miss Leigh had rebutted her advances and had chosen this slip of a girl. She had not even chosen another final year girl, but rather this pubescent fourth year one. No, Miss Leigh had totally disrespected the Circle's tradition and now she would pay.

'Will you still love me after I go away?' she heard Grace say.

'You'll never leave my side or my heart, I promise you,' said Miss Leigh.

Enraged, Elsa smashed her fist against a tree.

'I am sure I heard something, did you not hear it that time?'

'I told you my love, we're quite alone here. I have prepared it that way.'

If she was to retain the element of surprise she had to rush into the temple now. She felt the knife taken from the school kitchen in her grip and then picked up a sharp stone in her other hand.

Once inside the temple, she had immediately thrust the knife into the girl. She had fallen to the ground, the knife still in her heart. She had then turned on Miss Leigh and hit her with the stone. Blood had gushed from her forehead. Beside the teacher she had found a suicide note and small bottle. It seemed obvious what the glass bottle held: poison. Miss Leigh now groaned. Elsa knelt down beside the teacher and unscrewed the bottle's top. She squeezed open her lips and poured the liquid down her throat, which caused the teacher to involuntarily swallow. She had then ripped the golden key from her waist. It was all too perfect. With the note and poison beside the bodies, it would be thought that Miss Leigh had killed the girl and then taken her own life; the wound to her head no doubt inflicted by the girl as she tried to defend herself from Miss Leigh's murderous attack.

With the key in her possession and therefore a more clandestine way back to the school, she could leave the boat; so giving the impression the couple had rowed themselves across, rather than coming via the underground passage.

Returning to the present, Elsa now pushed the stone as hard as she could and finally felt it budge. She managed to get it far enough open to allow herself to step through and into the temple. She would now attempt to find out exactly what it was that she had left on the island. The temple was in semi-darkness as she entered. She saw the place where she had left the bodies; a tragic boating accident Miss Jennings had called it. She laughed. It did not matter, she had thought; if she could not be Miss Leigh's 'special girl', she would assume the Circle's leadership and choose her own.

As she moved toward the entrance, a voice spoke from the shadows.

'I am interested to know what you believe is here on the island which will incriminate you as a murderer.'

Elsa immediately turned back toward the passageway but Swann blocked her way. She turned again and ran out of the temple. Swann pushed the stone to its closed position and then headed towards the entrance himself. The only way off the island was by boat, and as that was moored on the other side of the lake, the girl he now knew to be the murderer of at least three people was therefore trapped on the island.

Swann had arrived at the school while the girls were inside the assembly hall, at prayers. He had found Miss Jennings in her office and informed her of the Circle of Sappho. They had then talked to Tom and Swann had told them exactly what to do. They had carried out his instructions to the letter, as Elsa was now on the island. Once the plans were set, Tom rowed Swann across to the island and then returned with the boat, leaving Swann there. He had tied the boat to its mooring on the school side again, so giving the impression the island was deserted.

The diary entries had confirmed his increasing suspicion that there was another way onto the island, other than by water; that suspicion having been aroused after seeing the second inscription against the far wall of the temple, and witnessing the apparent 'disappearance' of a person he believed he had disturbed whilst trying to unearth the diary.

On the way across the lake, Swann had finally discovered why Tom had been acting suspiciously. The gardener had been in love with Miss Leigh and although she was always friendly towards him, his love had been unrequited. After he had come across the dead bodies, and recovered from the shock, he had found the suicide note beside Miss Leigh. He could not believe what he read and in panic, had hurriedly put it in his pocket; he said he wanted to protect her reputation. Tom also confessed that he had seen the boat was missing during the morning – which Swann now assumed was actually taken by Elsa – and thought the teacher had taken it. Not wanting Miss Leigh to find herself in trouble, he had not mentioned it at the time to Miss Jennings, as he hoped it would be returned before the rest of the school returned from church. He had destroyed the letter, but remembered the essence of it, which he related to Swann as he rowed.

Swann had been waiting for an hour on the island, but the wait had proved worthwhile.

He now went through the temple entrance and out onto the island. It did not take long for him to find her. She had headed straight for the jetty, believing Swann had rowed the boat across in the time it had taken her to come the subterranean route. It was, of course, not there. She turned and saw Swann approaching down the path from the temple. She ran around the perimeter of the island trying to find a suitable place from which to dive into the water.

'There is nowhere to go,' shouted Swann. 'You might as well give yourself up.'

Undeterred, she continued looking until she found a little grassy outcrop, upon which she now climbed. By the time Swann caught up with her, she was in the process of discarding the dress she was wearing, realising the heavy material, once saturated, might drag her under the water. She now stood, naked, on the rock, her back to Swann.

'Do not jump, it is dangerous!' he shouted. 'There are rocks under the surface.'

His warning went unheeded and the next moment Swann saw the pale white body disappear over the edge. He ran forward to the outcrop and looked over. There floating in the water, face down, was the girl, a halo of blood starting to spread out beneath her. Swann assumed she had smashed her head against a submerged rock as she dived into the water. He broke off a branch from a nearby tree and tried to hook the body closer to the shore. As he touched her back with the branch, the body rolled over; as it turned face up Swann momentarily recoiled: along with two fully formed breasts, the body also displayed male genitalia. He had read about this kind of phenomenon – hermaphrodites they were called – but he had never seen one for himself. From what he could remember, the origin of the name had derived from the physical union between the Olympians Hermes and Aphrodite, and the name given to the resultant offspring: Hermaphroditos.

This was, Swann assumed, the 'condition' Miss Leigh had not revealed to Grace regarding Elsa, and, as much as the teacher had felt threatened by her, she had also perhaps felt sorry for her, which was why she had not told anyone about it.

Swann realised his efforts to retrieve the body would be unsuccessful and stood up to carry out the pre-arranged signal to Miss Jennings, the shooting of his pistol, which would bring Tom across to the island in the boat.

CHAPTER THIRTY-ONE

With the murders at the school resolved, Swann turned his attention to the next pressing matter; that of finding out the truth about his father. He believed he knew someone who might be able to help him. She lived about an hour's ride away, so he hired a horse, waited for it to be saddled, and then rode off.

Mrs Hunter had been the Gardiners live-in nanny for as long as Swann could remember. She would be old now, if still alive. Swann realised he had not kept in touch or seen her since she had retired and left the Gardiners' employ. He assumed if she had died, he would have been informed, given he owned the property in which she lived.

When Mr Gardiner had passed away and Swann inherited the majority of his adoptive father's property, the solicitor acting on behalf of the estate informed Swann about the provision which had been made for Mrs Hunter. Mr Gardiner had purchased a cottage near his former employee's birthplace, to be held in perpetuity – or at least for her lifetime – where she would live rent-free, along with a yearly allowance. When Swann had inherited the estate, including the cottage, he was asked by the solicitor if he wished for this provision to continue. Even though Mr Gardiner stipulated the arrangement was 'in perpetuity', the solicitor had said, somewhat conspiratorially, that if he wished to take back possession of the cottage there were 'certain ways and means' that could be instigated in order for this to be made possible. Swann immediately responded that the provision was to continue and no more had been said on the matter.

Despite this, the fact he had never visited Mrs Hunter made him feel guilty. She had played an important part in not only Mary's life but his own too as they were growing up, and he held affectionate memories of her kindness at the time of his father's death and in the period following it. Before his father was murdered Mrs Hunter had worked closely with him, therefore if anyone knew what his father was really like it would, hopefully, be her.

As Swann rode the horse through fields and over hedges, letting the animal have its head across the flat land, he determined that if he was going to die tomorrow, he would learn the truth about his father first.

On reaching his journey's end, Swann brought the horse to a halt, dismounted and tied the reins around a tree that stood outside the cottage. He had arrived at the village and asked the first person he had seen for directions. They pointed towards a small wood, beyond which the cottage stood. As he walked to the door of the cottage, he remembered Mrs Hunter's warmth, the way she used to stroke his head when he could not sleep in the days, weeks and months after his father's death. But now here he was, arriving unannounced to visit somebody he had not seen for many years. For all he knew she might not even remember him. He hesitated for a moment, then knocked. If there was something to find out about his father from Mrs Hunter, then he at least wanted the chance to learn it.

The door was opened by a woman in her sixties. She was younger than Mrs Hunter would be and he wondered for a moment if he had come to the right cottage.

'Can I help you?' she asked.

'Mrs Hunter?'

'Oh no, my dear, she is inside. Who shall I say is calling?'

'Jack. Jack Swann. I was adopted by the Gardiners, who Mrs Hunter worked for before she retired.'

'Wait here.'

The woman left the door ajar and went back inside. At least Mrs Hunter was still alive, Swann thought to himself.

The woman returned.

'Come on through,' she said. 'She has been expecting you.'

Swann paused momentarily. Expecting him? How could that be? He ducked his head under the front entrance and went inside the cottage. It was not too different to the one in which Mrs Leach lived, in Frome. In the corner, sitting in an armchair, was an elderly woman, but she was far too thin and frail-looking to be the robust, heavy-set Mrs Hunter he remembered.

'Jack, is that really you?' asked the old woman in a soft voice.

'You will have to go to her, my dear,' said the woman who had answered the door. 'She cannot hear very well and is almost blind.'

Swann went forward and knelt down in front of her. He touched her hand with his own.

'Hello, Mrs Hunter. Please forgive me for arriving unannounced.'

'You do not need to apologise, Jack,' she replied. 'It is so wonderful you are here.'

She put her free hand against his face and stroked his cheek.

As she did this, he sat and looked at this woman who had given him so much comfort and kindness when he had been growing up. He remembered her as a strong, capable woman, who would stand no nonsense but could always be charmed with a smile. But here she was now, her face drawn, her body shrivelled and the skin on her hand, which now stroked his cheek, was stretched almost translucent over a myriad of blue veins.

Now he was here, he did not know how to ask the question he had ridden all this way for. Although almost blind and deaf, she sensed there was something on his mind and she knew what it was.

'Your father was a good man,' she said.

'How do you know I am here about my father?' Swann enquired.

'Most of the time I hear snippets of information and once I put them all together I add my own dollop of wisdom and usually find the truth somewhere within that,' she said profoundly. 'I know you seek the people who killed your father.'

'But how; I have not seen you in many years.'

'I always knew what you were up to. I remember you would find your way to the servants' quarters,' she said, 'I would always find you there. From what Mary tells me, you have not changed. I …'

'You have seen Mary?'

'She comes to visit me once a week. How wonderful she has at last found someone and they are to be married. It was Mary who arranged for Mrs Bailey to live here and look after me.'

At this, Mrs Bailey stepped forward and offered Swann a drink. He thanked her but declined. Mrs Hunter asked for her usual. Mrs Bailey smiled fondly as she turned and went into another room.

'She used to come in to see me every day, then go home at night. When her husband died three years ago she moved in here permanently. It is much better, I think, and she looks after me well. Oh Jack, it is so nice to see you. I have thought of you often.'

She leant forward a little. 'After your father died,' she said, 'I told you that you could cry if you wanted to, but you never did. I am truly sorry about what happened to your father, Jack. I still blame myself for it after all these years.'

'Why do you blame yourself, Mrs Hunter? It was not your fault.'

'Your father should not have been in the house that night. If only my sister had not been ill, God rest her soul.'

Mrs Bailey returned with a tray which she laid on a table. She took the glass off it and placed it in one of Mrs Hunter's hands, guiding the fingers around it.

'A little drop of port never did no one no harm,' said Mrs Hunter, swallowing a mouthful of the dark liquid.

'I'll be in the back garden if you require anything, Mrs Hunter,' said Mrs Bailey as she left the room.

Alone once more, Swann took Mrs Hunter's hands and looked into her face.

'I need to know the truth about my father, Mrs Hunter.'

'You will have to speak a little louder Jack, I'm still as deaf as I was, but as I am almost blind I can no longer lip-read.'

'I said, I have to know the truth about my father,' Swann repeated loudly. 'Was he a gambler, did he have a sickness?'

'Do not think badly of your father, Jack. He was a good man with a kind heart. But yes, he did gamble, although I saw it as a weakness, not a sickness. He did not know when to stop, he always believed his luck was about to change and that he would win enough money to give the start in life he wanted for you. He only wanted what was best for you, Jack. He told me that himself. He didn't want you to go into service, like he had. If you want my opinion though, I don't think your father ever recovered from losing your mother. It was very hard for him bringing you up on his own, and I think he gambled to take away the pain.'

'Where did my father go to gamble?'

'I do not know exactly where your father went,' said Mrs Hunter, 'only that he would always return late, having lost all his money. Your father would always make sure you were asleep, once he had read to you, before he left. I would then hear him come back, several hours later. I would make him a drink and he would tell me his plans, for when he won a lot of money. He wanted to make a better life for himself, for both of you. He wanted you to become a gentleman. He said he knew he could not afford to do that on his wages – even though he considered himself well-treated by the Gardiners – so that's why he gambled. I am sorry you know the truth, Jack, but perhaps after all this time it is for the best. It does not take away what your father felt for you. He always made sure you were provided for first.'

'What about the night he was killed? Do you remember anything?'

'As you know, I had to look after my sister and so your father did not go out. I stayed the night with her, and when I came back the following day I heard what had happened. That's all I know.'

Swann's many years as an investigator meant he knew immediately that Mrs Hunter was lying.

'Mrs Hunter, please, I need to know the truth. You will probably not tell me anything I have not heard myself, it is just that I do not know whether to believe it or not.'

'Then believe it is not true.'

'What do you know? Mrs Hunter, please, I need to know.'

Mrs Hunter sighed and held one of Swann's hands again.

'One of the servants that worked for the family, he wasn't there long, he had certain relations that were a little bit on the … well, you know what I mean. He told me a story not long after your father was killed. I told him I did not believe him, but he said it was true. Your father used to gamble at the same club all the time – as I said, I do not know what it was called. What I do know is that it was run by some nasty types. Your father became heavily in debt to them, through his gambling, and they gave him a chance to pay them off. He told them Tuesday evenings were the staff's night off and the Gardiners always went out until late. The only ones in the house would be us and we would not cause them any trouble; you would be asleep and I would most likely not have heard them. What happened that night was never planned though, I am certain of that. It was just tragic your father did not go out that night.'

'If he knew they were going to break into the house, why did he try and stop them?'

'I do not know. Perhaps a change of heart, perhaps protecting you.'

There was a silence between them, both lost in thoughts of the past and comforted by the other's presence, once more, after all these years.

CHAPTER THIRTY-TWO

Swann was already inside the Fountain Inn when George and Bridges entered. He had arrived shortly before seven and ensconced himself in one of the alcoves. He had been in various drinking houses in the Avon Street district for the last hour or so, in disguise, listening out for any news or information regarding the Scarred Man's whereabouts, but had come to the Fountain without hearing any mention of him. It was the same response when he asked the two thief-takers.

'If this man you want is in the area, Mr Swann,' said George, 'no one is talking about him, at least not when we were about.'

Swann accepted this with quiet sanguinity. 'The evening is yet early,' he said, 'and so we may still hear something. The information I received did report he was due here *sometime* tonight.'

Bridges tugged George's arm. George nodded.

'Mr Swann, Bridges would like to say he appree … appreesh …'

'Appreciates?' injected Swann.

'Yes, sir. Bridges appreeshates what you have done for Rosie. It was a good thing you did for her, Mr Swann.'

'I was only too happy to assist, George, although I believe it will turn out to be mutually beneficial.'

'Mute what sir?'

'Mutually beneficial, George; it means that finding a room for Rosie might help me as much as it helps her.'

'What do you mean, sir?' For a moment George looked a little suspicious of Swann's motives.

'It is nothing like that, George,' Swann reassured him. 'What it means is that I have persuaded Rosie, in return for living rent-free, to help me in my work, like you and Bridges. There will be no danger involved for her though, I will make certain of that, but as a woman she may be able to gain access to places that you and Bridges might not.'

'How do you mean, sir?'

'Ladies' dressing rooms for a start, George.'

'I've been in a few of them myself, Mr Swann.'

'I am sure you have, George, but Rosie told me that along with playing the violin, she has acted in a few plays, back in Ireland, when she was younger. I may be able to use her talents.'

'If you ask me, Mr Swann, I don't think she'd be much good.'

'Why is that, George?'

'She's too well-known 'round here. Everyone would know her face straight off.'

Swann thought for a moment.

'You might be right, George. Perhaps I will have to rethink my decision.'

George nodded, pleased to have been able to help Mr Swann.

'So here is the plan for the evening,' said Swann, returning to the business at hand. 'I suggest, gentlemen, that we all take different parts of the district. George, you go across to Horse Street and then visit the public houses in Corn Street and Back Street; Bridges, you go as far as Peter Street and then make your way back, visiting any places you think might be worth going into. I'll take Avon Street itself, I'll start at the Duke of York and work my way back up to here. We will return here at the striking of the next hour with any information.'

There were nods of agreement from George and Bridges, then George said: 'If you're thinking of visiting all the pubs in Avon Street, Mr Swann, it will take more than an hour. There are a lot of pubs down here.'

'Thank you, George, although I have thought of that; I have asked someone to visit several of them as well. Ah here she is now. Hello Georgette.'

A grotesque-looking woman with a wart on her nose and an awful stench emanating from her clothes sat herself down next to George. George edged away from the woman.

'Georgette, this is George.'

'Oh did you 'ere that? Georgette and George; we'd make a right couple now wouldn't we love,' said the woman, nudging George as she spoke in her broad Somerset accent. 'Georgette and George, why that's a match made in 'eaven that is, if I do say so me-self.' She lifted her left buttock off the seat a little and let wind.

'Thinking about it,' said Swann, 'it might be more agreeable if we stay in pairs. I will go with Bridges and George, you can go with Georgette.'

Bridges nodded at this arrangement but George looked less certain.

Georgette nudged an increasingly annoyed George.

'That'll be nice, won' it? We can spend the dimmet together, jis you and me. We'll get comferbull somewhere and perhaps even get up to somefin' naughty.'

'I don't think that being in twos is a good idea, Mr Swann,' muttered George.

'Why not, George?'

'Because I, er … I …'

The woman leant in close to George and, reverting to her Irish accent, said: 'Ah, come on sweetie, you didn't think it was such a bad idea when you suggested it to me last year.'

George, having realised the true identity of 'Georgette', angrily stood up and stormed out. As he went he shouted, 'I'll see you all in an hour.' Swann, Bridges and Rosie burst out laughing. Rosie had signed to Bridges as soon as she had entered the inn, so he had been aware of the deceit from the beginning.

As good as his word, George was back in the Fountain at eight o'clock; his earlier anger now tempered by the various drinks he had drunk while visiting all of his allocated pubs. It was not long before Swann and Rosie entered, followed shortly after by Bridges. Once again, they had returned without any information about the Scarred Man.

'I am sorry for earlier, George,' said Swann, 'but I wished to prove to you how good an actress Rosie is.'

George reluctantly accepted Swann's apology, but would not look Rosie in the eye.

'I have an appointment at eight-thirty,' Swann announced. 'I suggest you have a drink or two in my absence and I will be back here at nine,' he placed several coins in front of George. 'No hard feelings I hope.' George looked at the coins and begrudgingly smiled at Swann.

Swann left the Fountain and made his way up to the East Gate, as he had done two nights previously. He reached his destination, only this time approaching it from the direction of the river. He hid in the shadows and waited. Ten minutes had elapsed since the time of their agreed meeting and it looked to Swann as if he had been double-crossed by Lockhart. He was not coming. Swann began to walk away, disappointed, when a voice whispered from the shadows.

'Swann, it is me, Edmund.'

'Lockhart?'

'I could not afford to be seen in your presence, even if you are in disguise, so I have taken precautions myself. That is why I am late.'

'Do you have the letters?'

'Yes, here they are.' Lockhart reached into his clothing and retrieved a packet of letters, tied with a piece of ribbon. 'They were not easy to obtain,' he said. 'I had to wait until Kirby left his office. When he finds out they're gone, I do not know what he will do.'

Swann took the letters and secured them within his pocket.

'I thank you for these Edmund and appreciate what you have risked for them. If anything happens to me tomorrow, promise me you will take good care of Mary. I may not have been in agreement with the wedding, but if I am to die, then at least I can do so knowing of your promise.'

'Of course, I promise,' said Lockhart.

There was an awkward silence for a moment before Swann turned and began to walk away. Lockhart went after him and caught his arm.

'Swann, tomorrow morning, when you fire first, do not aim for Kirby's heart.'

'What?'

'He is to wear a type of jacket that will stop your bullet, if fired there,' Lockhart said. 'If you wish to kill him, you must aim for his head. He intends to kill you, and will not miss.'

'Why are you telling me this?'

'Perhaps with Kirby dead, I can be free of all this,' replied Lockhart, more to himself.

'Free of what?'

'It is of no matter. Now I go back to Kirby's office to await his return.'

'Where is he now?' Swann enquired.

'He received a message from Wicks, about an hour ago. His London connection is here and he wanted Kirby to meet him.'

'What!' exclaimed Swann. 'Where are they to meet?'

'I do not know; possibly the Duke of York. Is it important?'

Swann did not answer as he had already turned and was running back toward the Avon Street district.

CHAPTER THIRTY-THREE

Bath, Saturday 31st March, 1804

I feel my faith is lost, my belief shattered. I now possess the truth I sought and it makes me sick. Mrs Hunter told me that despite his weakness for gambling and collusion with the burglars to pay off his debts, my father was a good man and, before losing his money, always made certain I was provided for first. But then she was not there the times my stomach was painfully tight from hunger because he had gambled our money away on one game of chance or another and had nothing left to buy food; my father finding a new excuse each time as to why he had lost.

Is this to be my last entry? Tomorrow is the duel with Kirby and I feel I have been trapped into taking part. I cannot let Fitzpatrick fight for me, yet I do not want to die. I have written a letter to Mary. At least she is to be married, even if it is to a man I do not trust. I surely cannot leave it like this.

I have scoured the streets for the Scarred Man tonight but he was nowhere to be found. Is he really in Bath? Did he return? I sense he is here, but am I fooling myself? Perhaps I have fooled myself my whole life through.

And why did Lockhart tell me about Kirby's jacket? Is it a double bluff or does he really want Kirby dead? With Kirby dead, Lockhart will not need to explain to him about the missing letters, yet if it is to be me who is killed, I will no longer be there to protect Mary from Lockhart's clutches. There are so many questions that remain unanswered, and may never be answered now.

How could you have done this to me, Father! I vividly remember the night you died. I could not sleep and woke from a nightmare. Something was not right. I called out for Mrs Hunter but you came instead. You stroked my hair and said how much you loved me. I could not go back to sleep and so you said to come downstairs with you. You were in a back room, polishing boots. You seemed nervous, on edge, but you looked at me and then took out the three cups. You found a dried pea and showed me the game you had done so often. 'You must watch for the pea,' you said. 'Always watch for the pea.'

Whether you meant it or not, I have taken it to mean to always look for the trick behind the illusion. There was no pea, or at least not under any of the cups. That is the answer – you are looking for something that does not exist. Is that what I am doing, chasing the Scarred Man after all these years; looking for justice that does not exist? I could not figure your trick out until later. And then the noise from elsewhere in the house came and the next moment you were gone.

CHAPTER THIRTY-FOUR

It was still dark as Swann left the house in Great Pulteney Street and stepped into the carriage organised by Fitzpatrick. He closed the carriage door and, as the horse trotted off, glanced up at the window where his sister lay asleep.

'Does Mary know?' asked Fitzpatrick.

'No. I wanted to tell her but it would have been too painful for her. I have placed a letter addressed to her on my bedroom table, in case I do not return. If I am killed this morning, perhaps you could enlighten her as to why I could not let her know.'

'You can rely on me, Swann,' replied Fitzpatrick. 'You look tired.'

'I must confess I have not slept. I was putting my affairs in order until the early hours and writing these correspondences.'

Swann handed his companion several letters, each one addressed separately.

'I would be grateful if you can forward these to their intended recipients in the event of my death. There is one addressed to you, Henry. I would consider it a great favour if you were able to fulfil the instructions enclosed within.'

'I will do my best,' replied the magistrate.

The carriage reached the end of the street and turned left, towards Bathampton Down. The journey was a relatively short one and as the carriage neared its destination it left the main road and travelled up a narrow, uneven track, the chassis bumping and shaking all the way. They reached the intended spot for the duel and the driver pulled on the reins to bring the horse to a halt. They were the first to arrive.

'Kirby is not here yet,' said Fitzpatrick, looking out of the window. 'I suggest we wait in the carriage.'

Swann agreed, although after a short while he decided to get some fresh air. He stepped down from the carriage onto the dewy grass and walked around. The sun had risen and its golden rays shone through the tree branches, casting dappled sunlight on the ground.

Fitzpatrick left the carriage and unpacked the pistol box, along with the required paraphernalia, in silence. He set up a small table on which he placed two pistols. He loaded each of them in turn and set them back down. He then busied himself by pacing out the space between where the two combatants would stand and marking the positions where each would turn and discharge their firearms.

A few more minutes passed and there was still no sign of Kirby.

'This is strange,' said Fitzpatrick. 'I thought he would have been here by now. Perhaps you have a reprieve?'

'I do not wish a reprieve,' said Swann. 'I wish honour to be restored and justice to be served.'

'And rightly so,' said a familiar voice. From behind the nearby trees a figure stepped out.

'Wicks!' exclaimed Swann. He instinctively reached for a loaded pistol.

'I would suggest you leave those exactly where they are. Several of my men are surrounding you at this moment and all have their weapons aimed at you.'

'What are you doing here? I cannot believe you have become Kirby's second.'

'Kirby will not be coming, as there is someone who wants to take his place.'

'My disagreement is with Kirby,' said Swann, 'and nobody else. I suggest this duel is annulled.'

'Do not be too hasty, Mr Swann,' said another man, stepping into view. His face was shrouded by a hood.

'Who are you?' asked Swann.

'I have many names, Mr Swann, but I believe you call me the Scarred Man.'

The stranger lifted his hood and let it fall back. The deep scar on his cheek verified his identity.

'Why are you here?' asked an increasingly bewildered Swann.

'I know you have been searching for me. Well, here I am. I have often wondered what happened to the boy from *that* night.'

Swann stared at the man in disbelief. 'I still do not understand,' he said.

'I am here to bring your quest to an end; that is what you want, is it not? Although I do not know why you think I am to blame. I did not kill your father; it was not me who ran the cutlass through his body.'

'You were there.'

'So were you. But then, of course, you also blame yourself.'

'What do you mean?' said Swann.

'You stood there and did nothing. You allowed your father to die just as much as I did.'

'I was twelve years old!' shouted Swann. 'What could I have done?'

'And what about this!' growled the Scarred Man pointing to his face. 'Look at what your father did to me.'

'It is only a scar. You still have your life, my father lost his!'

'I also lost the sight in my right eye. I do not bear a grudge, though. It has been more than twenty years; why don't you give up chasing me and stop tormenting yourself?'

'Never! You are my chance of finding Malone.'

'It will not bring you the satisfaction you seek.'

'I do not wish to kill him, merely to see that justice is served.'

'You cannot fool me. Admit it. You want to execute Malone; you want to watch the look on his face as you administer that fatal blow. You want him to suffer the way your father did. You know your father was to blame though, don't you.'

'What do you mean?'

'Your father was the one who told us about the house, whilst gambling. In return for his debts being cleared he told our boss about the property, about that particular evening in the week being the staff's night off and how the family would be out. How there would only be a near-deaf woman and a young boy left in the property.'

'I do not believe you!' shouted Swann as he grabbed one of the pistols.

The Scarred Man smiled. 'That's it,' he said, 'let us bring this matter to a close.' He stretched his arms out as if crucified.

'Remember though, if you do kill me, you will never find Malone. I am the only one who can lead you to him. If I die, you will lose your chance forever. I could lead you to him right now. We could go on foot, by horse, in a carriage. Malone changes his whereabouts as often as you change your mind about your father's character; was he a good, honest, respectable man or just some sad, compulsive, selfish gambler.'

Swann began to squeeze the trigger.

'If anything happens to me, Malone will be gone and your quest will be over, anyway. If you really want justice to be served, you have to play my game; you have to adhere to my rules. Do you agree?'

'No, it ends here,' replied Swann.

Swann discharged his pistol and watched it find its target; the Scarred Man's heart. The impact knocked his adversary off his feet and he fell backwards to the ground. Swann stood motionless. The Scarred Man was dead, but he felt no satisfaction; no fulfilment; no resolution. He had let his emotions have free reign again and now he had lost Malone forever.

Then incredibly, as Swann watched, he saw the body of the Scarred Man move; his arms; his legs; his torso. He brought himself up onto his knees and then onto his feet. The Scarred Man laughed and picked up his pistol from the floor and aimed it at Swann's heart. He squeezed the trigger and the pistol discharged. As Swann fell to the ground, Fitzpatrick ran over and knelt down beside his friend.

'Swann! Swann!' he said quietly. 'Wake up, Kirby has arrived.'

It took a few moments for Swann to realise he had been dreaming, that there had been no Wicks or Scarred Man, only Kirby and Lockhart, who at this moment were waiting outside. He stepped out of the carriage and approached the two men. Fitzpatrick followed.

The surgeon, who was there to attend to the participants, whether wounded or dead, was also to act as the adjudicator. Everything was ready.

'Gentlemen,' said the surgeon, 'on my signal you will walk the agreed twelve paces and then turn to face each other. Mr Swann, you will fire first and, Mr Kirby, you will fire second. It has been agreed this duel is to the death, so if neither of you are fatally wounded, you will fire again, this time together.'

Swann and Kirby nodded briefly to one other, then turned and stood back-to-back. They slowly began to stride out the paces ... one ... two ... three ... Swann felt his heart quickening ... four ... five ... six ... he could not shake his dream of the Scarred Man from his mind ... seven ... eight ... what if he was in the city right now? ... nine ... whatever his father might have been, he had loved him and owed it to him to seek justice for his death. He had tried to protect the property, after all, and through his death Swann had been given this privileged life ... ten ... he saw the Scarred Man manically laughing at him as he stood up from being shot ... eleven ... twelve ... Swann stopped and turned to face Kirby. He knew what he had to do. He raised his pistol and aimed it at his opponent. He focussed all his attention on making the shot count. His heart pounded, his throat was dry and the hand in which he gripped his pistol trembled slightly. Swann brought all to mind in that final moment before he fired; that fatal night; his father; the Scarred Man; Malone; Wicks; Lady Harriet; Lockhart; Kirby.

Swann thought he saw a hint of smug satisfaction on Kirby's face, but this vanished as he discharged his pistol, replaced by one of shock and disbelief as the bullet reached its mark.

The surgeon walked across to where Kirby had fallen and knelt down beside him. He looked up at Swann.

'He is dead,' he said.

Swann walked over and gazed down at the magistrate's face. Blood where the bullet had entered Kirby's right temple trickled down his face, collecting in a pool on the grass beside his head.

Swann turned and strode purposefully towards the carriage. As he did so, he exchanged a knowing look with Lockhart. He then entered the carriage and, once Fitzpatrick had joined him, drove off back towards the city.

CHAPTER THIRTY-FIVE

Bath, Sunday 1st April, 1804

So I have killed a man. I had no choice, what else could I do? The truth is that I had no choice but to go through with it, as I was caught up in an irreversible sequence of events arising from the moment Kirby insulted my father's memory. If I had not fatally shot Kirby, I know he would have mortally wounded me.

A thought has embedded itself in my mind; what if Lockhart was lying about Kirby, that he was not wearing a padded jacket, that it was all a plan to get me to kill Kirby? Certainly Lockhart had several motives to want him dead. I will ask Fitzpatrick to enquire of the surgeon as to the garments Kirby was wearing. Fitzpatrick has assured me that I will not stand trial over the death; he will make certain it does not happen. He will not say anything, nor will Lockhart; although their motives are different, with the latter choosing to remain silent for selfish reasons rather than through friendship. The story which will appear in the local newspaper, as reported by Kirby's fellow magistrate, Henry Fitzpatrick, will relay that Richard J. Kirby had financial problems and in a fit of despair drove himself to the woods at Bathampton and committed suicide by shooting himself in the head.

Although I would rather not have taken up my pistols in the first place, let us not forget that Kirby was corrupt and his death has also weakened Wicks' empire.

As for Lockhart, if, as he has said, he truly puts his past behind him now that Kirby is dead so he can lead an honest life with Mary, then I shall welcome him; after all, if what he said was true about Kirby's jacket, then I owe him my life. If he reneges on his intention then I shall once more endeavour to find out the truth about his past and put a stop to the wedding.

And what of the Scarred Man? As soon as I made my farewells to Fitzpatrick, I returned to my warehouse, changed into a disguise and walked the streets until exhausted, trying to find him. Whatever else my father might have been, or whatever else he may have done, he did not deserve to die in the manner he did. Supine on the floor, my father was at the mercy of Malone – he begged for mercy – and yet Malone ran him through brutally and mercilessly. And for that, Malone will pay. And to find Malone, I must continue in my quest for the Scarred Man. I shall speak to Huntley and attempt to find out what he knows. At the same time, I will aim to discover what involvement Lady Harriet has in all this. Somehow, however outrageous it might sound, I believe that Lady Harriet, Huntley, the Scarred Man, Wicks, Lockhart and Malone, as well as Kirby before he died, are linked in some way and by unravelling this mystery I will finally be able to bring my quest to an end and serve justice on those who deserve it.

I will also visit London and my father's graveside; whatever he may have done in his life he was my father and I loved him. He died so I could live.

Earlier I heard the sound of a violin in the street below. It was a familiar tune called 'A Begging I Shall Go', which I have heard many times at the Fountain Inn with George and Bridges. I looked out of the window and to my surprise saw Rosie and Bridges. I waved my candle back and forth several times and having seen me, they stopped outside the window. Bridges waved, while Rosie nodded her head appreciatively before they strolled off towards Pulteney Bridge, the music gradually fading until silence replaced it in the street once more.

POSTSCRIPT

As pressure for Henry Addington to resign as prime minister increased, William Pitt the Younger, his illustrious predecessor, at last added his voice to a growing number of dissenters. With the King's latest illness and the possibility of his dying becoming all too apparent, the former first minister realised he had to take action. Pitt began to make significant noises towards the latter's replacement. On St George's Day he rose in the House of Commons to ridicule the government's latest attempt at patching up its military policy, and two days later gave an epoch-defining speech which he believed encapsulated and therefore focused the attention of the House on what was the real issue at stake.

The consequences of these speeches were that the government literally collapsed and Henry Addington resigned. The King, now thankfully recovering from his latest bout of illness, tried to convince his prime minister to recede his resignation but when he realised it was a lost cause, called for William Pitt the Younger to form a new government.

Across the Channel another great change was at hand. At the very moment Pitt resumed his prime ministerial seat in England, the First Consul, Napoleon Bonaparte, was declared Emperor of France. The Frenchman (although born on the island of Corsica) had been able to elevate himself to this position through his exposure of the plot to assassinate him, which had seen various conspirators, in collusion with the British Government and its secret service, imprisoned. By giving this failed attempt the widest publicity, while showing himself as an innocent victim, Napoleon was able to gain the support of hitherto Republicans, who subsequently helped sweep him into this powerful and now unassailable position; culminating in his crowning in the cathedral at Notre Dame de Paris.

If there was one mistake the Emperor of France made, however, it was carrying out the execution of the Viscount Duc d'Enghien. As Lady Harriet's boss had rightfully concluded, the killing of this young Bourbon prince and legitimate heir to the French crown shocked Europe. As horrified as the English government were at this action, they were able to play the situation to their advantage. From then on the young conqueror, as Napoleon saw himself, could not set himself up as a law-abiding citizen and distance himself from the suspicions of Jacobean traits he might have. A consequence of these events in France was that the plan involving families going across the Channel was cancelled. The parents of Grace Templeton though, even if the plan had continued, had already been excused from duty, at least temporarily, so they could mourn the loss of their only daughter.

As for Charles Moorhouse, he would play no part in Pitt's newly formed government, or indeed any subsequent ones, having failed to become elected Member of Parliament for Knaresborough. The 'owner' of the borough, the Duke of Devonshire, ultimately decided not to switch allegiances, thus remaining Whig, replacing the ill-fated James Hare with one of his own relatives, twenty-one-year-old William

Cavendish of Savile Row, Middlesex, who, on assuming his seat, voted steadily against the administrations of Addington and then Pitt 'both by family and principles'.

Three months after receiving the letters back from Swann, Moorhouse indulged himself in another indiscretion and became a victim of blackmail once more. This time, however, his supporters deserted him and without their money to help pay off the blackmailers, the scandal became public and he lost not only any political ambitions but his family too; his pregnant wife returning to her parental home with their young son, resulting in his father-in-law issuing a challenge to a duel. Moorhouse did not live long enough to take part: riding to Hampstead Heath, having moved to London after the scandal became public, he put a bullet through his head.

The day Charles Moorhouse had taken his own life – Saturday, 23rd July 1804 – also saw the anniversary of the failed rebellion in Dublin, led by Robert Emmett. Although there were concerns – mainly in the Alien Office – over the possibility of another attempt, the day passed uneventfully. Lady Harriet knew nothing would happen, mainly because the 'grapevine' she had established had been quiet and she would have heard of anything being planned. This was no time to be relieved, however, as she knew that if there was to be an uprising, it would surely come on the actual anniversary of Emmet's execution; it was therefore to September that Lady Harriet now looked and to which all preparations were aimed.

As the summer progressed, the details of the wedding between Miss Mary Gardiner and Mr Edmund Lockhart were finalised. The ceremony, set for the 27th of October, was, as far as the two main participants were aware, going ahead, although unseen forces behind the scenes were working to make certain it did not happen.

As news of the school deaths eventually reached parents, gossip spread like wildfire. Despite the fact the school claimed they were tragic accidents, the sheer fact that three pupils and a teacher had died was enough to convince parents not to let their daughters return after the break. The consequence was that by the time the following academic term was due to start, Catherine Jennings found her school without pupils and short of fees. Lady Harriet offered to help in the short-term but the principal understood the long-term reality of the situation and regretfully closed Grove House School. Catherine Jennings subsequently became the main speaker for an organisation calling for the equal education of women, which Lady Harriet was in the process of creating.

Although the events at the school eventually faded from public memory, those who had been directly involved, including Swann, never forgot the Circle of Sappho.

About the Authors

DAVID LASSMAN is a scriptwriter, author, journalist and lecturer. He has appeared many times on television and radio, including BBC's *The One Show*, Radio Four's *The Today Programme*, *News at Ten* and *Good Morning America*. He currently teaches at the City of Bath College and for Frome Community Education. David was born in Bath and now lives in Frome.

Now a full-time writer, TERENCE JAMES is an award-winning editor (*Murder of Shirley Banks, Dangerous Music*) at ITV. Throughout an illustrious career he has held various roles on prestigious television programmes such as *Man Alive* (BBC) and *The Avengers* (ITV) as well as feature films at Elstree, Pinewood and Shepperton studios. He was born in London but has lived in Bath for more than forty years.